THE BLOODY CANVAS

KJ KALIS

Copyright © 2020 K.J. Kalis

eISBN 978-1-7334480-9-3

ISBN 978-1-7352192-0-2

ALSO BY K.J. KALIS

The Kat Beckman Thriller Series:

The Cure

Fourteen Days

Burned

The Blackout

The Bloody Canvas

Sauk Valley Killer

The Emily Tizzano Vigilante Justice Thrillers:

Twelve Years Gone

Lakeview Vendetta

Victim 14

1

Hailey walked slowly away from her last class of the day at the Savannah College of Art and Design, trying to stick to areas where there was still a little shade. She shrugged the black portfolio filled with her sketch-books higher up on her shoulder. The strap was digging into her skin.

Her phone vibrated in the pocket of her denim shorts. She pulled it out, realizing that she'd gotten paint on yet another piece of clothing. She shook her head and stared at the phone. It had stopped ringing before she could get to the call, the area code for New York City on the display. She smiled a little, wondering if it was another job. She'd reached out the week before to ask for changes to their business arrangement but hadn't heard back. Now, they'd have to wait for her.

Ahead of her was Calhoun Square. Savannah was littered with small parks celebrating important people of the South. There had to be more than twenty of them, each of them festooned with elaborate plantings, statues and benches. Calhoun Square was just one of the squares she walked through on the way back to her apartment each day. Her roommate, Missy Langford, who was from an old Georgia family, had taken Hailey on a tour of the squares when they first got to college. That was three years ago. It was hard to believe she was a junior already.

Hailey stopped at one of the benches that faced the green lawn in the middle of the square and sat down. She pulled a water bottle out of her bag. It rested on a post just below a sign that described Calhoun Square as the memorial park for John C. Calhoun, former Vice President of the United States. She took a long drink of water, using her free hand to thumb through her social media. She sent a quick text to Missy. "Stopping to sketch at Calhoun. Be back later." Her phone chirped almost immediately, a red heart on her screen.

Hailey glanced around the square. There was a City of Savannah truck at the other end, the whine of a weed eater bouncing off the buildings. A family passed her, stopping to read the sign. "Mom, Mom, can we mark that one off?" the little girl said. In the far corner of the square, there was a small group of boys. From where she was sitting, she couldn't see what they were doing, though they all appeared to be looking at something.

From inside her portfolio, she pulled a medium-sized sketchbook and a set of pencils. She kneaded the gray eraser between her fingers as she looked at the buildings, warming it up. Calhoun Square was one of her favorite places to sit and sketch. The arching trees and the buildings made for a depth of interesting angles and shadows. Every one of them had a story to tell.

Hailey chose a section of the Abercorn house to sketch. Built in the mid-eighteen hundreds, it had wrought-iron camellias on the railing of the upstairs balcony. Hailey's art history professor thought it was beautiful. Hailey thought it was weird.

As she started to rub the graphite gently onto the paper, she heard voices. Kids, rustling and jostling against each other.

There were always kids around in Savannah, everything from babies being pushed in their strollers to the wayward toddlers who tried to run from their families while on vacation. She shook her head but didn't look up, ignoring the ruckus.

She glanced up at the Abercorn house, choosing a darker pencil to build more structure into her drawing. As she pressed down onto the paper, she felt the air move as though someone was close to her. She looked up. The boys who had been at the other end of the park were now right by her, running by. One of them tugged at her bag. "Hey!" she said, standing up. "That's mine! You can't..."

Hailey didn't have time to finish her sentence. As she turned, she saw the glint of something metal coming at her as all of the boys, save one, ran off. The pain as she was stabbed in the stomach was paralyzing. With nothing but a groan, Hailey slumped back down on the bench, a pool of blood seeping out through her shirt and down through her shorts. She tried to make noise, to get someone to help her, but the drone from the maintenance equipment at the other end of the square drowned out her whispers for help.

With the last bit of strength in her body, Hailey reached for her phone, which had clattered just out of reach. She watched her hand as it moved in slow motion, trying to retrieve it, but for some reason, she just couldn't get to it. Numbness filtered throughout her body. She looked down, seeing the red patch expand on her abdomen, soaking through her thin t-shirt. She put her hand on it to try to stop the bleeding, but blood oozed out. Her head rolled to the side, toward the spot where she had tossed her sketchbook as the boys interrupted her work. She saw the lines of the Abercorn House beginning to take shape. They were lines that she would never finish...

2

The beeping of the police radios didn't bother Detective Carson Martino anymore. He was well used to them, as well as the baking heat of Savannah summers. He parked his car on East Gordon Street, one of the small roads that flanked Calhoun Square. Before he got out of the car, he straightened his tie and made sure his badge was hanging in the center of his chest.

The officers that had beat him to the scene had erected a line of yellow police tape to prevent visitors from sullying the area or getting a look at something that wouldn't exactly be considered southern hospitality. "Carson," the officer manning the tape nodded.

"Ginny, how are the kids?"

"Good."

"I'd like to come and see them sometime."

"Anytime you'd like."

Carson managed to have the whole conversation without breaking stride. In the Savannah Police Department, Carson was known to be matter-of-fact and focused. Maybe too focused. "Hey, Byron," he said, approaching the scene. "You beat me here."

Carson watched Byron Zachs, the county coroner, for a moment. He was a stick of a man, long and thin in every way from his arms to the length of his nose. He was peering at the body as if he were perched. His eyes didn't move to Carson until he started to stand up, unfolding his narrow limbs until he was a couple of inches taller than Carson.

"Yeah, I was doing a lecture around the corner. 'The Tales Dead Bodies Tell,' was the title."

"Fascinating. What is this dead body telling you?" He didn't want Byron to get off into one of his speeches on medical forensics.

Byron pulled his gloves off and pushed his glasses up on his nose. "Well, I can't know for sure until I get her back to the lab, but it looks like a stab wound hit a major artery. Which artery it was, I can't tell you."

Carson shook his head. He didn't care which artery it was. That was something that wouldn't help him solve the case. "Any idea what kind of knife."

Byron pursed his lips, staring back at the body. "Something about four to six inches long. I'll be able to tell if it was serrated once I get some tissue samples." He stared at Carson. "She didn't have a chance. If it was a severed artery, she bled out within a couple of minutes. Was probably unconscious in less than thirty seconds."

Carson looked at the pool of blood on the ground and all over the girl's clothes. "Yeah, that's a lot of blood."

Byron nodded, "Looks like a good chunk of her blood volume. We'll check that out when we get her back. You need a couple of minutes?"

"Yeah. Just want to get a better feel for what happened here. Five would work."

Byron nodded. "Let my assistant know when you are ready,

and we will pack her up and get her out of here. I'll be in the truck starting the paperwork."

"Thanks, Doc." Carson looked more closely at the scene as Byron walked away. Carson sighed. Coming to a new scene was never easy. He had gotten used to it as much as anyone could in his fifteen years on the job. He'd made his way to detective after only three years with the Savannah Police Department. It was a record. Savannah needed more beat cops than detectives with the number of vacationers in the area. But Carson's chief had seen the detective in him, and he was added to the bureau, solving his first case just a week into his new placement.

Carson lifted his eyes to look across the square. He had walked Calhoun Square many times before with its perfectly maintained planter beds and painted benches. Back to the body, he told himself. He started his mental rundown. That's what he called it at least. Finding details was what made him good at what he did. The girl looked to be somewhere between eighteen and twenty years old, blonde hair, a single braid hanging down. She was wearing a blue t-shirt that had a picture of a zebra on it and a pair of cutoff jeans shorts, the rims of the pockets hanging down below the seams. On her feet were a pair of canvas tennis shoes, no laces, with paint spatter on the toes. A portfolio was on the ground next to her, a sketchbook nearby, the pencil she had been using on the ground near her phone. It was a lonely scene.

"We have an ID on her yet?" Carson said to Byron's assistant, Adam, who was hovering nearby waiting for Carson to be done.

"Not yet. I'd guess she was a SCAD student. As soon as you are ready, we can start going through her things to see if she has an ID on her."

"Did you take pictures?"

Adam nodded.

Carson stood up. "Let's do that. I'm ready." He took a step

back and waited, while Adam started to move items toward Carson. Carson pulled a pair of blue gloves out of his pocket and started going through the bag that was nearest the body. He found a set of keys on a long lanyard. A SCAD ID was attached. "Hailey Park." Carson handed the keys over to Adam, who put them in a bag that had a strip of red adhesive at the top. There was no telling what they'd find on any given piece of evidence at the scene, hair, DNA, spatter. It paid to be overly careful in case they needed it in court, that was, if they could find the killer. "Says she's a junior." Carson shook his head. "Now the question is what happened…"

As he pulled the blue gloves off of his hands and stepped away, letting Byron and Adam take over moving her body, Carson's eye saw something across the square. In the alcove of the entrance for the Abercorn House stood a man in the shadows. He was too far away for Carson to make much out about him other than he seemed to be of average height and was bald with glasses. "Hey," Carson said to the officer that was nearest him. "That guy been here long?"

The officer shook his head. "I think I saw him when I got here. Has been just kinda hanging out there. Hasn't made a move."

Carson looked at the man again. His gut told him there was more to the man staring than just curiosity. What the connection was, he didn't know. Carson took a couple of steps forward, lifting the yellow tape. As he did, the man in the alcove moved off, hands in pockets, head down. Carson stopped. The guy was too far away for him to catch up to unless he started a foot chase. "Strange," he muttered to himself. He motioned to the officer, "Keep an eye out for him, okay?"

"Will do, detective."

A shout caught his attention. "Over here!" A uniformed officer was waving to Carson. "I've got something!"

Carson walked to where the officer was standing. On the

ground, lodged between two plants in an immaculately maintained planting bed, was the glint of something metal. Carson knelt down and pulled another pair of blue gloves out of his pocket. Byron had followed. "Let's get a picture of this before I move it." Adam took a couple of pictures, the click of the shutter the only break in the silence. "Done?" Carson asked. He wanted to make sure the pictures were good before he moved anything.

"Yep. All good."

Carson brushed some mulch off the metal and picked it up. It was a six-inch hunting knife, the kind that folds in half to make carrying easier. The blade was blackened with blood and mulch. "Looks like we have our murder weapon," Carson said, dropping it into an evidence bag.

"Well, we can't know for sure until we test the blood and the wound..." Byron said.

"I know, Doc. I know." Carson shook his head. Byron, ever the scientist, was a bit of a stickler for details to the point it was annoying.

Carson shrugged his shoulders as he stood up, the bag in hand. They had a body; they had the weapon. The question was, who was Hailey Park? And who would want her dead?

He glanced back at the Abercorn House, the entry now empty. The man who had been watching them was gone. Was he connected to the case? Carson sighed, rubbing the bottom of his nose. It itched from the pollen of the summer blooms in the park. It was going to be a long couple of days ahead, probably ones without much sleep. It was always that way with the cases he landed. The images stayed with him until he had it solved.

CARSON WAS SITTING at his desk when his email chirped. The forensics report on Hailey Park was ready. He took a sip of lukewarm coffee and opened the email. The cause of death was exactly as he expected. The knife had punctured her hepatic artery causing massive blood loss. He clicked on the next page, looking for more information when Ginny Thompson walked up to his desk. "Get any more information on the murder from today?"

He and Ginny had gone through the police academy together and had a brief fling before she met her husband Dan and had two kids. Pregnancy had put her on a desk for a while, but she quickly rebounded. Carson knew that she aspired to become a detective someday, but raising the kids came first. He didn't look at her, still staring at the screen, "Report just came back. Stab wound cut an artery. She didn't have a chance."

"Must have been a wickedly sharp knife."

Carson clicked on the report details. The forensics team had run a standard test protocol on the knife. As he scanned the report, he saw they had confirmed that it was Hailey's blood on the blade. He clicked over to the next page, hoping they had been able to pull fingerprints. "You've got to be kidding me..."

Ginny leaned forward in her chair, staring over Carson's shoulder. "What? Something come back?"

"The prints on the knife belong to a kid."

3

"Beckman! Wait up!" Kat Beckman turned just in time to see Zara Reid running up after her. Their session at the National Conference for Independent Journalists had just let out. Kat had sat on the panel, answering questions about her work and her methods. She stepped off to the side, letting people pass, some of them mouthing "thank you" or "good job" as they walked down the hallway, rushing to their next session.

"Good job back there," Zara said breathlessly.

Kat and Zara had met earlier in the week in the buffet line. Zara was an aspiring journalist who was just getting started on her career. Whether their meeting was by chance or designed, Kat wasn't sure. Either way, it had been nice to have someone to pal around with while she was at the conference. "Thanks," Kat said. She glanced down at her phone, seeing that Van had tried to call a few times. "Listen, I've gotta run up to my room. My husband just called."

Zara panted, "Sure! I'll catch up with you later. Meet up for dinner maybe?"

"That's fine. Just send me a text."

"Yes, I'll do that! Thanks! Maybe we can talk about your process of finding a story? Like how you found out about the guy that was setting the wildfires, right?"

Kat paused. She didn't know if Zara was more of a stalker or just someone who needed to talk. She smiled. "Sure."

"You broke that story, right?"

"I did."

"Great. Can we talk about that later? I'd love to pick your brain."

Kat glanced down at her phone again, feeling anxious to talk to Van. "Look, I really gotta go. You know, when the editor calls..." Kat started moving before Zara could say anything more. She heard a shout of "I'll text you later!" as she walked away.

The chime of the elevator told her it was time to get out. As she put the keycard into the slot in her hotel room, she pushed the redial button on her phone. Van picked up after one ring. "Were you sitting by the phone waiting for me?" Kat asked.

"Kinda."

Kat couldn't tell if he was flirting or serious. "Are you making a pass at me, sir?"

"I wish. Except that you are in New York City and I'm in California." Kat and Van had been married for two years. Their son, Jack — it was really hers from her first husband — was ten.

"Somehow I don't think that's the entire reason for your call."

There was silence on the phone for a minute. "It isn't."

Kat sat down on the edge of the bed, the flowered comforter sinking underneath her. "Is everything okay? Jack?"

"He's fine. He's at school. Has a big math test today. He said he wished you were home to study with him."

Knowing that she wasn't around when Jack needed her made her heart ache. Though she knew he was okay, and that Van would take care of him — it was in his Marine training to do so, not to mention that she knew he really loved Jack — she was sad. "I wish I was too, but my mean boss made me come to this conference." Kat liked to tease Van about his double role as her husband and editor-in-chief of *The Hot Sheet*, the online newspaper that Van had started when he left the military. The success had been noted by an investment group who bought the paper and moved Kat and Van to California, promoting him to Editor-In-Chief. It was a win-win. She had the flexibility to do the things she wanted to do, but going to the conference hadn't been her idea. The organizers wanted her to come and speak about her stories and her career. Van thought it was good visibility for the paper. Now she wished she had said no.

"He's fine. There's something else going on though..."

Kat could immediately hear the darkness in his voice. "What's wrong?"

"There's a story that broke. Thought you might want to have a look."

"What happened?" There was a pause. Kat could hear papers shuffling in the background.

"I'm just starting to see some information on this now. Looks like an art student in Savannah was murdered."

"Murders happen every day. Why this one?"

"It's not the person that has been murdered that's the problem. It's who they think did it that is..."

"What do you mean?"

"There are some initial reports coming out of Savannah that it was a ten-year-old boy that stabbed the art student. She was about twenty. I'm waiting to get the final information on her age. I've got a call in."

"A kid? Jack's age?"

"Yup. I think there's a story here, Kat."

Kat chewed her lip. There were still two days to go at the conference. She was scheduled to speak on three more panels. After that, she wanted to go home. She wanted to hug Van and

Jack and play with their dogs, Tyrant, and Woof. She was ready for a normal life again. "So, what are you asking me?"

"I'm asking you to go to Savannah and figure this out."

"Can't you send someone else? I mean you have a whole stable of journalists."

"We don't have anyone else to send."

"What does that mean?"

"Everyone else is out on other stories. I need someone who can do the work, someone who isn't going to give up if the story takes a turn."

Kat got up and walked to the window, looking at the bustling streets of New York City below her. It seemed that no matter the time of day, there were people moving. Cabs filled the road below and a constant stream of people walking congested the sidewalk. Lights from the stores flickered on and off even though it was just approaching evening. The night before, Kat sat up for a few hours, watching the people go by. She had no desire to join them. "You are seriously telling me there's no one else in your vast stable of journalists that can go? I'm sure this is nothing."

There was silence. Kat knew by the silence Van was giving her a moment to think. He wasn't the kind to snap at her. She was grateful for that. "I'll do anything for you, Van. I just don't know how I'm gonna get out of this conference. I've still got appearances to make."

"They will do without you. Think about it. Send me a text when you decide. Stephanie will get you a flight if you want to go."

As Kat ended the call, she started to pace. She really just wanted to go home, to leave the Zara's of the world at the conference and go back to running with the dogs and working at home. She knew she was out of her comfort zone, something her therapist told her was good for her. She had been counting on going home in a couple of days, but now Van needed her.

She sat down at the tiny desk the hotel had put in the corner of her room and opened her laptop, searching for information on the murder in Savannah. There were only sketchy details and only from local outlets. No national media had picked up the story yet, though it was early. A picture of the girl that had died, Hailey Park, was on the page header. The name of the child that had been accused of stabbing her hadn't been released. The first line of the article read, "Fingerprints from a ten-year-old were found on the murder weapon, but the Savannah Police Department hasn't released the name of the child yet."

Kat closed her laptop, her mind wavering. If she said no to Van, she knew he wouldn't be mad. She'd arrive home probably more disappointed in herself for not taking a chance than in him for asking her to go. She leaned back in her chair, shrugging her shoulders forward, hoping to release the tension in her back. She pushed a lock of blonde hair behind her ear and reached for her phone. "I'll go," was all she wrote.

By the time Kat was packed, Stephanie, Van's assistant, had texted her flight information for the quick jaunt from New York City to Savannah. She checked the times and realized she needed to get moving. Her flight was scheduled to leave in just over three hours. With New York City traffic, she'd need every bit of it to get to the airport. She checked the room one more time to make sure she hadn't left anything behind and let the door click closed behind her.

As she rolled her suitcase through the lobby to the front desk to check out, Zara found her. "Where are you going? I thought we'd have dinner together!"

"Sorry, duty calls. Hey, have you seen Margaret?"

Zara, her eyes wide, looked across the lobby for the conference organizer, who was usually flanked by at least two assistants and a pack of people who wanted to get a word with her. "She's over there."

"Any chance you can go and snag her for me while I check out?"

"Yeah, sure."

Kat finished her checkout just in time to see Zara pushing her way through the throng and pointing to Kat while talking to Margaret. The throng moved toward Kat as she stepped away from the reservation desk. "Are you leaving us?" Margaret said, her thin lips covered by crinkled red lipstick.

"Duty calls. I'm so sorry."

"You were supposed to speak on how many more panels?" Margaret turned to one of her assistants, who was madly flipping through information.

"Three," Kat said, saving the assistant from looking.

"When we invited you to come, it was for the entire time. Our attendees will be disappointed."

Kat frowned. Guilt trips weren't her thing. Living with Van had broken her of that. "And my editor will be disappointed if I don't do my job."

"You are married to your editor."

"Which makes it even worse. Listen, I'm sorry about this. Not my intention. Sometimes stuff happens."

"I'm not sure we will be able to extend you an invitation to come next year if you leave so suddenly," Margaret said, her lips pressed together. Kat noticed her assistants made the same faces as she did.

"That's okay. I'm not a big fan of New York City anyway..." Kat walked away, her heart pounding in her chest. As much as she had tried to sound confident, she didn't feel it. She didn't like to break the rules. When she made a commitment, she really tried to stick to it. All she could do was to keep moving. Outside of the hotel, the fresh air hit her like an oven. New York City in the summer was miserable. High heat and even higher humidity. She immediately felt sweat start to form on the back of her neck even though it was well after dinnertime. The doorman hailed a cab for her, and she got in, heading for the airport.

THE FLIGHT to Savannah took just over an hour. Kat tried to sleep a little on the plane, listening to relaxing music on her headphones, but restless thoughts kept her from drifting off. Why was this story so compelling to Van? She understood that a child committing murder wasn't ordinary, but she still couldn't get a read on why he felt she needed to go. She rolled her head from side to side, trying to loosen her neck. She opened the bag of pretzels they had given her, putting a few of the stale pieces in her mouth. She'd find out soon enough.

The landing into the airport was about as different from New York City as you could get. There was barely an airport in Savannah, only a few gates. What there was of it was done impeccably, serving both Savannah and Hilton Head, South Carolina. It was clean and bright even though it was dark by the time they landed. As Kat walked through the terminal, the wheels on her suitcase clattered over marble floors. She passed posters of well-dressed people golfing and playing tennis, others showing off the historic parts of the city. The people that passed her looked like they could have been in any of the images that she saw hung on the walls. It took just a minute to get outside. As she walked out in the sultry evening air toward the rental car agency, she could smell the ocean.

Within a few minutes, she was on the road. There would be nothing to see in the dark, so Kat headed the car to the hotel that Stephanie had reserved for her.

THE NEXT MORNING dawned bright and early, the long southern days streaming light into her room before six in the morning. Kat got up and went for a quick run to get the aches out of her bones. She went back to the hotel, returned the wave from the woman manning the front desk, and went upstairs. After a shower, she sent a text to Van, not wanting to wake him up with the time difference between Georgia and California. "Heading out soon to see what I can find. I'll call later."

As she walked away, heading into the bathroom to dry her hair, her phone chirped. "Miss you. Call me with an update when you get a sec." Kat smiled. She was surprised Van was up. The time change would have put it nearly in the middle of the night at home.

After a quick breakfast in the hotel, Kat got into her rental car, a red four-door sedan, and drove into town. The first place she wanted to check was the square where the murder had taken place. She plugged in the address and started to listen to the directions, music playing in the background. The windows of the sedan were down, the ocean breeze rustling its way through the car.

Savannah was a charming city. Kat could see that after driving for just a few minutes. The city planners must keep a tight rein on development, she thought, driving past a historic railway station that now housed the visitor's center. She pulled in the parking lot and chose a spot, deciding to take a brief detour before going to Calhoun Square. The heavy wooden door was already open, a few families inside even though it was just after eight o'clock, their bright eyes glistening with vacation excitement. The building had expansive ceilings and rough brick walls. A young man in a red vest approached Kat, "Hi, welcome to Savannah. How can I help you?" he said with a drawl.

Kat looked past him at racks of brochures of things to do in the city. "I'm not sure. Do you have any historical information? Anything on Calhoun Square?"

"Certainly, right over here."

Kat followed him to a rack that was in the corner of the

room, walking carefully over uneven planked floors that she thought were probably original to the station.

"Here's a bunch of information on all of the squares in Savannah."

Kat frowned, "How many are there?"

"Roughly twenty-two," the young man said. "They were originally built to give Georgians a place to gather and sell their goods. There were even some squares that were used to train the militias."

"Really?" Kat said, her eyebrows raised. "I didn't know that."

"Yes, ma'am. You'll find a map for a walking tour if you want to take a look at them. You can also take the trolley."

Kat furrowed her brow. "How far is Calhoun Square from here?"

"About a mile, ma'am. Should take you about fifteen to twenty minutes to walk there depending on how fast you move."

Kat nodded and said thank you. By the time she headed back outside, the temperature had inched up a few degrees. It was sure to be a hot day. Kat got back in the car, turning on the air conditioning. She looked more closely at the map, unfolding it and draping it across the steering wheel. He was right. The city was dotted with squares. As she studied the map, she saw the Savannah College of Art and Design noted near where she was parked. That would be her first stop, she decided. Kat put the car in gear and pulled out of the lot, turning right and heading down the street. The college was just a few blocks down on the left, according to the map. Kat drove slowly, looking at the small shops that dotted the side of the road, offering everything from coffee to ATV rides. The mix of community and tourist life was interesting. Unlike New York City, where the tourist areas seemed to be cordoned off in certain sections, Savannah had mixed them up within the daily life of the city.

At the end of the street, Kat turned the sedan to the left and immediately saw the signs for the college on the right side of the road. She pulled off to the side to get her bearings. From the map, it looked like the buildings were dotted over a large area, like most college campuses. She looked up the college on her phone. Tapping the about page, it said that SCAD was housed on what had originally been a large plantation. She put the car in gear. Driving through the campus, she saw a few students scurrying to class, portfolios slung over their shoulders. Others carried things that looked like toolboxes. Maybe for supplies, Kat wondered? Some students walked together chatting and smiling. There were other students who stared straight ahead and moved with purpose toward their next class.

Kat sighed. Hailey Park had been one of those students. On a telephone pole near the intersection that would take her out of the campus, Kat stopped for a red light. Something caught her eye. It was a poster with flowers on the edge, the words Hailey emblazoned on the bottom of it, a picture in the center. The memorials had started already. Kat shook her head and took a deep breath, her thoughts spiraling. What had happened to Hailey? Why was she a target? Kat pushed the thoughts aside and started toward Calhoun Square.

The square was about a three-minute drive from campus. The GPS took Kat through side streets and quickly announced her arrival. Kat pulled the sedan off to the side of the road, finding a parking spot in front of a building that was now used for historic candle dipping, according to the sign. She got out of the car and looked left and right. The square wasn't enormous, not like the squares that were in places like Washington D. C. In fact, it was pretty small, maybe half an acre, with sidewalks that went around the perimeter and cut across the middle in a diagonal pattern. Much of the area was grass, but large trees drooped over the green areas, providing shade for people who had come to the square to get out of the sun. Kat started walking, not sure where Hailey's death had happened. The buildings were crowded up to the edge of the square, so close it felt like they were leaning over. In the center of the square, there was a statue of a man. Kat guessed it was Vice President Calhoun. As she turned the corner, past a pile of shrubs that had been carefully trimmed and shaped, she saw a bench ahead of her, flanked by a sign that she imagined described the historic significance of the area. On the bench were flowers.

Kat's steps quickened, realizing she had found where Hailey Park had been killed just about twenty-four hours before. She approached the bench, slowing to a stop. Whatever had happened, the day before had been washed away. There was no sign of blood, or struggle, or pain. It was as if Hailey had never stopped there to sully the Savannah square. Kat stared at the bench, taking in the wilted bunch of flowers. A brown teddy bear sat in the middle of the patch of flowers. On the ground were petals from flowers that were shedding from lack of water and the suffocating heat. Kat looked to the side of the bench, trying to imagine how Hailey had been sitting. Frustration tightened her chest. There was no way to understand what the scene had looked like without more information. Kat stood up and looked at the edges of the square, trying to imagine where the boy who had stabbed her had come from. She shook her head. The news reports hadn't revealed much information. Whether that was because it was an ongoing investigation or they had sanitized the information because of Savannah's pure reputation, Kat didn't know.

Kat stood back, folding her arms over her chest, one hand on her face, a finger crooked over her lip. What was she seeing here? There wasn't much of a story to tell, she realized, at least not based on the location. It was an open area. Literally anyone could have come up and stabbed Hailey and quickly disappeared in the crevices between the buildings that surrounded the area.

Questions started to form in Kat's mind. She started to walk, wanting to get a full sense of what the square looked like from all angles. As she moved from the scene, she glanced back, trying to get a better sense of where the bench was compared to the entry and exits from the square.

A full lap of the square only took Kat five minutes. She walked slowly, looking for any ideas that might come to her. There weren't any. It felt like a wild goose chase. Shaking her head, she walked back to the bench one more time, taking stock of what had been left there. Drooping flowers, a teddy bear, a few pictures of Hailey with people that must have been her friends. Kat picked one up, staring at it. Hailey was blonde, with long hair and brown eyes. In the picture, she had her arms around another girl, paint dabbed on their faces as though they had just finished an art class. Her smile was wide and genuine. There was no doubt she was a beautiful girl, fully of life and personality. Could that have been the motive for her murder? A jilted boyfriend? Could someone be wrong about the ten-year-old that was accused?

Kat flipped the picture over. It was blank save for a strange mark down in the corner. Kat squinted at it, wondering what it was. A circle had been drawn with several different shapes in the center. It was so small that it was hard to make out what it was. Kat turned the picture back over and shoved it in the back pocket of her jeans. Seeing what Hailey looked like sent a surge of sadness through Kat as she walked back to the car. She wondered what Hailey's life had been like, who her friends had been, what she thought of as the life left her body.

The ring of the trolley bell broke through her thoughts. The announcer started her spiel, telling the passengers all about Calhoun Square. Kat was sure she would skip the part about Hailey's murder. In some respects, she was surprised the city allowed the memorial to her. It would be interesting to see how long they let it stay.

Kat left. There was nothing else she could do without information and she didn't have any. She drove to the center of Savannah, feeling hungry. It was lunchtime and she hadn't had anything since breakfast. She parked the car and left the air conditioning running, sending another quick text to Van letting him know about the memorial. She took a picture of the image of Hailey she had found at the memorial and sent it to him. "She looks so happy," Kat typed. "No idea what happened yet."

"You'll figure it out," was the reply from Van.

Kat decided instead of texting back to call. Jack answered Van's phone. "Hi buddy, how are things?"

"Good mama. Getting ready for school. When do you come home?"

"In a couple of days, pal. How are the boys?"

"The dogs? They are good. Tyrant ate the corner of my book. I think she misses you."

Kat laughed. "Sounds like it. Can I talk to Van?"

"Sure, Mama."

A second later, Van's voice broke through the silence. "How's it going?"

"Doing fine. Not sure why I'm here. Doesn't seem to be much of a story yet."

"Thanks for checking on this one for me. What's the plan for the rest of the day?"

Kat shook her head, "I have no idea. I've got no leads and no contacts. Not sure I'm going to be able to make any progress."

"There any other media around?"

"No."

"Well, that could be good news. At least you are the only one following up. They've probably played it out already." There was a pause. "I miss you..."

"Miss you, too. It's just my horrible editor sent me to Savannah."

"Sounds like an awful guy. Come home soon, okay?"

"I will." Kat ended the call and decided to walk through the commercial district to see a little more of Savannah while she was there. Using the GPS on her phone, Kat found River Street and started walking. There were a couple of paddle boats docked to the side and a bank of buildings that had clubs and restaurants that were already open for the day. Kat walked up a hill and turned right onto East Broughton Street. Both sides of the road were filled with restaurants, stores — both local and national chains — and trinket stores. Above the stores were floors and floors of what Kat thought might be either offices or apartments. The ringing of wind chimes caught Kat's attention, and she noticed there was a small cafe on the corner. Realizing how starved she was, she went in, hoping to get some lunch.

Unlike some more touristy parts of Savannah she had seen, the cafe looked to be one that was used by locals. A small bell on the door rang when she entered. At the far end of the cafe was an order counter, the menu displayed on the wall above it. She stepped to the counter, a woman with dry wrinkles saying hello. "What can I get for you, darlin'?"

"I'll have the turkey sandwich and an order of hummus. And a coffee, too, please."

"I'll bring it to you as soon as it's done. You just go have a seat. Want some water?"

Kat nodded and walked away, choosing a booth toward the back of the cafe. The waitress came over with silverware and a napkin. "What brings you to Savannah?" she said, setting the items down on the table.

"Work."

"What kind of work?"

"I'm a journalist."

"Really? You lookin' for a story or you already have one?"

Kat sized up the waitress before answering. Though her face was wrinkled, her eyes had a sparkle to them, her black hair tied up on the top of her head. "I'm here about the art student that was murdered yesterday."

"Really? That's interesting." The waitress glanced over her shoulder. "I'll be back in a minute with your order."

Kat was grateful the waitress had moved off. She pulled the picture out of her back pocket and looked at it again. Some people might have thought she was insensitive to take Hailey's picture from the memorial, but Kat needed to see who she was writing about. Pictures like the one she had found were more helpful than the sterilized ones that the media usually put out. Kat flipped the picture over again, looking at the mark on the back of it. She tilted her head. It looked to be a tangle of letters, but she couldn't be sure. It was probably something one of the art students had done.

Just as she put the picture back in her pocket, the waitress came with her food, the sandwich so big it tilted precariously toward the edge of the plate. "I still gotta get your coffee. Be back in a minute."

Kat dug into the hummus and the sandwich, feeling better almost immediately. When the waitress brought the coffee back, she set it down in front of Kat, dropping a couple of creamers next to it. "So, which paper are you with?"

"*The Hot Sheet*. It's an online paper."

"Seriously? I read that all the time!"

Kat looked up from her sandwich, chewing. She wiped her mouth. "You do?"

"Absolutely. It's fresh. The reporting is to the point. No messing around."

Kat shook her head, "I'm glad you like it."

"They've had some good stories over the last few years. There was one about how the journalist got blackmailed for the cure for cancer. Can you believe that? Was so glad they got that guy... There was another about a church that had burned down in England."

"Yeah, I know something about those stories," Kat said, watching the woman, a surge of amusement running through her. "I wrote them."

"You're Kat Beckman? What? Right here in Savannah?"

Kat held up her hands. "Listen, it's no big deal."

"Are you kidding me? It's a huge deal. You do great work!"

"Thanks." Kat started to feel uncomfortable, as though someone had swung a giant spotlight onto her. It wasn't something she enjoyed.

The waitress, who didn't seem to be leaving any time soon, pursed her lips. "You said you are here following up on Hailey's death?"

The change in her tone caught Kat's attention. "Yeah, my editor sent me here to check it out. You know something?"

"Naw, I don't know her, but I have something better."

"What's that?"

"My brother is running the investigation. Carson Martino. If you go to the police department tell him we met. My name's Anita. He'll help you out. I'll shoot him a text to tell him to keep an eye out for you."

"Thanks, Anita. I really appreciate your help."

"No problem, sweetie. You just keep doing what you do best." Anita sauntered away, her apron swinging in front of her.

The frustration that had been dogging Kat since she landed lifted a little. At least she had a lead. It was only one, but it was better than nothing.

4

K at finished her lunch and gave Anita a wave before she left. The Savannah Police Department was her next stop. The building was low, heavily land-scaped, and clearly designed to look like part of the community. It was barely noticeable nestled into the trees except for the modest sign that was close to the corner it stood on. Kat parked the sedan in the lot and went to the front desk. "I was wondering if Detective Martino is available?"

The officer behind the desk, a tall woman with a tight bun at the back of her neck, looked her way. "Who are you?"

"My name is Kat Beckman. His sister, Anita, sent me."

The woman nodded, her long fingers pushing buttons on the phone. Kat heard her mutter a few words but couldn't make out what she said. The woman stood up, her birdlike features unfolding, "Come with me."

The door in front of Kat buzzed and Kat followed the woman, who hadn't introduced herself, toward the back of the building. Kat looked around as they walked. Like everywhere else in Savannah, the design of the department was hospitable and friendly. Warm wood desks arranged neatly in small groups flanked by pictures of historical sites in Savannah on all the walls hardly made it look like a police department.

The woman opened a door to an office. "He'll be with you in just a moment. Wait here."

Kat walked in and stood at the back of what was Carson Martino's office. It was the neatest office she had ever seen. She chuckled to herself for a moment, remembering Henry Nash's office at Scotland Yard. There were so many things jammed in it, she couldn't even sit. Detective Martino's office was exactly the opposite. The adage "everything has a place, and every place has a thing" rattled in her head. She smirked and sat down in an upholstered chair in front of Carson's desk. There was only one pile of files, a box of tissues, and a cup of pens and pencils on the surface. Kat guessed that he cleaned his own office each week, though she hadn't even met him yet. There was a two-drawer lateral file behind where his chair had been pulled in, three pictures sitting at attractive angles to each other on it. On the wall was a picture of downtown Savannah at night. Kat guessed the department had put it up long before Carson ever got the office.

"My sister said you might stop in," a low voice said, entering the room.

"Hi, yes, she said it would be okay." Kat stood up and offered her hand, "I'm Kat Beckman."

"Nice to meet you." Carson sat down at his desk, adding a file to the top of the pile. "Anita said you are following up on the death of Hailey Park."

"That's right. I'm a journalist." Kat took a moment to look at Carson. He was of average height with a stocky build. His dark hair was the same color as Anita's, though he looked to be more tan than she was. He had large square hands that took up much of the space on the desk and sharp brown eyes.

"Anita made me fully aware of your work when she called. Impressive."

Kat could hear the sarcasm in his voice. "Just doing my job. I wanted to see what's going on with the Park case."

Carson shifted in his chair. "It's an ongoing investigation. I can't really discuss it."

"Can you at least confirm that the suspect is a ten-year-old boy?"

"Listen, Ms. Beckman, I understand that you are doing your job. I invited you back to my office because of my sister, but I really can't discuss the leads we are following. You are welcome to talk to the information officer. She might be able to give you the details that you are looking for."

"Yes, I understand that you can't tell me much about what's going on. I was just hoping you could tell me a little about the scene, maybe something that you saw."

Carson stood up, "Ms. Beckman, I'm afraid this discussion is a waste of both of our times." His phone buzzed, a scowl on his face. "I'm sorry. I've got to go. Please see yourself out."

Kat walked out of his office, not feeling any better than she did when she entered. She knew nothing more than she did when she arrived. She stopped at the desk for the information officer, but he was out for the afternoon. Kat left her name and number.

Frustration filled her. Kat was ready to text Van to tell him to get her on the next plane home. She should have stayed at the conference. As she wove her way through the desks back and went out the front entrance, the humid Savannah air washing over her, she saw a couple coming out the back entrance, their arms around each other, faces pale. Carson was escorting them. Kat wheeled around, realizing they were probably Hailey Park's parents. From the reporting that had already been done, she knew that the family was from Bloomington, Illinois. Could they just be arriving now? Is that why Carson got her out of his office so fast? It was possible, she realized, depending on the flights that were available and if they had anything they had to take care of at home before they could come down. Should she wait?

Kat had just started the car and turned the air conditioning onto full blast when she saw the couple walk toward her to get to their car. She got out, her heart beating in her chest. She trotted over to them as they made their way to their waiting vehicle. "Excuse me? I'm sorry, are you the Parks?"

The man was helping his wife in the car. He looked at her with sunken eyes and said, "Yes. Can I help you?"

"My name is Kat Beckman. I'm a journalist. I'm sorry for the loss of your daughter."

Mr. Park pursed thin lips, "I'm sorry. This is an awful time for us. I don't really want to speak to a reporter."

"I can imagine. I'm a mom, too. I can't begin to know what you are going through. Listen, I left a conference in New York City because my editor thinks this is an important story. We want to get the information out so this doesn't happen again." Kat knew she was on slippery ground, "Can you at least tell me the name of your daughter's roommate? Is there anything you'd want people to know about Hailey?"

The woman spoke, her voice soft. "Sam, it's okay. Why don't you talk to her for a minute? I'll just wait here." She pulled the door closed. Kat could see her dab at her eyes with a tissue.

Sam Park held up his hands. "Just for a minute. My wife is fragile right now. We wanted to come down yesterday — we're from Illinois — but she was so fraught the doctor had to give her medication to calm her down. I can't believe Hailey is gone."

"Was she your only child?"

Sam nodded. "She was an amazing artist. Was since the time she was a little girl." He leaned against the car. "We've got no one else. The rest of our family is gone. Losing Hailey may just kill my wife..."

Kat swallowed. The line between being a journalist and a

human was blurry sometimes. "Have some faith. I know this is a horrible time for you, but you may be stronger than you think. I've had to learn that myself."

Sam Park looked at Kat, "You seem like a nice person."

"Nice for a journalist?"

He offered a weak smile. "You could say that. What would you like to know?"

"I just have two questions: what did the police tell you and where was Hailey living?"

Sam shook his head, a scowl on his face. "Apparently, they have someone in custody. A boy. They've got no idea why he'd do this. Can't tell us anything, other than Hailey died of massive blood loss." He looked away for a moment, "We are on our way to the coroner's office now. As for where Hailey was living, she had a roommate in an apartment somewhere near here. Missy Langford is the girl's name. I can give you the address."

Kat pulled a notebook out of her pocket and wrote it down. "Thank you, Mr. Park. Did you want me to follow up with you to tell you what I've found?"

"No need. Just let the police know, okay?" He turned to open the car door and doubled over, his hands on his knees, choking sobs coming from inside of him. Kat instinctively put her arm over his shoulder, sadness welling up inside of her. Her mind focused on Jack. She couldn't imagine the pain of walking in the house knowing he wouldn't be coming home ever again. The loss, the fear. It was palpable, hanging over her and Sam as he wept. "I'm sorry," he said, straightening up. "We were supposed to go to Hawaii this week for our anniversary. Now we are planning a funeral for our daughter."

Kat could barely swallow. "I can't imagine."

Sam pulled a handkerchief out of his pocket. "You said you are a mom. Please do what you can to find out what happened to our Hailey. My wife, Nora, she's never going to be the same, I'm afraid."

Kat put her hand on his shoulder, looking him square in the eye. "I will. I'll do what I can. I promise." She pulled a business card out of the back of her notebook. "Here. If you need anything, let me know."

Sam nodded and got in the car. Kat stood off to the side, her arms folded over her chest. She gave them a small wave as they pulled away.

5

W hy Anita had sent a journalist over to his office, Carson had no idea. He didn't have time to deal with reporters. He scowled. What could he say to her anyway? That his only lead was a prepubescent tween they spent all night trying to find? Carson got up from his desk. It was time to try to question the child.

Carson walked to the back of the department's building where the holding cells were. Getting the child's fingerprints off the knife had been easy. Finding him had not. A couple of officers had found him overnight, but Carson hadn't talked to him yet. The Park's were in the building. One problem at a time.

The officer on duty nodded at Carson as he approached the holding area. "Can you bring the kid into interview one?"

"Sure."

Carson went into the room and sat down, straightening his tie, setting a bag with a breakfast sandwich in it on the table. He flipped open the file in front of him. On the left side was information about the child whose fingerprints had been found on the six-inch hunting knife. Carson leafed through what they knew, which amounted to a picture and three lines of information from child services. Miles Nobesky was the child's name. The only information they had on him was that he was an orphan and had been placed with a foster family a few months before. He expected the foster family to be filing in at any minute, demanding to see Miles. Child services had been called the minute they brought him in but hadn't shown up yet. It has been hours. Carson shook his head. Legally, all he could do was make a soft pass at the kid until some adults arrived to represent him. As much as he didn't like it, that was the law.

Within a minute, the officer on duty in the holding area had Miles in the room. He looked disheveled, his hair flopping around his face. "Miles, come on in, pal. I brought you some lunch. Thought you might be hungry. They don't give a good breakfast in the back." The boy didn't make any eye contact, but he nodded. "Your foster parents are on their way in. We can talk once they get here."

Carson looked at the boy. The officers that had picked him up found him at a park near his home. His foster family had spent the night out looking for him when he didn't come home. Officers had called the house when they found him explaining he was wanted for questioning.

"Miles!" A woman burst into the room, looking disheveled, wearing leggings and a t-shirt. Her pasty face made it look like she hadn't been out of the house in months. "We have been so worried! Where have you been?"

Miles didn't look up. "Out."

A man walked in the door quietly behind the woman, "You have a curfew. We were up all night looking for you."

"So?"

Carson watched as the man clenched his fists and walked out of the room. The woman stayed, sitting in a chair next to Miles, running her hand down the back of his head. "You have no idea how scared I was. Why didn't you come home?"

"I had things to do," Miles said between bites of sandwich.

The woman sat back, her eyebrows furrowed. "You had things to do? Like what?"

Carson had the feeling that things were going to degrade if he let the foster parents talk much more. "Miles, how's the sandwich?"

"Good."

"Can you tell me about yesterday?"

"Nope."

"Were you at Calhoun Square?"

"I don't know."

Carson had the urge to pull the pictures of Hailey's dead body out of his file folder but decided against it. He didn't need the foster mom getting upset and trying to defend Miles. Instead, he pulled a picture of Hailey out that they had grabbed from her social media. "Do you know this girl?"

The foster mom leaned forward, "I'm sorry. What is this about? I thought we were here because Miles ran away last night?"

Carson sighed, "That's part of it."

"Part?"

"How about if we step outside for a minute while Miles finishes his breakfast?"

The mom followed Carson out of the room. He closed the door with a quiet click, "We haven't really had a chance to meet. I'm Detective Martino."

The foster dad, who had been sitting on a bench outside of the room got up and extended his hand, "I'm Ken McRaney. This is my wife, Barb."

"I appreciate you coming down to the station. Can I ask you, do you know this girl?"

They both peered at the picture and shook their heads no. "I'm sorry, we don't. Who is she?"

"Her name was Hailey Park. She was stabbed yesterday at Calhoun Square."

"How awful!" Barb breathed.

Ken looked at Carson, "I'm sorry. I don't understand what that has to do with us."

Carson shifted his weight and looked at them, wondering for an instant how they were going to take the news that he was about to give them. "The knife we recovered from the scene had Miles' fingerprints on it."

"What?" Ken said, staring at Carson. "That's not possible."

Carson tilted his head. "I wish it weren't, sir. Miles' fingerprints are in the system since he was placed in foster care. It's standard procedure. According to the forensics report, we've got three solid, full fingerprints that match Miles' exactly."

Barb shook her head from side to side as if she were trying to get the facts to line up in her brain. "You think Miles stabbed this girl, whoever she is?"

"It was more than a stabbing. She's dead."

Silence filled the air for a moment. Carson didn't say anything. He was waiting, watching. He'd worked enough cases over his career that he knew much of investigating was what was left in the blank spaces. What people didn't say. What they didn't do. He saw Ken look right at him and then at Barb. Carson couldn't tell by their expressions what they were thinking.

"Excuse me..." a man with a briefcase approached from behind the group. "Are you Detective Martino?"

"I am, but as you can see, I'm busy at the moment."

The man, tall and thin with a square jaw and brown hair, pushed up his glasses and extended him a business card. "I'm Alberto Soza. I'm here to represent Miles Nobesky. The foster center sent me." He turned to look at the foster parents. "You must be Ken and Barb. We should have a conversation outside. Why don't you head on out and I'll meet you in the parking lot?" He held up one finger at the parents before they walked away, "Please don't answer any questions from anyone unless I'm present, okay?" The McRaney's walked away, nodding.

Alberto fished around in his briefcase and handed Carson a sheaf of papers. "This is paperwork to get Miles released from your custody. You can see it has been signed by Judge Nicastro. That should give you enough authority to send him out with me."

Carson frowned, "We haven't even had a chance to question him."

"I'd be happy for you to question him at another time, but for now, I do need him to be released. You see, Miles is in a sensitive psychological state. There's an affidavit from his psychiatrist, Dr. Oskar Kellum, that states that keeping him at the police station could be detrimental to his mental health and long-term viability as a healthy child." Alberto leaned in closer to Carson. Carson smelled something like strong mouth-wash. He refrained from wrinkling his nose. "Miles has been through a lot. I'm sure you can imagine. Foster care is a last resort. Dr. Kellum said he's been making such great progress that we don't want to interrupt that." Alberto closed his brief-case and opened the door to the interview room, "Miles, son, it's time to go. Dr. Kellum sent me to get you. Let's go home."

Carson didn't say anything. He had the urge to ball up the papers that Alberto had given him and launch them into the closest wastebasket but didn't. "At what point can we question Miles?"

Miles had come out of the room. Alberto put a hand on his back. "Call my office and we will set up a time." He looked around, "We probably won't meet here, though. Might not be healthy for Miles." Without another word, Alberto pushed Miles forward and they disappeared among the cluster of desks and officers.

Carson stood in the same spot in stunned silence. He stared

at the business card that Alberto had pressed into his hand. Alberto Soza, Attorney at Law, Soza, Clark and McGinnis.

Lisa McAllister, another detective, walked by. "What was that?" she asked, putting one hand on the butt of her gun, resting it there.

"I have no idea. That lawyer just showed up, stuffed a bunch of paper in my hand and walks off with my suspect."

Lisa frowned. "The papers are legit?"

"Signed from Judge Nicastro. Guess the kid has some mental problems."

"Who sent him?"

"He said it was the foster center."

"Not sure I believe that."

Carson turned to look at her. He had always liked Lisa. She had joined the police department about five years before, assigned to the cold cases they had to get them closed. It was hard work, but she had earned herself a reputation as a dogged investigator. He could respect that. "Why?"

"He works for the foster care system and he wears a three-thousand-dollar suit? Just his briefcase alone is probably worth more than the amount I pay for my mortgage each month." She poked at the business card in his hand. "And, he's a partner in a law firm. One that has offices downtown. My guess? Someone is paying for his services."

Carson stared at the type on the business card, taking in what Lisa said. "The question is... who?"

6

K at was shaken. Once Hailey's parents had pulled away, she had driven back to the parking lot where the visitor's center was. It was the only familiar place she had to go, other than the hotel. Her hands gripped the wheel as she made each turn, the faces of Hailey's parents playing over and over again in her head, their ashen color, the way that Sam Park had nearly collapsed with grief.

Kat knew about grief. From the loss of her parents while she was in college, to the loss of SEALs that were the result of her giving in to a blackmailer, Kat knew what it felt like. She pulled into the parking lot by the visitor's center and took the first spot she could find. She didn't get out. She sat, her eyes closed, taking deep breaths. Seeing Sam and Nora devastated by the loss of Hailey was more than Kat could take. Images of her parent's funeral ran through her head, the way the caskets had been placed next to each other, the silence from her brother, the family members she hadn't seen in years trying to comfort her. Kat swallowed hard. Losing a child wasn't natural. The parents were supposed to go first.

Kat's mind flashed to Jack. What if she died while out on

some investigation and Jack was left alone? Her breath became shallow, her heart pounding in her chest, a couple of tears running down her face. She couldn't bear the thought of Jack losing her. She belonged at home. She reached for the gear shift, ready to put the car in reverse, drive to the hotel and get the first flight home. She stopped, watching a family pass her car, a mom and dad and two little kids circling their parents paying some version of tag. The mom and dad were laughing, holding hands and dodging their little ones. Kat wondered if Sam and Nora Park had those kinds of memories to hold onto. Certainly, the last twenty-four hours had changed that. Kat wiped her eyes and gritted her teeth. She couldn't leave Sam and Nora without answers. She needed to go home to Jack and Van knowing that she had done what she could to help them. She sighed. Whether she could find those answers, she didn't know. But she had to try.

KAT GRABBED her phone and her notebook and typed the address for Hailey's apartment into the GPS. It was a seven-minute drive from the visitor's center parking lot. Kat put the car into gear and headed out, hoping to find the answers she needed.

The apartment building, constructed of wood and stone, gave off the feeling that it was craftsman inspired. The front door, surrounded by stone, didn't feel as much like Savannah as maybe a more rustic town, but it looked attractive next to the old Georgian brick buildings. Kat looked around. There was certainly plenty of shopping, places to eat and clubs for Hailey and her roommate.

After parking her rental car in the back lot, Kat walked to the front door and buzzed the apartment from the call box by the tall wooden door. "Yes?" a girl's voice answered.

"Hi, I'm Kat Beckman. I'm a journalist. I wanted to talk to

you about your roommate if that's okay?" Kat paused, not sure if Missy would let her in. A moment later, the door vibrated. Kat pulled on the handle, surprised by its weight.

Inside, Kat took the steps to the second floor, moving down the hallway to the back of the building. The smell of fresh paint followed her. Everything about the building seemed to be new. Kat furrowed her brows. Certainly, this wasn't the lifestyle of college students, she thought. She didn't have time to follow that train of thought, though. The door to Hailey's apartment was at the end of the hall. Kat knocked.

When the door opened, Kat saw a small girl with jet black hair. "Come on in." Kat glanced around. The room was spacious, with two-story windows in the back and a picturesque view of the park behind the building. The floor was covered in stone and a few throw rugs, furniture placed carefully around the perimeter of the room.

"I'm Kat. Thanks for seeing me. You must be Missy."

"I am. You said you are a journalist?"

"Yes, from an online paper in California." Kat pulled a business card out of her notebook. "I'm so sorry about Hailey. Quite a shock, huh?"

"Yeah." Missy shifted from side to side, her hip jutting out from the side of her leggings. She pulled a tissue out of her pocket, wiping her nose and sniffling. "She was just here and then she was gone."

Kat noticed there were some boxes in the corner. "Are you packing Hailey's stuff up already?"

Missy walked into the living room, "No, that's my stuff."

"Are you moving out?"

Missy nodded. "Yeah. This place is Hailey's. She bought it. I figured the family would want me out."

Kat furrowed her eyebrows. An apartment like that had to be more than three hundred thousand dollars in an upscale market like Savannah's. How could a college kid afford that? "It's awfully nice for college kids."

"Yeah." Missy plopped down on the couch. Kat sat across from her in a leather chair. The glass coffee table in front of her was strewn with art magazines and rings left from cups.

"I just gotta ask, how did Hailey afford this? Did her parents buy it for her?"

Missy curled her legs underneath her, wiping her nose again. "No. It's so funny..." she looked out the window, "...everyone thought I was a trust fund kid." She looked straight at Kat. "I'm not. Hailey let me live here for free."

"Really? Can you tell me a little about that?" Kat retrieved her notebook as Missy started talking.

"Yeah, we met during freshman year in a drawing class. Sat right next to each other." Missy paused for a moment looking far away. She sighed. "Became friends right away. Besties. Hailey was from Illinois."

"Yeah, her parents said Bloomington."

"That's right. She got a partial art scholarship and her grandma picked up the rest of the bill until about halfway through our freshman year."

"Her parents didn't help with tuition?"

Missy shook her head. "Didn't want her to be an artist. Knew she had the talent, but man, they were not into it. Said she'd never get a job."

"You said her grandma helped with the tuition?"

"Yeah, until she died. Hailey thought she'd have to quit school and go back to Bloomington. I went there once. Nothing there. Definitely not the place for an artist."

"What kind of art did Hailey do?"

Missy pointed to an enormous canvas hanging on the wall, filled with images of children playing. The colors were alternately light and bold, the figures barely defined. It looked like they were playing in the fog. "She did oils, mostly. Liked

Expressionist artwork. That's where she found her inspiration."

"It's beautiful." Kat looked back at Missy, "So, did she sell some of her artwork to help with bills?"

Missy frowned. "Sort of. She had something going with one of the art professors, Dr. Roux."

"What kind of thing?"

Missy shook her head and crossed her legs. "I'm not really sure. All I know is that it let Hailey stay in school. Paid for everything."

"You weren't ever curious about what she was doing?"

"A little, but I've got my own stuff going. And she let me stay here free. I didn't want to pry. You know, that old 'don't look a gift horse in the mouth,' or whatever."

Kat nodded. "What's the name of the art professor again?"

"Dr. Roux. She's over in the Mannheim Building, I think."

Kat got up and headed for the door. Missy followed. "Thanks for the info, Missy. I appreciate it."

"No probs. I'll be here if you have more questions."

Kat stepped out into the wide hallway and ran down the steps, thinking about what Missy had said. How could a junior in college afford an apartment that looked like the one Hailey bought? The job she had gotten with Dr. Roux had to be lucrative, that was for sure. Kat got into the car and stopped for a moment, pulling up an online map and looking for the building Missy had mentioned, the Mannheim Building. Finding it, Kat started the car.

THE BUILDINGS on the campus of the Savannah College of Art and Design ranged from completely modern to as traditional as could be. As Kat drove, she passed one building that looked as if it had been formed from sheets of molten metal. Another looked like it could be housing Confederate soldiers. The contrast was startling. Even though it was summer term, there were students peppered across the campus, toting their art equipment to classes. She saw a few students laying on blankets in the sun, one man tossing a frisbee to a dog.

The Mannheim building was a two-story modern building, with sides of brick and a black, sloped roof. Kat guessed it had been built in the 1970s. It fit right in with the range of building styles on the campus adding to the helter-skelter design of the architecture. Kat parked and headed into the building, the air conditioning hitting her in the face like a wall as soon as she opened the door. Inside, there was a long hallway running left and right and another running down the center of the building. She smelled a faint odor of solvents probably from studio classes in the building, she guessed. A sign posted near the door had a list of professors and their offices. Kat ran her finger down the list, finding Dr. Roux second from last.

Her office was down the hallway to the right at the end of the line of name placards that dotted the hallway. A job as an art professor had to be a fairly good one, she realized. Professors would have a stable income, health insurance and probably even have time to work on their own art on the side.

As Kat reached the end of the hallway, she noticed all the office doors were closed. Dr. Abibi Roux's was no exception. Kat knocked and waited, staring at the engraved placard. "Professor of Art Technique and Mastery." There was no response, no stirring from inside. She pulled out her notebook and checked to make sure she had the right name, then knocked again. Still no response.

From the door across the hall, a young man came out, a rainbow of paint on his hands, one earbud in his ear. He slammed the door behind him, clearly unhappy, his face red. He stopped when he saw Kat, "You looking for Roux?" Kat nodded. "Next door at the installation."

"Thanks. You okay?"

The kid shook his head. "Idiot," he pointed back to the office. "Shouldn't be allowed to teach."

Kat didn't get a chance to reply. The young man marched down the hallway and out the door without looking back. She looked around and decided to go back out the way she came into the building. Outside, she realized there were two options for next door. A large plantation-style building and another, a smaller ultra-modern white stucco building that sat low to the ground. Kat headed toward the white building, hoping to find Dr. Roux there.

As soon as Kat walked into the white building, named the Glass House, she knew she was in the right place. Working as a miniature museum, the bright entryway opened up to a large room where canvases hung on the walls and pillars displayed sculptures. A student sat at a reception desk next to the front door, staring at a textbook. "Is Dr. Roux here?" Kat asked. The student nodded without answering, pointing into the exhibition space. Kat wandered forward, looking at the art and for Dr. Roux at the same time.

The space was as bright inside as it was outside. Skylights filled the room with the harsh afternoon light of a southern summer. Walls were placed strategically throughout the center of the space to move traffic through and provide wall space to hang art. The entire interior was so white that everything appeared to be glowing. Kat passed a few pieces of art that had been hung on the walls, small black plates affixed to the wall below each piece giving credit to the student. Kat passed a few more pieces, weaving her way through the space, slowing down to look at what was on display. From the back of the space, she could hear banging and voices. She walked a bit more quickly to see what was going on.

As she rounded the corner at the back of the hall, there were five students taking down art and setting up new ones, like the changing of the guard. An instructor, dressed in batik clothing of yellow, reds and oranges from head to toe stood to the side, her arms folded over her chest, her black hair piled high. "Dr. Roux?" Kat said, approaching from the side, avoiding the area where the students were working.

"Yes?" The woman turned to face Kat.

"Hi, I'm Kat Beckman. Missy Langford suggested I come and find you."

"About Hailey Park, I'm assuming?"

"That would be the case." Kat pulled out a business card and passed it to her. "I'm a journalist from California. I came to learn more about Hailey and her story."

Dr. Roux narrowed her eyes and then waved Kat forward. "Walk with me," she said, taking a few steps forward. "James, make sure this is done correctly. I'll be back to check." The words came out of her mouth deliberately, as if she were pronouncing each syllable individually. As they moved through the room, Dr. Roux looked at Kat, her black eyes unblinking, "What is your interest in Hailey?"

"Well, Missy Langford shared some information about her with me, particularly about how talented she was."

"She was indeed. Hailey had a raw, yet refined talent that was a joy to work with. It's awful what happened to her. We are all just sick about it." Dr. Roux stopped in front of a landscape scene.

"Missy also said that she thought you may have helped her when her grandmother died. Something about finding her a job so she could stay in school?"

"Before I answer that question, can I ask you one?"

"Sure."

"Why are you here, Kat Beckman? Why come the whole way from California to research this story?"

Kat felt startled at her question. Other than telling her she was doing her job, what could she say? "Well, I think it's fair to say that this story is different from so many other violent crimes. The location, the method and the accused all make it something that we think our readers can learn from."

"Learn from..." The words coming out of Dr. Roux's mouth lingered.

"Yes." Kat started to feel a little defensive. "There are lots of journalists that just take the facts and send them out. They don't look at the layers of the story. The motivations. Why things happen. That's what I do."

"Layers..."

"Like artwork," Kat suddenly felt uncomfortable, as though she was preaching to an unwilling audience. "Art has layers. It's not always what you see, but what you don't that makes a piece interesting. The same is true in journalism."

"And where did you learn this philosophy?" Dr. Roux turned to face her, her long fingers clasped in front of her.

"In the Middle East. I was embedded with the Army in Afghanistan. I was there to tell the stories of the people, not just the facts."

"A noble pursuit." Dr. Roux unclasped her fingers and sighed, "All right. I will tell you what you wish to know. Come."

Kat followed Dr. Roux toward the back of the exhibition hall again. "We can talk over here while I watch these students."

"What are they doing?"

"We are putting up new art for the show that starts tomorrow."

Kat tilted her head and looked at what had already been hung on the wall. They were large pieces of canvases, at least three feet by three feet each. Landscapes, portraits and religious scenes were included. "These look like old masters, Dr. Roux."

"Please, you may call me Abibi. They aren't old masters, per se. They are 'after' old masters."

Kat furrowed her brow. "What do you mean?"

"The task for the students exhibiting in this show was to take the work of an old master and reproduce it exactly, from the colors to the composition to the brushstrokes."

"I have to say I'd never know the difference between their work and the originals."

Abibi smiled. "That's the point. These are graduating seniors. They do this work for this show in particular because it helps them to get jobs. Not all artists need to do their own work, you see. Some of them need to be available to understand the work that was already done. We will have representatives from galleries, churches, museums and private collections come through this coming weekend to assess the talent of the students. Many of them may get job offers based on their final project."

"That's fascinating. Speaking of jobs, that brings me back to my original question. Missy Langford said that Hailey's family wasn't necessarily supportive of her art career."

"That is correct." Abibi took two steps forward, her flat sandals moving noiselessly on the white marble floor. "James, tell me what is wrong with that?"

James, a tall young man with dark hair that hung over the edge of his glasses, swung his head toward Dr. Roux and then back to the painting. There was a pause. "Sorry, it's not straight."

"Use the level, please. That's why we have it. Your eye will lie to you." Abibi looked back at Kat. "I feel as though I say the same thing over and over again to these students. One day I'm hoping they will retain the wisdom."

"I'm sure they will," Kat said, watching James fidget with the level.

"You were asking about Hailey's family?"

"Yes."

"To answer your question, no, they weren't particularly supportive of her talent. It was a shame, really. She had an incredible eye and could identify nuance in a way that just couldn't be taught. So, when she lost her grandmother, yes, I helped out."

"In what way?"

"Hailey came to me as her academic advisor. She told me that her grandmother had recently died, and she didn't have the money to continue at SCAD. She was devastated. She felt the loss of her grandmother and her dream very deeply. I offered her a way out."

Kat turned to look at Abibi directly, "And that was?"

"I gave her a job of sorts."

"Could you tell me a little about the job she had?"

"Do you remember a few minutes ago when I told you that many of our students go on to work in restoration?" Kat nodded. "I simply connected Hailey with someone I knew that would require such services." Abibi sighed. "I'm sorry, but I must cut this short. James is moving at such a slow speed that it will be next week before we get this show hung."

"Of course," Kat said. "By the way," Kat called after her, "Who was Hailey working for?" Abibi turned back, smiled over her shoulder and kept moving, her dress skimming around her ankles. Kat watched for a moment as Abibi pulled students off to the side and spoke to them quietly, almost in a whisper. She didn't answer Kat's question.

Kat left the exhibition hall wondering. She didn't have a background in art. The information that Abibi Roux gave her sent her in a direction but wasn't really concrete. Who Hailey was working for might be the thread that pulled the entire story apart.

7

A bibi Roux looked over her shoulder, waiting for the reporter to leave. "James," she beckoned him closer with long fingers and orange nail polish. "I need to make an urgent phone call. I shall return in thirty minutes. I expect perfection when I come back." James nodded, his eyes wide.

Abibi walked out of the building through the back entrance, her sandals making a quiet crunching sound on the dry grass. She used her key fob to enter the back of the Mannheim building, unlocking the door to her office. Inside, she held the knob so there would be no noise as she shut it. She didn't need any students to hound her.

The interior of Dr. Roux's office looked like a miniature art studio. In the corner were two bookshelves butted up against each other, the shelves filled with volumes of art reference books. The books were held in place by things she had collected in her travels, a replica of a prehistoric pot she purchased in Morocco, a small statue of Buddha she found in a flea market in India, and a brass compass she brought back from London. In front of the bookcases were two well-worn leather chairs and a small, round coffee table. She preferred to have comfortable seating for her students rather than the desk in between them. The college had furnished her with a wide wooden desk. On it was three neat stacks of papers, one pile things she had to grade, a stack of art history magazines and a pile of miscellaneous papers that Abibi had yet to file or throw away. In the other corner of her office was an easel, standing almost completely vertical. On the ledge of it was a pad of heavyweight white drawing paper, two pencils, a stick of vine charcoal and a kneaded eraser. She kept the pad handy in case she needed to demonstrate a concept to a student coming in for help.

Abibi stepped behind her desk and stood in front of the window, one hand holding her cell phone up to her ear, the other crossed in front of her chest. She waited as the call connected.

"Yes?" a low male voice answered the phone.

"I had a visitor today." Abibi stepped away from the window and started to pace the small space of her office, exactly four steps across.

"Who was it?"

"A reporter from California."

"Name?"

Abibi pulled the business card out of a pocket in the skirt that she wore, "Kat Beckman."

"Thank you. I'll take care of it."

The call disconnected before Abibi said any more. There wasn't much more to tell even if he had asked. Abibi went back to the window for a moment and watched a young couple walk across the quad behind her office. They were holding hands, one of them toting a large tube that looked like it could carry blueprints. The sun caught the planes of their faces. They were smiling at each other. Abibi turned away and sighed. She reached into the drawer of her desk and pulled out a tube of lipstick, running it over her lips. Smoothing the fabric of her skirt over her legs, she put the lipstick back in the drawer and sighed. It was time to go back to work.

8

The next morning dawned early and hotter than the day before. After a quick run, Kat was back in her hotel room. She had more questions than answers. She dialed Van. "Did I wake you?"

"No, I was up. Waiting for your call."

"How did you know I was going to call?"

"That's the job of a husband."

Kat smiled. She still liked it when he said the word "husband." They had only been married for a few years and it was a completely different experience than when she had been married to Jack's dad. Steve had been moody and difficult. Van was exactly the opposite.

Van's voice interrupted her thoughts, "How's the investigation going?"

"It's okay." Kat relayed to him the information she had found so far, the background on Hailey's family, the visit with the roommate, and the trip to the exhibition hall where she'd met Dr. Roux.

"Any news on the suspect?"

"Nothing yet. I did meet the detective on the case. His name is Carson Martino. I figured I'd head back to the police department this morning and see if I can trade him some information."

"That sounds like a good idea. Think he'll bite on what you have to offer?"

"I have no idea. All I can do is see."

"We've had luck with that strategy in the past."

Kat knew what Van was saying. On other investigations, Kat and Van tried to work with law enforcement, giving them all the information they had in order to get access to the full story. Something in Kat's gut told her that Carson Martino might be the exception, not the rule. "I'm gonna give it a try. No promises."

"That's all I can ask."

"I'm heading over there now. Kiss Jack for me?"

"Will do. Check in later, okay?"

"Sure." Kat ended the call and finished getting ready.

The drive to the police station took just a few minutes. Kat pulled into the same spot her rental car had occupied the day before. The same long woman was sitting at the desk. "Is Detective Martino in today?"

"I am, but I'm on my way out the door." Carson emerged from just past the first set of cubicles carrying a cup of coffee before the woman at the front desk could call him.

Carson breezed past Kat without saying anything. Kat followed him out the door. "What can I do for you?" he asked, opening the door to a blue unmarked car.

"I wanted to check in on the Hailey Park death. Any news on that?"

"You can talk to our PIO if you want an update."

From hanging around enough police departments, Kat knew PIO stood for Public Information Officer. "I'll do that, but I wanted to pass on some information I found."

Carson put his cup on the roof of his vehicle, "That is?"

Kat could tell by the tone of his voice that he was impatient to leave. "I stopped by Kat's apartment yesterday and talked to her roommate, Missy Langford."

"Yeah, I talked to her on the phone."

"Have you gone over there?" Kat knew she was taking a risk. If Carson hadn't, he'd either be irritated at the idea she was calling him out for not doing his job or he'd be curious. She hoped it was the latter.

He opened his mouth and then pursed his lips before he said, "I haven't had a chance. The Park murder isn't my only open case."

Kat held up her hands. She didn't want him to get the wrong idea. "Of course. I found something interesting."

"What would that be?"

"I'm not sure if the parents told you, but they weren't supportive of Hailey's desire to be an artist. From what her roommate said, her grandmother was paying her tuition until she died."

"So?" Carson's eyebrows knitted together.

"The apartment Hailey lived in is probably worth several hundreds of thousands of dollars. Not exactly what you'd expect for a college student."

Carson shifted his weight from one foot to another. "Meaning?"

"The place is decorated like it came out of a magazine. The roommate said that Hailey let her live there for free."

"So, what you are saying is that there might be another motive? Is that it?"

"Maybe."

"Well, maybe Hailey got an inheritance from the grandmother when she died. Who knows?" Carson checked his phone. "Listen, I appreciate the information, but I've gotta go."

Kat slipped around the side of the car as he got in. "Did you have a chance to interview the suspect? The kid?"

"No, some fancy lawyer showed up and bailed him out." Carson slammed the car door but rolled down the window. "I appreciate you coming to tell me about the apartment, but I don't think there's much of a story here. You might want to head on back to California."

The car window rolled up and Kat was left standing in the parking lot, her arms hanging limply down her sides. Another flood of frustration filled her, images of a grieving Sam and Nora Park running through her mind. They deserved to know what happened. Kat could feel there was a bigger story to be told. The question was, could she find the answers that she needed in order to bring it out into the open?

She left the police station and headed out in the red sedan. Kat drove a couple of miles, weaving through the summer tourist traffic that was in Savannah enjoying the sights. She pulled the car around the back of a small shopping area and went into a local gallery that she had found online. It was almost as white as the exhibition hall she had seen the day before when she tracked down Abibi Roux. "Excuse me," she said to the woman at the desk. "I'm just curious if you have anyone working here who knows about old master's art?"

The woman, wearing a pair of white capri pants and a yellow off-the-shoulder shirt, wrinkled her nose. "That's not very popular here. We certainly don't have anything like that."

Kat glanced around. The majority of the art in the gallery looked to be beach scenes or images of the Savannah coastline, probably painted by people who were hobby artists. There were no serious pieces of art in the gallery anywhere. "Of course. Might you know if there is another gallery somewhere that would have that information on those pieces?"

The woman frowned and pulled on her top, exposing a bit more of her overly tanned skin. "You could try the antique shop down on Fourth Street. It's a block down on the right-hand side. They might have something there. We don't sell that kinda stuff. No one wants it."

Kat nodded and left. She walked down the block, feeling frustrated. Whether there was a link to Hailey's murder and her art, Kat didn't know. It did seem strange that Dr. Roux quickly walked away when Kat had asked her who Hailey was working for. And, a child committed the murder? A chill ran down her spine as she passed a small restaurant and a shop where Savannah memorabilia was being sold. If it was true, Hailey had been killed by someone who was the same age as Jack.

Kat's thoughts floated to Jack as she walked the last half a block to the art store the woman had recommended. She tried to imagine him taking a knife and plunging it into someone. She felt a wave of nausea wash over her. Jack was certainly strong enough, even at his young age, to stab someone, but why? What could make a child commit a murder like that? She shook her head as the sign for the antique store came into focus. Kat walked to the front door, the windows dim and dirty. The words Savannah Art and Antiques were painted in script on the front door in gold paint. There was a small sign, a clock with moving hands, that said that they would return in an hour. She put her hands up to the glass, covering the sides of her face so she could see in.

From her spot on the outside of the store, Kat couldn't see much. Shelves with items rescued from someone's home or estate sale crowded every surface of the store. A few pieces of art hung on the walls in gilded gold frames. It was impossible to tell from the street what they looked like. Kat stepped back, ready to leave when a voice stammered, "Are you looking for something in particular?"

Behind her, holding a large ring of keys stood a small man. He wore wrinkled khaki pants and a short-sleeved plaid shirt with a light blue vest over top. His hair was gray with streaks of black, wiry and wild, a pair of small glasses perched on his nose. The keys jingled as he unlocked the door, their song met by the chiming of clocks that were set to sound on the hour.

"I'm looking for someone who knows something about old master's art."

The man walked into the store without a word. Kat followed.

The scent of old things filled Kat's nostrils, reminding her of how her grandparent's basement had smelled when she was a child. What made that odor, she wasn't sure. She glanced around at the stacked shelves. Lives had been lived in front of the things that were in the store — babies being born, families losing a loved one, the tragedy of war, and the comfort of peace. If only the items could talk, Kat thought.

The man walked behind a glass-topped case that served as the counter, thumbing through some papers that were stacked at the corner. "You said you are looking for someone who knows a bit about old master's art. What exactly are you looking for?"

"I'm doing some research on the art world, but I don't have a background in it. The lady down the street at the other gallery said she thought you might be able to help." A knot formed in Kat's stomach. She braced herself. It seemed that at every turn someone said no to her, wanting to keep their information to themselves. Savannah was a town of secrets.

"Which gallery did you go to?"

"The one over on Sandstone. They had a lot of beach scenes on the walls."

"Yes, I know this gallery."

Kat hadn't noticed before, but the man had an accent. It sounded like he was from somewhere in Europe, but Kat couldn't figure out where. She tried to prod him on by adding, "The lady wasn't too interested in old art, or too friendly for that matter. She seemed to only have more modern items."

The man looked up from the stack of papers he'd been looking at. He blinked several times and pushed the glasses up on his nose. "Why do you have an interest in old art?"

Kat sighed. Where this was going, she didn't know, but she wondered if she was wasting her time. "I'm investigating the murder of Hailey Park."

"Yes, yes. The art student from SCAD."

Kat nodded. "That's right. It turns out she was incredibly talented in replicating old master's art. I think part of the story is about her art, but I don't know enough in order to understand that."

The man nodded. "Come to my office. I'll make tea and you can tell me what you know."

Kat followed, leery about going with a man she didn't know into the back of an empty store. A lump formed in her throat as she followed him behind a red velvet curtain that separated the showroom from the office.

The back offices of the antique shop were nearly as crowded as the display area. There was a row of shelves and several filing cabinets jammed up against the back wall, a small red sign that said exit glowing in the darkness above a metal door and a desk. The man turned on several lamps, the click of their knobs bringing the room into focus. Against the wall to the left was a small cabinet, a sink and a counter. There was a hot plate plugged in. The man ran water into an old tea kettle and set it on the hot plate that started glowing red. A folding table draped with a tattered tablecloth covered in yellow fruits was in front of her. "Here, sit," the man said, clearing a pile of papers from the chair that was closest to the front of the store.

Kat sat down, unsure what else to do. "I'm sorry. I didn't catch your name."

The man turned from the tea kettle, his movement slow and deliberate. "I am Eli. Eli Langster." He pulled two mugs out of a metal cabinet that had been attached to the wall, dropping tea bags in each of them. "And you are?"

"Kat Beckman."

"It's nice to meet you, Kat Beckman. Where are you from?"

"California."

Eli raised bushy eyebrows above the rims of his glasses. "California? That's a long way to come for a simple story of murder."

Kat tilted her head. "I was in New York for a conference when Hailey was killed. My editor asked me to come and take a look."

Eli nodded ever so slightly. The tea kettle started to whistle. Eli poured the water over the tea bag and moved the mugs to the table setting one in front of Kat. "Sugar? Honey?"

"No, thank you."

Eli turned away, putting honey in his own tea, "Suit yourself."

Kat's nervousness had turned into curiosity. Who was this man that had offered her tea? "Can you tell me a bit about your store?"

"There's not much to tell. My own father started it in the 1950s. Came here from Europe. Thought the people living here would like antiques for their homes. He was right. It's not the same anymore, though." He stirred his tea, the spoon making a tapping noise on the inside of the cup. He looked up at her. "How can I help, Ms. Beckman?"

"I think there is more to the story of Hailey's death. I don't know why. It's just a feeling right now except for one thing."

"And what is that one thing?"

"Hailey seemed to have some sort of side job that earned her a lot of money, or at least that's what I think."

Eli raised his eyebrows. "You think this is more than just a random killing?"

"I don't know Mr. Langster..."

"Please, call me Eli."

She nodded. "I'm not sure. I have a ten-year-old son. I can't imagine him stabbing someone to death. There's that, too. And the detective I talked to said they haven't even had a chance to interview him. He got bailed out right away by some fancy attorney."

Eli tsked. "People these days think that any attorney can get them out of trouble." He looked at Kat, "What you are telling me is that things are not adding up."

"That's right." Kat felt a sense of relief cover her. All of the frustration she'd been feeling had come out. "There are all of these pieces. They don't fit together."

Eli smiled. "And you are someone who likes to have them fit together..."

9

D r. Oskar Kellum opened his office door to see yet another child sitting and waiting for him. The woman sitting next to the child gave him a curt nod, "Miles, come on in."

The child stood up and walked into Oskar's office, quickly finding a seat on the couch, his feet barely touching the floor. Oskar watched him for a minute from the padded chair behind his desk. The child seemed to be the same as he had been for the last two years he had been treating him. Quiet, sullen, introverted. Oskar picked up a notebook and a file from his desk.

Oskar's office was like many other psychiatrist's offices. A desk, a few comfy chairs and a couch, a box of tissues. The light from outside streamed in through a privacy curtain so that no one could accuse him of violating his client's rights. He sat in silence, waiting on Miles.

Miles had come to him having problems adapting to his foster parent's home. His file from the Department of Child and Family Services of Georgia was fairly complete, thick with documentation. He'd been abandoned at the age of three after being abused by a sometimes-present boyfriend of his mother, who was mostly strung out on some combination of opioids and alcohol. The child protective workers found him hiding in a closet, holding a dirty blanket, humming to himself the night he'd been taken from his mother, who had overdosed once again. She barely said goodbye to him when she'd been taken to the hospital. He'd never seen her again.

After a few rocky placements, he'd found a home with a pair of foster parents who were concerned for his mental state. They'd come to Dr. Kellum at the recommendation of their pediatrician, who was concerned that there was some underlying mental illness that had been triggered by Miles' start to life. The pediatrician was right.

Initial testing and conversations with Miles were difficult. Dr. Kellum had tried everything from art therapy to bringing in a service dog. Miles finally opened up when they read a book together. Words were still fewer than normal, but Miles had managed to make a few friends at school and was doing better at home. Dr. Kellum knew that he'd never be what anyone considered normal, though.

"Miles, tell me about the last few days. Your mom said things have been busy."

"Foster mom."

"Yes, of course. Foster mom. I heard you had a visit to the police station?"

Miles nodded, staring at his hands. They were clasped together, knuckles alternately white and blood-red as he gripped and ungripped his hands. "They were nice."

"Why did you go there?"

Miles looked at Dr. Kellum and blinked, a wash of confusion over his face. "I'm not sure," he stammered. "I don't remember."

Dr. Kellum crossed his legs, a feeling of relief relaxing his entire body. He didn't remember. That was good. "That's okay,

Miles. No one remembers everything. Can you at least tell me about your trip to the park with your friends?"

Miles turned his head toward the window, "I went there with a couple of other boys from school. Foster mom said I could go to play basketball, but I had to be home on time."

"What happened then?"

"We played. I got a basket."

"That's good. Did you have fun?"

"Yes."

"Then what happened?"

"We walked to Calhoun Square. We still had the basketball with us."

"Is there a court there?"

"No, we were just bouncing it around."

"Then what happened."

Miles looked back at Dr. Kellum, his eyes vacant, his brows furrowed. "I'm not sure. The next thing I remember is that I was home."

Oskar leaned back in his chair, pulling his notes closer to him. "What's the first thing you remember after you got home?"

"Foster mom told me to go take a shower." Miles shook his head. "I'm sorry."

"Why are you sorry, Miles?"

"Because I don't remember."

"Are you worried I'll be mad?"

Miles glanced up from under his bangs and nodded.

Oskar made a few notes on the pad of paper in front of him and looked at Miles. "I'm not mad. I'm not mad at all. In fact, I think you've made great progress."

THE REST OF THE SESSION, Oskar spent time with Miles playing one of his favorite card games. Keeping his hands busy seemed to unlock the words in his head. Oskar glanced at him. There weren't many to be found, that was for sure. Because of the way that Miles had been abused, it was almost as if a part of him had been locked away when he was in the closet. Even with all of his years of experience, Oskar wasn't sure he could find a way to help Miles get out.

At the end of their time together, Oskar called Miles' foster mom into the room. "We've had a good session today," he announced, touching Miles on the shoulder. Miles winced.

Miles' foster mom, a round woman named Barb, whispered, "Did you figure out what happened at Calhoun Square?"

"I don't know how his fingerprints ended up on the knife, but he certainly didn't do anything. Based on what I know of him, he's not capable of violence. The police will have to dig a little deeper."

Barb relaxed but didn't say anymore. "Same time next week?"

Oskar nodded. "See you then."

As soon as Miles and Barb had left the office, Oskar's next patient walked in. Oskar told him to take a seat, "I'll be with you in a moment. Just need to make a couple of notes before I forget."

Oskar closed the door to his office, picking up the cards he and Miles had been playing. He put them back on his desk and grabbed his cell phone. It only took a moment for the call to connect. "Yes?" a voice on the other end answered.

"It worked."

"Does he have any memories?"

"No."

"How long is the gap?"

"From just before until he got home." Oskar hoped the man at the other end of the line would understand what he was saying.

"I understand. Thank you."

The call ended without any other conversation. Oskar let out a deep breath, as though he'd been holding it in for weeks. That was how he felt. He wiped his glasses with the hem of his shirt, took a sip of water, and tucked his shirt back into place. Scanning the office, he realized he'd left Miles' file on his chair. He quickly picked it up and put it in a locked drawer in his desk, not in the filing cabinet that flanked the back of the office with the rest of the patient files. He'd have to remember to take it home, though he had another copy there, just in case.

"Come on in," he said to the young girl waiting for him as he opened the door. "How are you today...?"

10

A fter two cups of tea, Eli agreed. He needed to see Hailey's work in order to help Kat. Eli stood up, took the two cups and put them in the sink. "One moment, please." From the front of the store, Kat could hear the front door locking again. "We will go out the back door," Eli said, suddenly moving much faster than he looked like he was capable.

Kat followed Eli out the back and into the hot summer sun. "You can ride with me if you'd like," Kat said. Eli nodded.

As they got in the car, Kat sent a quick text to Van telling her that she had met someone who might be able to help. She sent Eli's name and the name of his shop along to Van just in case. Eli didn't seem like a threat, but Kat had learned that even people that didn't seem like a threat could be.

Over tea, Eli had shared with Kat that in addition to owning an art store, he was an art historian. In his early years, he'd gone to college and gotten his undergraduate degree in art and then gone on to get his master's degree in art history from Columbia University. He smiled when he said it, his thin lips pulling back from the corners of his mouth, "Not that I've had the career my father wanted for me. He wanted me to work for a museum and use our gallery to procure pieces. Sadly, that didn't happen."

Kat interrupted, "I want to take you to Hailey's apartment." At a red light, Kat found the number Missy had given her and sent her a quick text. Before the light had changed, Missy had replied, saying she was home, and they were welcome. "She already replied. Gotta love those college kids and their phones."

Eli smiled. "I'm quite old school myself, but in this case, I'm happy about it."

They drove in silence over to Hailey's apartment. Kat could tell Eli wasn't much of a talker. He had settled into the passenger seat of her rented red sedan and simply sat with his hands folded in his lap staring straight ahead. That was fine with Kat. Fatigue crawled through her body. Leaving the conference and going straight to Savannah, running down leads as she found them had left her tired. Probably more mentally tired than physically, she realized.

Once they got to Hailey's apartment complex, Kat buzzed the front door and told Eli to head up the steps. She walked behind him as he took each step carefully, setting one foot at a time on the treads. At the top of the steps, he fell in behind her. The door to the apartment was cracked open. "Missy?" Kat called, pushing the door lightly until it barely moved.

"Come on in," a shout from the back of the apartment answered.

Kat opened the door. Eli followed. She heard him murmur under his breath, "Well, now." Before Kat could ask Eli what he meant, Missy padded out from the back of the apartment.

"Hi, again."

Kat nodded. "Missy, this is Eli. He's an art expert. He wanted to see some of Hailey's work if that's okay with you."

"Yeah sure. Let me show you her bedroom. I can't get into

her studio though." Kat chewed her lip, but she didn't ask what Missy meant. They followed Missy down a short hallway. "This place has three bedrooms. I've got one, Hailey had one and she used the other for her studio."

Kat stepped around a stack of boxes pushed against the wall as they walked down the hallway. It looked like Missy's art was displayed on those walls. There were framed drawings that were highly geometric in nature, almost like fractals. Looking carefully Kat could see the image of a woman in one.

"Here's Hailey's room and there's her studio. As I said, I don't have the key." Kat saw a room at the end of the hallway that had a padlock on the door.

Eli sniffed. "Would it be all right if I had a friend of mine come over to assist us in getting the door open?"

Missy frowned, "You mean like break-in?"

"Not quite. He's particularly good with locks."

Missy tilted her head. "I guess that would be okay. Hailey had some of my supplies in there for a piece she was working on. I need to get them, anyway."

Without saying another word, Eli stepped away from Kat and Missy. Kat watched him. He pulled an old flip phone out of a pocket of his loose khaki pants. He put the phone up to his ear and a minute later he put the phone back in his pocket. "My friend is on a job. He'll be here as soon as possible."

Missy nodded. "Stay as long as you like. I've gotta pack. There's food in the kitchen if you get hungry."

Kat pointed to Hailey's room. "Why don't we take a look in here first. Maybe we'll find something that will let us know who she was working for?"

Eli nodded and followed Kat.

Hailey's room was spacious with large windows facing the park, just like the great room. She had a queen-sized bed pushed up against the wall and a nightstand with a tall lamp next to it. Kat walked over to the nightstand. It was covered with books, some novels and some magazines on art. Leaning up against the wall was a pile of canvases. Eli was looking at them one-by-one. "What do you think, Eli?"

He pursed his lips, "I'm not sure. She's definitely into oils. On some of these, she looks like she was practicing her brushwork." He stopped for a moment. "That's strange."

"What?" Kat leaned over to see what he was looking at as he pulled one of the canvases out of the pile. It was a still life of a bowl of fruit. In the middle of the painting, there was a blank spot, as though the paint had been erased.

Eli pointed, "See that spot right there?"

Kat nodded.

"It looks like Hailey was practicing removing oils from the canvas." He picked up the picture and walked over to the window. Kat followed. "Oh yes, just what I thought."

"Did you find something else?" Kat leaned closer, her eyes searching the canvas.

"See right there?" Eli pointed to the section of the painting in the upper left-hand side. "See how the paint is dull?"

Kat tilted her head. She could see how the paint had lost some of its luster. "How would that happen?"

"It looks like Hailey was practicing removing varnish from oil paints." Eli set the canvas down. "Was she doing this for class, perhaps?"

"I don't know."

"Well, in any case, she was working on not only putting oils on canvas but taking them off."

Kat rolled her head from side to side, trying to get the tension out of her neck. She thought back to her conversation with Dr. Abibi Roux. "I spoke to one of her professors. She told me that many of the students are hired by museums, churches, or private collections. Could that be why she was practicing?"

"Maybe. You mentioned she had a side job?"

Kat thought back to how cagey Dr. Roux had been when she asked who Hailey was working for. She didn't answer the question. Kat shook her head, "I don't know for sure that she did have a side job. Her professor didn't answer me when I asked."

"Surprising."

"Why?"

Eli shrugged his shoulders. "Most people in the art world are more than happy to talk about their accomplishments. Being associated with someone who is successful is almost as good as being successful yourself." He offered a weak smile and looked back at the canvas that he had found. He shook his head. "This almost looks like a painting by Floris van Schooten. He was a Dutch painter from the 1500s if I remember right." Eli leaned over and flipped the canvases toward him, leaning them against his knees so he could look at the next one. His brow furrowed, "In fact, a lot of them do."

"Hello?" Kat heard a male voice call into the apartment. "Eli Langster, are you here?"

"Ya, Niels. We are in here."

Kat followed Eli out of Hailey's room. Coming down the hallway was a tall stringy man. His hair hung down to his shoulders and looked like it hadn't been washed in quite a while. He had on saggy beige joggers, slip on beige shoes and a beige t-shirt. With the dirty blonde of his hair, he was nearly one color from head to toe.

"Niels, thank you for coming."

"Happy to help, Eli. What's going on?"

Eli looked at Kat, extending his hand toward her, "Niels, this is Kat Beckman. She's a journalist from California working on the Hailey Park case."

"Hailey Park, the art student?" Niels looked Kat up and down, "You don't look like you are from California," he said with a thick European accent.

"Really?" Kat tilted her head at him, "And, what do people from California look like?"

Eli quickly jumped in the middle of the conversation, "I'm sorry, Kat. My friend has lost

his manners. Niels, let's stick to the work at hand. Chit chat gets you in trouble."

The two men walked down the hall. Kat could smell the wake of cologne coming off of Niels. Eli pointed to the padlock. "We need to get in here. Can you open it?"

"Ya," Niels said, lifting the lock. "I'll get my kit from the car." Niels walked back down the hall, his body slumping side to side with each step.

Eli pursed his lips, "My apologies, Kat," he said, pushing his glasses up on his nose. "Niels is a bit rough, you might say."

"I've dealt with worse, Eli. Don't worry about it." Kat looked down the hall and then back at Eli. She smiled, "What's his story, anyway?"

"Niels? His name is Niels von Hammond. He came here from Holland about ten years ago. Got into some trouble and spent a couple years in jail. He helps me with projects from time to time."

The fact that straight-laced Eli Langster hung around with someone like Niels von Hammond struck Kat as strange. Eli seemed so restrained in everything he did, so careful, that it was hard for Kat to reconcile the fact that someone he worked with was an ex-con. Interesting, she thought. Maybe there was more to Eli than it seemed.

Within a minute, Niels was back with a small bag of tools. Out of it, he pulled a flashlight and a set of small picks. "Hold this, will you?" he handed Kat the flashlight. Kat shone it on the bottom of the lock. Niels inserted two picks in the slot where the key should go. He turned the picks and moved them into position. As he twisted, the lock fell open.

"What are you doing?" Missy called.

Kat looked back down the hallway. Missy was standing in the doorway of her bedroom holding a pile of clothes. "Just getting the lock open. You said it was okay, right?"

"Yeah." She looked at Niels. "Who are you?"

"Niels."

Missy nodded and walked away before Niels finished. Kat stared after her in part wondering why she'd let three strangers into her house to rifle through her roommate's things. She shook her head. College kids.

Kat heard a pop. Niels took the lock off the door and pulled the flange apart. As he turned the knob and opened the door, sunlight flooded down the hallway. Kat peered in, following them in.

The room must have been what was originally designed to be the master bedroom. It was spacious, with high ceilings and exposed brick that went from floor to ceiling. Natural light poured into the room. To one side there was a set of doors. Kat walked over and looked inside. A full bathroom with a walk-in shower and tub flowed right off the space. The floors in the bedroom were wood and looked to be reclaimed from an older structure. In the center of the room was the largest easel Kat had ever seen. On the wall behind her were two large shelving units, filled with art supplies, brushes, large containers of paint, and even a box with rags and gloves. A portable fan stood tall in the corner near the window. It was running at low speed, the blades barely moving. In the corner of the room, a wash sink had been installed. On the edge were three brushes that looked like they had been set there to dry. Eli and Niels had gone to the far wall of the room, where there were more canvases leaning against the wall. As she walked over, Kat realized there had to be thirty of them, some of them larger than others, but mostly about four feet by four feet. Hailey had certainly liked her large-format works, that was for sure.

"Interesting, very interesting," Eli said, looking through the canvases. While Kat had been investigating the room, Eli had been focused on the art piled in the corner.

"What do you mean?"

"Well, every piece of art I've found is the replica of an old master. If they weren't sitting in this apartment, I'd have a hard time figuring out whether they were real or a duplicate."

Kat frowned and leaned over, looking at the canvases. "They are that good?"

Eli nodded. "They are."

Missy stood in the doorway. "Oh, you guys got in. Good. I just need my brushes and pencils." She reached over onto the shelf where the supplies were and took what she needed. She left Eli, Kat and Niels still looking at the paintings.

"Eli," Kat looked right at him, seeing the smudges on his glasses, "Could this be what she was selling? Could this be the side job that kept her at school?"

Eli pressed his lips together and nodded. "Indeed."

KAT TOOK a few pictures of the room and the artwork and followed Eli and Niels out. Kat called to Missy, "Thanks. We left the room unlocked for you."

Missy came out of her room again, staring at them. "Is that it?"

"Yes."

"Okay." Missy turned away from them and walked back down the hallway.

Kat closed the door behind her as they left. Outside, Niels wandered away without so much as a goodbye. Eli got back in the car with Kat. "You can just drop me off at the front door." He looked at an old-fashioned watch on his wrist. "My wife will be expecting me for dinner soon."

"Do you want me to drive you home?"

"No. I'd prefer to walk."

Kat hadn't realized the time until Eli had mentioned dinner. Just getting the door open and finding the art in Hailey's apartment had taken up the entire afternoon. As she pulled up to the front of the shop, Kat looked at Eli. "Thanks for helping out today."

"Certainly. Stop back if you need more information. That was quite interesting." Eli got out of the car, muttering to himself as he walked away.

Kat pulled away from the curb and headed to her hotel. She needed time to think.

11

D r. Oskar Kellum left work at precisely seven o'clock every night. His last patient was always at six o'clock. With his psychiatry sessions running exactly fifty minutes, that meant he had ten minutes to close the office and start his drive home.

The evening was humid and hazy. Parking in Savannah was challenging, so he typically left his blue Mercedes down the street in a municipal parking lot, leaving another spot open in the parking lot for his building that his patients could use. As he walked, he thought back on the day. He'd seen six patients, renewed prescriptions for four of them, and did an intake on one new patient. As he shifted his briefcase from one hand to the other, his mind drifted to Miles.

There was no doubt in Oskar's mind that Miles had the makings of a psychopath. His mind had been so injured as a child that Oskar doubted that he would ever be much of a functioning adult. He'd likely just barely get through school and take a low-paying job at a store somewhere. Relationships would be nearly impossible for him and the urge to express his psychopathology would haunt him. Oskar hadn't seen a lot of cases like Miles' in his career, mostly working with kids who had depression, suicidal ideation, or even anxiety. A true psychopath wasn't something that many psychiatrists dealt with except in cases of incarceration.

Oskar turned the corner to get to his car. He had taken the long way today, wanting to get some fresh air. The medication cocktail that he had prescribed for Miles had worked exactly the way he thought. There were two parts to the plan — the short term medication that Oskar had used for the last three months in the office with Miles that left him suggestible and with a case of memory loss and the change in dosage he had prescribed in his daily medication just last week. While he seemed to be mild-mannered enough every time Oskar saw him, his foster mom and the reports from child and family services told another tale. Miles was easy to deal with unless he was challenged. If he felt threatened in any way, he became like a wild animal. His efforts to survive at a young age had begun to turn. Instead of just isolating himself and withdrawing, his mind had become aggressive. Barb, his foster mom, had confided to Oskar that she was becoming afraid of him.

Oskar got into the deep blue Mercedes coupe and started it up with one touch to the button, feeling the surge of cool air coming out of the cabin's ventilation system. He put the car in gear and pulled out, away from the parking lot, driving down the street. He decided to take the riverfront back to his condominium. There was no hurry to get home. There was no one waiting except for his cat, Ralph. Ralph had been his father's name.

As he passed the riverfront, he saw couples walking to dinner. It was dusky now, the shadows long on the sidewalks. Each restaurant's front window glowed with celebratory lights even though it was the middle of the week. That was normal for Savannah with the tourist vibe. Oskar had no desire to join in what other people thought to be fun. All he wanted to do was go home, make a proper cup of tea using his mother's finest teapot and the spiced loose tea he found online at a specialty shop.

Behind him, the traffic merged and swayed, cars jockeying for position as they got to the stoplights. Out of the corner of his eye, he saw a black SUV cutting it a little close. He gripped the wheel and jerked the car into the other lane. As soon as he did, he heard a popping noise and felt the car jolt. The front end of the Mercedes, normally highly responsive, was sluggish. It felt like he had a flat tire. He turned up an alleyway to get off the congested road, frustrated. All he wanted was his cup of tea.

Oskar threw the Mercedes into park and jumped out, anger flowing through him at what he expected would be nothing short of a long inconvenience. His mind was already racing ahead to tow trucks and the inevitable delay in getting home. As he stared down at the left front tire, he saw that it was beyond totally flat. It was shredded. He looked back at the street corner and saw a metal strip with tacks on it, a man wearing a baseball cap leaning over to pick it up and move it off the street. So worried about his tires, Oskar never saw the second man behind him.

A hand clamped over his mouth and pulled him backward. Oskar struggled, mostly because he felt like he was going to fall backward, his arms and legs flailing, fear surging through his body. His eyes were wide, his heart pumping at near double the rate it normally did. He couldn't breathe. As the hands pulled him into the building next to the alleyway, he saw a man get into the Mercedes and drive off. Oskar was sure the rims of his precious sedan would be dented and destroyed.

The person behind him slammed him down in a chair in the middle of the room. Another set of hands, from where he wasn't sure, held him to the chair and taped his wrists and ankles. "Wait! What is this? I don't have any money!" he protested. The two men said nothing, just putting another line of tape across his mouth. They walked away, leaving him in the dusky darkness of the building.

Terror ripped through Oskar's chest, cold sweat forming on his brow. His chest was tight. He felt like he could hardly breathe. He was alone. He tried to access the rational part of his brain, forcing himself to take long, deep breaths out of his nose. The pounding of his heart hardly responded. He felt the sweat run down the back of his neck and onto his collar. It itched. His guts were churning. Nausea flooded over him. He looked every direction, trying to calm down, though he knew with his own weak constitution, that would be a futile effort. His mother had always told him he was weak. At that moment, he knew she was right.

After a few minutes, Oskar was able to slow his breathing, his vision broadening. The building he was in looked abandoned. Dust and dirt on the floor could have been there for a decade or more. The space was open, two stories of the skeleton of a building. Oskar guessed there had been some sort of manufacturing operation where he now sat. He grunted and mumbled, hoping someone would come and free him.

"You've calmed down a bit now, Oskar?" a man in a baseball cap walked toward him out of the darkness. Another man followed. Oskar guessed the second man was the one that pulled him into the building. Baseball hat leaned over and tugged at the tape on his mouth. "If you make any noise, other than answering our questions, I'll put this right back on. You understand?"

Oskar nodded.

Baseball hat pulled the tape off of Oskar's mouth, the adhesive stinging as it separated from his skin. "What do you want?" The question had slipped out of Oskar's mouth faster than he could hold it in. Before the words even formed for him to apologize, he felt a fist connect with his face, his head twisting violently to the right. He felt dizzy, tasted blood in his mouth.

"I think we've made our policy clear. Do you understand?"

Oskar nodded, pain surging in his head.

Baseball hat knelt down in front of Oskar. "This will go more smoothly if you just answer our questions. Then you can go home and do whatever you want to do, okay?"

Oskar nodded again, licking the blood from his lip.

"The boy. Remember the boy?"

Oskar nodded.

"What does he remember?"

"Nothing."

Another fist crashed into Oskar's face shattering his nose, blood streaming down his face.

Baseball hat said, "It's important that you are truthful with us, Oskar."

Oskar gagged from the stream of blood running down his throat. "I am. Why would I lie?"

Baseball hat stood up and started to pace, "Oh, I don't know, maybe so we don't keep beating you?"

"No, really. You can check the notes in my office. The medication worked perfectly. Miles doesn't remember what happened. He's got no idea that he stabbed that girl. No idea at all."

A fist slammed into Oskar's stomach. He felt his ribs crack. He started to wheeze. "Please stop. I'm telling the truth."

"Who else knows about this, Oskar? Who else have you told?"

"No one. All of the notes are secured. No one will look for them, I promise."

"Where did you hide them?"

"In my desk," Oskar dropped his head, unable to keep it up. There was a copy at his condo, too, but he didn't say that.

Baseball hat started to laugh, "In your desk? Like no one

would ever look in your desk for paperwork, right?" He looked at the man that was delivering the punches, "The stupidest thing I've ever heard. The boss isn't going to be happy."

"But I've done everything you asked!"

Baseball hat came close and grabbed him by the shirt collar with one fist. "Not quite, Oskar. Remember the eighty thousand dollars you owe us? Did you forget about that?"

MEMORIES OF SITTING at the poker table flooded his mind. A friend from his golf club had invited him to join in the fun one Friday night. Not that sociable, Oskar decided to push out of his comfort zone — how could he not, when it was advice he gave to his patients all the time? He popped an Ativan to keep him calm and went. It was in the backroom of a restaurant that he enjoyed, so he figured it would be good fun.

That night he won. It was the last time.

He'd kept going to the poker tables, hoping for better luck. The man who ran the game, Steven Smith, or at least that was what he called himself, was more than gracious for a few weeks. But, as Oskar lost more and more, Mr. Smith became impatient. One night Mr. Smith and one of his men showed up at Oskar's office as he was leaving.

"I need a favor, Oskar."

"I'd be happy to talk to you, but I don't have time right now."

"Yes, you do."

Mr. Smith, wearing a tangerine short-sleeved shirt, white pressed shorts and loafers, settled into one of Oskar's chairs and crossed his legs. "You owe me a lot of money."

"Yes, I do. I'm sorry. I'll pay you back. I have a new contract coming in..."

"I have another way that you can help."

"What's that?" Oskar sat down, tightness in his chest, unsure of what Mr. Smith might say.

"There's a threat to a colleague of mine. I need to have someone taken care of. It has to be discreet. Think you can help?"

"I can't murder someone! Are you crazy?" Oskar shot up out of his seat, fear ripping through him. He wondered if they would kill him for saying that.

"Relax, doc. We don't need you to kill anyone. We just need you to prime the pump, if you know what I mean."

Oskar sat back down, feeling faint. "What are you asking me to do?"

Mr. Smith stared at his hands, "I'd like you to motivate one of your patients to help. You don't have to do the killing. That's good news, right?"

Oskar could barely breathe. "How would I do that?" He looked at Mr. Smith, who seemed to be perfectly relaxed and wondered how many of these negotiations he had done. Oskar knew it wasn't really a negotiation, though. "I have no idea how to do that! I, I've never done this before. Nothing like it!" Oskar got up again and started to pace.

"Sit down, Oskar." Mr. Smith said, his tone turning serious. "Here's the reality. Unless you want to take out a home equity loan on that pathetic little condo you have with your cat..."

"How do you know about that?" Oskar plopped back down onto the nearest chair.

"You owe me a lot of money. The number gets bigger each and every day that you don't pay me. What I'm offering you is a way to get rid of the whole debt in one fell swoop. That would be good, right?"

Oskar nodded.

"I'm going to call you in twenty-four hours. When I call you, you are going to tell me which one of your patients you are going to use and how you are going to do it"

"Even if I know, it could take months."

"I realize that. That's why I'm coming to you now." Mr. Smith stood up and held up his hands, "See, I'm a reasonable person, Oskar. I'll call you tomorrow."

THAT NIGHT, Oskar didn't sleep. He canceled all of his appointments the following day and spent the time blockaded in his office going through files and research. Choosing a patient to do what Mr. Smith said was preposterous. But after calling his bank, he realized he had no choice. Even if he could get a loan, he knew Mr. Smith would insist that Oskar do what he'd asked. He dug through pharmaceutical books and tried to determine what drugs he could use to make a child suggestible and violent at the same time.

At the end of the day, Oskar had narrowed his choices down to two kids: Miles and a teenager named Samson. Both had tendencies that Oskar had helped them to control. Miles was clearly psychopathic after his abuse. Samson had gotten in more fights at school than anyone Oskar had ever worked with.

The call came in at precisely six o'clock. "Oskar, what did you decide?"

"I, ahhh," Oskar started to stammer.

"I need to know you've made a decision."

Oskar didn't know what to say. He couldn't predict whether the child he chose would be capable of doing what Mr. Smith wanted. He also knew that if he didn't choose, he'd face more problems than he wanted to think about. "Umm, I have a boy here. His name is Miles."

"Good. You think he can do the job?"

"Yes, I'm relatively certain with some work that we can get it done." Samson was unpredictable but violent. Miles was predictable and violent.

"You'd better be. I'll call you in two weeks for a progress

report. And, if you give me good news, I'll stop adding interest to your hefty bill."

"Oh, okay. Well, thank you. I'll do my best..." Although Oskar was still talking, the call had ended.

The next day, between patients, Oskar had gotten together the medication that he needed to start working with Miles. Before their session, he had called Barb, Miles' foster mom, into his office. "I'd like to try something," he said, crossing his legs in the chair, "With your permission, of course."

Barb furrowed her brow. "What did you have in mind?"

"Well, I think that if I use hypnotism, I can help Miles to not only remember his past but to move through it."

"Hypnotism? I thought that was a joke?"

Oskar nodded, "I can understand why you'd think that way. In fact, there is a heavy scientific basis for the process. The mind is powerful. If I can get Miles to relax, he might be able to speed up his progress through the power of suggestion."

Barb shrugged. "Sure, do what you've got to do."

"Great. I just have this little form for you to sign that we are adjusting the treatment plan to include it." Oskar wanted to have all of his paperwork in order. The situation was spiraling out of control.

Barb scrawled her name, the pen scratching across the paper. She handed it back to Oskar. "Here you go. When will you start with him?"

"Right now, if that's okay with you?"

Barb nodded, stood up and headed out of Oskar's office.

"Barb, one more thing... Miles might be a little sleepy after our sessions. Hypnotherapy can make people drowsy."

"No problem."

What Barb didn't know was that Oskar had gotten some flunitrazepam ready for their session. Impossible to find in any drug test after a few hours, flunitrazepam would induce relaxation and loss of inhibition. Oskar had no idea if Mr. Smith's plan would work, but he had to try.

Miles came into Oskar's office just a moment after Barb went out. "Hello, Miles, how are you today?"

The boy nodded.

"Listen, I talked to Barb and she said it was okay if we tried something new today. Is that okay with you?"

Miles nodded again, still not speaking.

"What I'd like you to do is to drink this juice for me and then we will begin, okay?" Oskar had smashed a dose of fluni-trazepam and put it in a small cup of orange drink.

Miles took the cup and drank down the liquid, smacking his lips a little.

"Okay, Miles, now I'd like you to lay down on the couch and just relax. We will talk like we normally do, but just with you laying down."

Oskar watched as Miles leaned back, settling himself on the pillows. "Now what?"

"I'm going to talk. You are going to listen. You might fall asleep. That's okay. All I want you to do is to focus on my voice."

THEIR SESSIONS, increased to twice a week because of the pressure from Mr. Smith, proceeded exactly the same way each time. Miles would drink the orange drink laced with the fluni-trazepam and then he'd lay on the couch. Oskar would spend the next half hour making suggestions to him that took advantage of his naturally violent personality. "Think about what it would be like to take a knife and slice through someone's skin," he'd say, or "Imagine yourself finding the anger you see in Barb and cutting it out of her." Though he hadn't shown it yet, Oskar was certain the more he worked with Miles that he'd do anything he was asked to.

"Now Miles, I'd like you to picture yourself holding a knife.

Can you show me how you'd do that?" Miles lifted his hand up from where it was resting on the couch.

"Very good, Miles. Can you show me how you would stab someone with the knife you are holding?" Miles made a few gestures that looked like stabbing motions.

"Miles, how do you feel?"

Still in his drug-induced stupor, Miles smiled.

THE PAIN in Oskar's body brought him back to the warehouse. Oskar whispered, "If you kill me, I can't pay you back."

Baseball hat looked at him. "Don't you think I know that? This is a warning."

"I thought my debt would be paid when the girl got killed."

"Mr. Smith is considering his options. What do you think he should do?"

"Let me go."

"That's not quite the right answer." Before Oskar could reply, a baseball bat hit him in the side of the head, the pain piercing every inch of his face. Blows covered his body, everywhere from his legs to his arms and chest. Oskar tried to cry out but found that he couldn't make any noise other than groan.

A few minutes later, he came to, still taped to the chair. He could barely move, his left eye swollen shut. He felt the tape being released from his wrists and ankles, strong hands pulling and dragging him into a vehicle. He couldn't make his mouth move. Pain pulled and tore all over his body. There wasn't an inch of him that didn't ache. He whimpered and tried to roll over, but the pain in his chest was too severe.

"Okay Doc, we are going to drop you off. It's gonna be a bit of a rocky departure, but it'll be good."

The van they had put Oskar in slowed down, the side door rolling open. The man who had done the beating shoved Oskar's body out onto the sidewalk in front of Savannah

Memorial Hospital near the main entrance. They sped off before Oskar's body even hit the ground.

"Oh my God," Oskar heard a voice that sounded female. "Someone get a doctor!"

That was the last Oskar remembered.

12

K at got back to the hotel feeling unsure of herself. She went upstairs, unlocking the door and tossing her backpack on the bed. She ordered room service, a BLT and a side of fries. Staring around the room, she wasn't sure what to do next. Finding Hailey's locked art studio had been interesting, but how was it connected to her murder?

Kat frowned and picked up her phone. Maybe calling home would make her feel better. "Hi, honey," she said. "How was your day?"

"Good," he said, his mouth full of some sort of food. "I just got back from school. The dogs are being bad."

Their two dogs, Woof and Tyrant, were just as much a part of the family as the people in it. Woof had been rescued from the man who had kidnapped Jack. They had been inseparable for years. Tyrant, a beautiful Belgian Malinois, had joined the family two years before when her police handler had died. Kat smiled. The dogs were always up to some sort of shenanigans. "What are they doing?"

"Remember that ball you picked out for them?"

"Sure."

"They have pretty much torn it in half."

Kat chuckled. "Well, that sounds pretty typical. How are you doing, buddy?"

"Good. Van is making ribs for dinner tonight."

"Wow, that sounds good. I'm jealous."

"When are you coming home, Ma?"

"Couple of days. Is Van there? Can I talk to him?"

Jack mumbled an uh-huh, his mouth still full of food. Van came on the phone. "How are things?"

"Okay, I guess."

"What does that mean?"

Kat spent the next few minutes explaining to Van about Eli and the artwork that had been locked up in Hailey's apartment. She told him that the boy accused of stabbing her had left the station without being interviewed by the police.

"That sounds strange. Why did they let him go without an interview?"

"Honestly, I'm not sure. I'm not making much progress with the detective."

"Think there is a story here?"

Kat sighed. "I'm not sure. I'm just so frustrated. It feels like there is something going on — I mean what motive does a ten-year-old boy have to stab a college student?"

"That would be the question, wouldn't it?"

KAT TOSSED and turned all night. Dreams of her family stayed in her mind. She woke up the next morning determined that she needed to resolve the case one way or the other. She couldn't wait any longer. There either needed to be something to investigate or she needed to get on the next plane home. She got out of bed, took a hot shower, and headed back to the police precinct. Once there, she looked for Carson Martino.

"You're back?" he said, sipping a cup of coffee. She had found him in his office.

"Yes, I think there's something you should see." Kat had decided on the way over to the precinct to talk to Carson about the art that she had found the day before with the help of Eli.

"And what's that?"

"I made another visit to Hailey's apartment yesterday. There is a locked room that has more art in it than I've ever seen in any place in my life before. I'm wondering if her side job is what got her killed..."

"Kat, we still have no idea what motivated someone to kill Hailey. This is an ongoing investigation. I'm not sure what you're hoping to find here."

Another wave of frustration covered Kat. She felt her face flush. All she had been doing since she got on the ground in Savannah was trying to help solve Hailey's murder. It seemed like every direction she went the doors were closed and locked, especially when it came to Carson Martino. He didn't seem to understand that she was just trying to help. "Listen, I'll make you a deal. All I need you to do is to come with me over to Hailey's apartment and see what's in that room. If you don't think there's a connection after that, I'll get on a plane and be on my way this afternoon."

Carson nodded. "Okay, you win."

Kat followed Carson out of the police station. She got into his unmarked vehicle with him and they rode silently over to Hailey's apartment. She sent Missy a quick text. When they got there, Kat pressed the button for Hailey and Missy's apartment. Missy's voice answered, "Who's there?"

"Missy, it's Kat. I brought a detective with me. Can we come up?"

"Sure."

Kat and Carson went up the steps and pushed the door open calling for Missy. Carson had met Missy before but didn't know anything about the locked room with the art. "So, Kat tells me that Hailey had a room that was locked with a bunch of art in it?" Carson stared at Missy.

"That's right. It's her studio." Missy disappeared around the corner. She padded down the hallway and opened the door for Carson and Kat.

As soon as she looked inside, Kat could tell something had changed. Instead of all the art stacked against the side wall, there was nothing there. The art was gone.

"What happened? Where did all the art go?" Kat asked. She looked around the room and nearly every piece had been removed. "Missy? Did someone come in and take the art last night?"

Missy stood in stunned silence. "I didn't let anyone in! I left to get dinner with some friends for a little while. That was all! Someone must've broken in." She walked around the room and seemed to be looking for something in particular, her color pale. "There had to be thirty pieces of art in here yesterday," she said. "Why would someone come in and steal all of this art? They were just pieces for her classes."

Kat watched as Carson glanced around the room. He didn't say anything. He walked over to the windows and looked carefully. Kat guessed that he was trying to see if there had been forced entry. He walked back to the group, shaking his head. "I don't know what happened here, but this seems strange to me." Just as he finished the sentence, his phone rang. "Excuse me for a moment."

Kat stood with Missy for a few minutes waiting for Carson to come back. She couldn't hear what he was talking about, but she had bigger problems. Missy was shaking. As she comforted the girl, Kat overheard Carson answer whomever he was speaking to in short, clipped sentences. Carson came back into the room, his shoes padding on the carpet that ran down the hallway, "There's been a development in the case. We just found the psychiatrist for Miles, the child whose fingerprints we found on the knife that stabbed Hailey. He's been beaten. He's in bad shape. I have to get over to the hospital." He looked at Kat, "Do you want to come, or should I drop you at the office?"

Kat could tell he'd rather leave her at the police station, but she quickly said, "I'd like to come to the hospital." She felt a combination of excitement and trepidation as she followed Carson out of the apartment. They said a quick goodbye to Missy with the promise that Carson would send more officers and an investigative unit over to the apartment to see what else they could find and what evidence they could gather. She was on the phone with friends already.

Kat followed Carson out to the car and got in without saying a word. Once he pulled out of the parking lot Carson glanced at her, "Do you always help the police departments when you follow a story?"

"That's how I prefer to work. My husband was a Marine and I was deployed to Afghanistan as an embedded journalist. It's a tough job to work in law enforcement. But my job is no different from yours. I'm out to get the facts. You just get to prosecute them."

Carson nodded and smiled. "That's good to hear."

"So, what happened with Miles' psychiatrist?"

"I don't have all the details yet. What I do know is that he was found beaten in front of our local hospital. Someone rolled him out of a van and dumped him right on the front sidewalk. Sounds like his injuries are pretty bad. I'm not sure if he has any connection to the case but I wouldn't be surprised if he does."

Kat nodded. All of a sudden it seemed that the case was starting to come into focus. Hailey's side job, her locked room, the boy that was accused of stabbing her and now the beating of his psychiatrist — it all seemed to be linked. The motive was still a question, though. "If you had to guess, what do you think is going on here?"

"Off the record?"

Kat nodded, "Yes, of course." She could tell Carson didn't want to answer, but he was trapped in the car with her.

Carson sighed, gripping the wheel a little tighter. "I don't have all the pieces figured out in my head yet. I think I still have more questions than answers. But it doesn't seem like Hailey's death was an accident."

"I thought you had already established that her death was a murder?" Kat didn't understand what Carson was driving at.

"Sorry. That's not what I meant. What I meant to say is that Hailey's death was a murder. The question that I have in my mind is why? Other than a random act of cruelty why would a ten-year-old child kill a college student? It just doesn't seem to make sense."

Kat stared out the window. The streets of Savannah weren't very full yet. She imagined families still waking up on vacation taking their time and eating breakfast together. Her thoughts drifted toward home. She wondered what Jack and Van were doing. She turned to Carson, "You think there is a connection between Hailey's death and the art being stolen?"

"It certainly seems that way." Carson frowned, "I feel like an IRS auditor that is trying to make sense of a million receipts tossed around in a paper bag. We have facts, but they don't seem to make any sense. Maybe things will come into better focus when we hear a bit more about what happened to Oskar."

Kat nodded. The fact that Miles' psychiatrist had been beaten and dumped in front of the local hospital added something to the story that she didn't quite know how to process. More questions than answers flooded her mind. Why would Oskar be a target? Did he have any connection to the case? Or maybe it was a random act of violence and unrelated to Hailey's murder? Kat didn't know.

Carson pulled the police unit up to the front of the hospital and parked in a spot that was marked for emergency vehicles only. Kat got out and followed him into the emergency room. The call had only come a few minutes before they arrived, but by the looks of the hustle and bustle in the emergency room, it was a busy morning. Nurses and doctors seem to be darting everywhere in the white hallways of the hospital. Carson walked to the front desk and showed his badge. "I'm here to talk to Oskar Kellum, please."

The triage nurse, dressed in light blue scrubs wearing a pen on a string and an ID around her neck pointed down the hallway, "I'll open the doors for you come on back. He's in bay seven."

Kat followed Carson down the hallway. The hospital smell and the shiny linoleum floors reminded her of when her mother-in-law, Laura, was in the hospital being treated for cancer. For some reason, all hospitals seem to smell the same. Kat shook the thought from her head, not wanting to remember what she had been through, the blackmailer kidnapping Jack and Kat having to kill him in order to save her son. The only good thing that had come out of the incident was that she and Van had developed a deep relationship that led to marriage. For that, she was grateful.

"Do you know anything about Oskar's condition?" she asked Carson.

"Nothing, really. Just that Oskar was dumped. The rest we need to figure out."

Kat nodded. There was a tightness in her chest and stomach she couldn't explain. Was she nervous? Excited that things were starting to move in a better direction? She couldn't tell. Carson led her to Oskar's room. By the looks of it, the doctors had moved quickly once Oskar was dumped on the sidewalk. He was wearing a light blue hospital gown covered in a small diamond pattern. Blankets had been pulled up to his chest and an IV and oxygen were attached to him.

"Oskar? I'm Detective Carson Martino. I wanted to come and ask you a few questions about what happened to you."

Oskar turned his head to the side. "I don't have anything to say."

"Can you at least tell me how you ended up here?" Carson asked, pulling a pad of paper out of his pocket.

"I don't know."

Kat didn't know if she should speak. It was Carson's case after all. She sat down on the chair next to Oskar's bed and pulled close to his face. "Oskar, I'm Kat Beckman. I'm a journalist." She glanced at Carson, hoping he wouldn't be angry with her. "You took a pretty severe beating. What happened?"

Before Oskar could answer, a doctor came to his bedside. He looked at Kat and Carson, "I heard there were people here looking into Oskar's case. Could I have a minute?" The doctor nodded his head as though he wanted them to step away from the bed. Carson nodded, and he and Kat followed the doctor away from Oskar.

"You're treating Oskar? Carson asked.

The doctor nodded. "I'm Dr. Blake. I'm the head of the emergency department here." He pulled up images from a tablet he was carrying and pointed to them. "Normally, I wouldn't be quite so forthcoming with the information on a patient, especially without a subpoena, but this is a pretty severe case. Since you are doing the investigation, I wanted to give you a heads up on what you are looking at." Dr. Blake pointed to his tablet. "From what we can tell from the surveillance video, a blue van pulled up in front of the hospital and barely stopped. They slowed down enough just to open the door and toss Oskar out onto the front sidewalk. Luckily, our security guard was standing right there and was able to quickly get medical help for him.

"Was a security guard able to get a license plate?" Carson was holding his pad and paper at the ready. Kat could tell he was hoping for more information.

The doctor shook his head. "Unfortunately, the van was unmarked. There were no license plates our security guard could see. You can, of course, go and talk to our chief of security and look at our front door surveillance."

Carson nodded, "That would be helpful."

The doctor nodded, "I'm hoping that you can see by the x-rays I have here, that Oskar's injuries are fairly significant. He has four broken ribs, a lung contusion, bruised spleen and many lacerations to his face. We are waiting for the swelling to go down in his left eye to see if there's been any retinal damage." The doctor turned the tablet off. "I have to be honest. I haven't seen a beating like this in many years. Whoever did this had a bone to pick with him." The doctor shook his head, "I'm just telling you this because I don't want to see more patients like this show up at my hospital." With that, the doctor walked away.

Kat didn't say anything. It was clear that Dr. Blake was frustrated by the fact that Oskar was dumped right in front of the hospital. His turf. It was a bold move by whoever had done it, one that she wasn't sure how Carson would handle.

Kat waited for a moment while Carson jotted a few notes in his notebook. He looked at her, "Let's go back and see if we can get Oskar to tell us anything more."

Kat followed Carson back to Oskar's bedside. "The doctor tells us that you have quite a few injuries," Carson said. "I won't take a lot of your time, but I do need to let you know that your name came up in another case."

The way that Carson said it, Kat knew that he was trying to get a reaction out of Oskar. It worked. Oskar turned and looked at Carson, his one eye nothing more than a bloated red ball on his face. "What case is that?"

"I'll bet you can guess." Carson stared at Oskar. "I'll save you some time since I'm sure you're in a lot of pain. The Hailey Park murder. Your name came up as connected to the suspect we are looking at."

"And who would that be?" As Oskar tried to push himself up in the bed a little bit, his face shrunk into a mask of pain.

"Miles Nobesky."

"Miles? Why would Miles be involved in your murder case?"

"That's what I'd like to know," Carson said. "I heard he was a patient of yours."

"I can't talk about it unless you have a court order." Oskar adjusted himself in the bed again and turned on his side, away from them. Kat could tell that he was tired of talking already. She wasn't sure how much more they would get out of him.

Carson took a breath. It seemed he wanted to say something else. As he did, a nurse came into the room and said, "I'm sorry. This patient needs to go downstairs for additional testing. You'll have to come back later."

13

The fact that they had to wait to talk to Oskar while he was in testing sent a surge of frustration through Kat. She stepped out of the way as his bed rolled by. Just as she did her phone rang. "Hello?"

"Kat? This is Eli."

"Eli? What's going on?"

"I was wondering if we could meet? I have some more information I think might be helpful."

"Sure," Kat wondered what he could possibly have found out, but was curious. "Are you at the store?"

"Yes. Can you come now?"

"Yes. Right now, I'm at the hospital. I'll be there in the next twenty minutes."

"Are you okay?" Eli sounded panicked. "You aren't injured, are you?"

"No, no. I'm fine. I'm just here following up on a lead with Carson, the detective that's working on the case."

"Oh, okay. I'll see you in a few minutes."

Kat looked at Carson. He had moved down the hallway a bit, furiously scratching notes into his notebook, a frown on his face. She could tell that he was as confused by this case as she was. There seemed to be too many stories happening at the same time. It was almost impossible to see how they were tied together. A surge of frustration drove its way through her chest. She pushed it aside, hoping that Eli would be able to shed some light on what was going on. It seemed unlikely that he would be able to. After all, he was just an antique dealer here in Savannah. What could he possibly know? "I just got a call from my art source," Kat said. "He wanted to meet with me. He said he has news on the case." Carson had stopped writing and was staring at her. "Want to come?"

"Well, since I drove you to the hospital, I guess I'll have to," Carson said, shoving the notebook back into his pocket and tugging on the front of his sport coat. As Kat followed him out of the hospital, she noticed that everything Carson did was with a certain level of precision. His haircut, his clothes, even the way his badge hung around his neck showed that he cared about his appearance. Details seemed to matter to Carson. Like Carson, Kat hoped Eli could provide a layer of details that would help them figure out the next step in the case.

They were both silent on the way over to Eli's art gallery. Kat watched the traffic pass and saw more people walking on the sidewalks. It seemed there was a never-ending stream of people touring through the city no matter whether it was morning or night. It didn't take long for them to drive over to Eli's gallery. As soon as Kat pushed the door open, she could smell tea brewing. If nothing else Eli was hospitable. "Eli?"

"Back here!"

Kat wove her way through pieces of old furniture, easels with musty paintings on top of them, and shelves of everything from old brass tea kettles to clocks that no longer worked. She walked behind the counter and pushed aside the curtain. Eli stood at the makeshift kitchenette in the back, pouring tea into three mismatched cups, "Hey Eli." A new tablecloth had been smoothed on top of the old table. There was a small plate of what looked to be Russian tea cakes in the center of the table with bowls of creamer and sugar and small silver spoons at each place setting.

"Thank you for coming," Eli put two cups of tea on the table and then reached for a third before sitting down. He looked at Carson, "You must be the detective working on the case." Eli extended his hand.

"Yes. Carson Martino. Nice to meet you."

"Make yourself at home."

Carson sat down across from Kat. Eli sat at the head of the small table. Kat said, "You said you had information?"

"When you work in the art business for as long as I have, you develop relationships all over the world. Out of curiosity, I made a couple of calls about the art that we saw at Hailey's apartment. I think I found out something interesting."

Carson pulled his notebook out of his pocket and set it on the table. He placed a pen right next to it. "What would that be?"

I heard from a contact in New York that a large shipment of old master's art was headed for London. It should be landing there sometime today."

Carson furrowed his brow. "And, why would that be interesting? How does that relate to Hailey's murder?"

Eli threw his hands up in the air. "I'm not the detective, but the fact that an entire load of old master's art is headed to England isn't normal."

Kat chewed her lip. "What do you mean, Eli?"

Eli used wrinkled fingers to smooth the fabric he had laid across the table. "There just aren't that many pieces of old masters art. I asked my friend if he knew who the collector was and that was the strange thing, he didn't."

"It would be normal for someone's name to be attached to a collection like that?" Kat tapped her fingers on the table.

Eli nodded. "While there are some collectors who are private about what they own and where they display it, the vast majority of collectors want to be seen and known. The art world is filled with braggarts." Eli looked away for a moment and then looked back, "It's strange for such a large number of pieces to be in one place."

Carson flipped open his notebook. "How many pieces were in the shipment? Did your friend say?"

"Thirty."

"How many would be normal?"

Eli scratched his head. "In my experience? Three to five."

Kat stopped to think. There had been about thirty pieces in the pile that had been left in Hailey's apartment. Now they were gone. She looked at Carson, "Do you think there's a connection between this large shipment and the missing artwork from Hailey's apartment?"

"Missing artwork?" Eli asked. "The artwork that was in Hailey's apartment is gone?"

Kat nodded.

"Well, that changes things. I thought we were talking about another shipment, but it's pretty apparent what happened," Eli said.

Carson stood up and started pacing near the small table where he had been sipping a cup of tea that Eli had given him. "I'm not sure I understand. You think Hailey's art was stolen out of her apartment and now it's on the way across the world?"

"That's exactly what I'm afraid of."

Kat furrowed her brow. "Afraid of? What do you mean?"

Eli stood up and walked over to the sink. Kat could hear the sound of water being poured into his teacup even though his back was turned. When he turned back, she could hear the clink of the spoon hitting the sides of the inside of the cup as he stirred. "There's a lot that goes on in the art world that is good and pure. There is also a lot in the art world that isn't."

"Like what?" Kat asked.

Eli turned back. "For centuries, people have been killed, kidnapped and punished on the darker side of the art world. It makes sense if you think about it. When a piece of art goes on the market – particularly from someone who's famous – it's priceless. Van Gogh, Rembrandt, Michelangelo. The list goes on and on. There are a lot of things that people are willing to do to get their hands on something that valuable."

Kat's mind started to turn with questions. She folded her hands on the table and looked down at her lap searching for their next move. Carson interrupted her thoughts. "If what you're saying is true, Eli, then this is a much bigger case than simply the murder of an art student here in Savannah."

Eli nodded. "That's why I wanted to talk to you in person."

"If that is the case, then we are going to need help on an international level," Kat said.

Carson nodded. "That might take me a little time. I have plenty of contacts in the area, but not many that work on an internationally."

Kat pulled her phone out of her pocket. "I think I might be able to help. Give me a minute." Kat got up from the table and walked back through the curtain into the showroom area. The smell of mustiness and attics permeated the store. Although she wasn't a fan of antiques, all the things that surrounded Eli seem to fit him perfectly. She stared at her phone and went to her contacts, pulling up one name that she thought might be able to help.

"Kat, is that you?"

"Hi, Henry, how are you?"

Henry Nash worked for Scotland Yard. More specifically, he worked for the counterterrorism unit within the department. He had been Kat's contact when she was in England investigating the cathedral fire. They had formed a friendship and Kat had ended up taking his ex-wife's dog, Tyrant, home with her after Bev's death. If anyone had the international contacts to help figure out where the art had gone, it would be Henry. And, if he didn't know it himself, he'd know who to talk to. It was the only idea she had. They had to solve the mystery of where Hailey's art had gone. In her gut, she knew that was key to figuring out who had killed Hailey and why.

"Kat, it's so good to hear from you! I'm doing quite well, thank you for asking. How's Tyrant?"

"She's amazing, Henry. She's become quite a part of our family."

"From the sound of your voice, Kat, it sounds like you are calling with an agenda."

"You'd be right." She paused for a moment wondering how much to tell Henry. After all, he wasn't really part of the case. Neither was she. She didn't want to upset Carson and have him block her out of any information that might come in. At the same time, the more she told Henry the more he would be able to help her. "I'm working on a story right now and have run across some information that I am not sure to do with. I was wondering if you'd be able to help?"

"Of course, love. What are you up to?"

Over the course of their time together, Henry and Kat had become good friends. It didn't start out that way. Kat had been sent to England under the guise of being a US Army contractor looking into a cathedral fire that had destroyed a communications hub for the government that was located under the cathedral. The Brits didn't know anything about the American hub. Her contact in the Army, Hannah Carter, had introduced her to Henry. Henry had been her guide during her entire time in England and had accompanied her back to the United States as they solved the case. By the time they were done, Henry had saved her, and she had saved Henry. A friendship had been born. They'd stayed in touch once Kat got back to the United States. "I'm in Savannah, Georgia, right now. I'm working on the case of an art student that was murdered."

"That sounds like a local issue," Henry said.

"I know... but it has turned out to be something more, or at least I think it will be something more."

"What do you mean?"

Kat could hear Henry fumbling in the background. In her mind, she imagined him in his office at Scotland Yard. The way she remembered it, it was filled to the brim with paperwork and coats and equipment and file drawers. She imagined he was pushing things around on his desk to try to find a piece of paper to write notes on. "What brought me down here in the first place was that the suspect is a ten-year-old child. He's accused of stabbing a twenty-year-old student from the Savannah College of Art and Design in the park. She bled out on the scene."

He whistled through his teeth, "But there's more?"

"Yes. In the process of trying to put the story together, I went to her apartment. In it, there was a locked room that had approximately thirty pieces of art — replicas of famous paintings — that are now missing."

"And what makes you think that Scotland Yard would be interested in your art student?"

"Well, I ran into a local art expert, Eli Langster. He did a little digging for me and said that one of his contacts told him that a large shipment of art had just been sent out of New York on its way to London."

Kat could hear Henry tapping on his computer keyboard. "Hold on for one moment. Let me see something." Another moment passed, and Kat could hear Henry typing more.

"What are you looking up?" Kat said.

"For years, I worked on customs enforcement. Somehow, the name Eli Langster sounds familiar to me."

A shiver ran down Kat's spine. Could the mild-mannered

man in the next room have some connections she wasn't aware of? In her most logical moments, it always surprised Kat how danger seemed to pass everyone so closely. Most people never suspected that the people around them could do them harm, not to mention what they might be capable of if pushed.

"Yes, yes. It's right here. We have had some dealings with Eli Langster before. Looks like he was a rather good informant. What did he tell you?"

"Nothing more than what I just told you. He said he had a contact who mentioned that a shipment of art was on its way to London. Eli said that shipping thirty pieces at one time was unusual." Kat glanced back toward the curtain that separated the showroom from where Carson and Eli were having tea from where she was standing. She eyed it suspiciously, wondering what her next step should be. "Henry, let me ask you, is Eli a problem?"

"Oh, I don't think so. Based on what I can see here he just passed information along to get himself out of a scrape. Can't say for sure, but I think you'll be okay."

Kat took a deep breath and started to relax a little bit. Knowing that Eli was just passing information made her feel better. She had been in too many situations that had violence attached to them. Her PTSD was finally under control, or at least she thought it was, and she didn't want to go back to living the way that she had been.

The tapping on the keyboard continued. "Here's what I was looking for," Henry said. "We keep shipping manifests in our files. They are for merchandise that is coming into London and the things that go out. Let me take a look at these and give you a call back."

"Thanks, Henry, I appreciate it." Kat walked back to the kitchenette, pulling the curtain to the side. She found Eli and Carson still sitting at the table. Carson had a pastry in front of him and was breaking it into small pieces with his fingers. She realized he probably didn't want to get anything on his suit. "I made a call to a friend I have at Scotland Yard." She looked directly at Eli, "He seems to know you."

Eli's cheeks reddened, "Really?"

"He said you had provided information to them in the past." Kat sat down at the table and pulled the plate closer to her. She chose the pastry that was on the top and put it on her plate.

"Anything I should know about that, Eli?" Carson said, his mouth full. He wiped his hands on a napkin and looked directly at Eli.

Eli's face flushed even more deeply. "There are a lot of good people in the art world. There are also a lot of bad people in the art world. During my career, I've bumped into many from both camps."

Carson raised his eyebrows. "If Scotland Yard knows you, then it sounds like you run into your fair share of bad eggs."

Eli stammered, "I got myself into a scrape with several gentlemen who wanted to move art. I just provided information to Scotland Yard."

It was Kat's turn to raise her eyebrows. "I'm guessing you traded information so that you wouldn't get into trouble?"

Eli nodded. "As I said, there are lots of good people in the art business and lots of bad ones, too."

"Is this contact that you got in touch with, is he one of the good ones or one of the bad ones?" Kat asked.

"He sort of straddles the line..." Eli immediately looked down into his lap. Kat had the feeling that he wasn't telling them the whole story and that the part he wasn't telling them he was a little ashamed about. She didn't want to push him. The last thing she needed was the information to dry up all of a sudden.

"Those are sometimes the best sources," Kat smiled. She could tell by Eli's reaction that he was a little embarrassed that his past had been exposed. She didn't know the extent of it.

She hoped Carson didn't decide to dig too deep and scare Eli off.

"So, where do we go from here?" Carson asked standing up from the table and pushing his chair in.

"I'm just waiting for my contact at Scotland Yard to get back to me to let me know what's going on." She looked down at her phone, "He's usually pretty fast."

"While we are waiting, how about if you tell me a little bit more about this art that you saw at Hailey's apartment?" Carson asked, looking at Eli.

As they started to talk, Kat walked back out into the showroom, wandering the tightly packed aisles, waiting for Henry to call her back. Impatience surged through her system. She pulled her phone out of her pocket and sent a text to Van. "Source here says paintings may have been shipped to London."

Van texted back right away. "Are you going?"

Kat's stomach clenched into a small ball. Going back to London would inevitably remind her of the last time she was there. While there were good things that came out of her trip — finding a missing Navy SEAL and bringing her girl, Tyrant, home — there were also a lot of other memories that she would prefer not to relive. Things like how a blackmail list that she had turned over to criminals had gotten the Navy SEALs in trouble in the first place and how it all linked back to her time in Afghanistan. Sometimes she felt like she walked around with a cord that tied her to her past. She could only go so far before she bumped up at the end of it. Tears started to form in her eyes. She quickly turned a corner around a stack of old antique books and wiped her face. The last thing she needed was to have a complete meltdown.

Her phone started to vibrate. She looked down and recognized it was Henry's office calling. "That was fast," she said, wiping the last tear from her face.

"Well, you know how we work here at Scotland Yard. We are efficient about once a year. You happened to get lucky."

Kat laughed, the tension melting from her chest. Despite what she had been through she had made a lot of good friends. She counted Henry Nash as one of them. "Don't keep me waiting. What did you find out?"

"Well, there is a shipment of art that is on a plane to London right now. According to the manifest, there are approximately thirty pieces in the collection. Sound familiar?"

Kat's heart started to beat a little faster in her chest. The fact that Henry had found a shipment with the exact same number of pieces of art in it gave her hope that they had found Hailey's work. "What do we do now?"

"I've put a notice on the customs manifest to hold it for additional screening when it arrives. If we don't find anything though, we'll have to let it go."

Kat chewed her lip. Why would student artwork get shipped across the world? It just didn't make sense to her. "Henry, I just don't understand. If it is Hailey's art why send it the whole way to Europe?"

"There's a lot of money in forgeries, Kat," Henry said. "We see it all the time. Some fakes are better than others, but no matter what, they always command a lot of money. There is an entire division that's devoted to just looking at forged art. It's a big deal here in Europe."

Kat did a quick calculation. If the pieces that were on the plane were actually Hailey's work, someone could buy them not knowing that they weren't real. "How much do you think those pieces of artwork are worth?"

"It's hard to tell. But the whole group together? It could be worth hundreds of millions of pounds."

Kat shook her head. The idea that Hailey's work could make it across to London and disappear frustrated her. Even worse, Kat thought about the collectors, museums and churches that could easily be duped into spending millions of dollars for work that had been painted by a student artist. Not that the work wasn't beautiful, Kat realized. She had seen the pieces herself. It would be nearly impossible for an average person to notice they weren't originals, but if someone was paying for an original and didn't get one, that would be quite the heist. "How long will you hold the shipment for?" An idea began to form in her head.

"We can hold it for up to forty-eight hours. That is, unless we find something. Then all bets are off, as you Americans say."

"Hold that shipment for me, will you? I'm on my way." The words were out of Kat's mouth before she realized what she said. She committed herself to flying the whole way to England to follow up on the delivery of art. It could be a wild goose chase. She instantly regretted saying that she would. Toughen up, Kat, she told herself. See the story through.

Kat walked back toward the table where Carson and Eli were still chatting. The redness in Eli's cheeks had returned to normal, so she guessed that they were talking about something other than Eli's checkered past. They both stopped and looked at her as she walked in. "I just got a call from my contact at Scotland Yard. There is a delivery of art on the way. I'm going to London."

Carson and Eli both raised their eyebrows simultaneously. Eli stood up. "How will you know what you are looking at?"

"I think I can remember the ones we saw." Eli's comment felt like a punch in the gut. Kat was no art expert. Could she remember?

"I'll go with you." Eli stared at her, "After all, I'm the only one of the three of us that has any art expertise. I'm also the only one that saw all the pieces of art in Hailey's apartment and would be able to remember which pieces they were. You need me. Plus, I've got some connections that might come in handy."

Kat didn't say anything for a moment. She was surprised

that Eli would want to go the whole way to London. "What about the shop?"

Eli shook his head. "My wife will run it. It won't be a problem."

Kat considered his offer. "Are you sure? This could be a complete waste of time."

Eli stood up a little straighter. "I haven't had a good adventure in quite a while. It's time I get out of Savannah for a bit."

Kat stared at Eli for another moment. His slumped posture had straightened up and there was a sparkle in his eyes. She tried to imagine how he had been ten, fifteen, or even twenty years earlier before the gray had permeated his hair. She wondered about the time that he had worked with Scotland Yard and how he knew Henry Nash. Who was she to deprive him of an adventure? The reality was that she wasn't an expert in art and could definitely use the help. And he was right about one thing, he was the only one who had seen all of Hailey's art before it had disappeared. She had been busy looking at the apartment. He would be their best shot at positively identifying that it was her work. Kat nodded, "You're right. I'm not sure I would know what I was looking at."

Carson stood up, putting his notebook back in his pocket. "That settled, then. Keep me in the loop once you get to London."

Kat sent a quick text to Henry and purchased two tickets to go to London. She sent another text to Van to let him know what was going on. It was research, so the newspaper would pick up the cost to go. "Want to drive me back to the hotel so I can get my things?" she asked Eli.

Eli nodded. "Sure. I don't need to stop at home."

Kat tilted her head, "You're already packed?"

"When I heard from my contact, I figured there was a chance you might want to go and see for yourself. I'm prepared," Eli smiled.

She followed him out to the car, hearing the click of the lock as he closed the shop. Her mind raced, veering between what she was doing right now and what she had done in the past. Thoughts of being in London and walking through the rubble of the Stratham Cathedral fire, the smell of smoke still in her nostrils. She turned to Eli, wondering where this journey would take them. As he started the car and pulled out of the parking lot, she swallowed hard. Did she really want to follow this? Wasn't it enough that Henry knew that the art was on its way to London? She shook her head, not saying anything. The words of her therapist floated through her head, reminding her that if she would give it a few minutes, the thoughts would clear, and she would be able to move forward. She hoped that was the case this time...

14

D r. Abibi Roux finished teaching her classes for the day, not without some level of distraction. The visit from the day before from the journalist was still rattling in her mind. The woman had seemed nice enough, but her questions weren't something that Abibi was expecting. The fact that someone was looking into Hailey's art and her side job was troubling. The last two years had been exciting and profitable. She didn't know what might happen now that Hailey was dead. She needed to make a phone call.

"Yes," a male voice answered.

"I'm calling because I have some concerns."

"What might those be?"

Abibi had met Christopher Lavaud at an art auction two years before. She pictured him in her mind as they spoke. He was tall and blonde. She had watched him at the auction. He stood at the back of the room, his hands in his pockets, his eyes moving not only across the art, but across all the people. It looked at the time like he had been taking stock of nearly everything.

The art auction had been held in New York City, in the

plush room of a hotel in upper Manhattan. Most people assumed that the best art auctions were held in places like Soho, the bohemian center of the art world in New York. It just wasn't true. The people with the money to buy the most expensive pieces of art didn't like to have to stray too far from home, no matter what anyone else thought. With the traffic always being a challenge in New York City, the auction organizers decided to host it at a hotel that would be close to their clientele. It was a smart move.

The night of the auction, Abibi had watched Christopher as he watched everyone else. It was curious to her. Most people when they attend an auction were either busy chatting with people they knew or looking at the art. That wasn't Christopher. She watched him over the shoulder of a colleague from another art school as he moved around the room. He would look at a piece of art and then look around the room. He repeated the cycle several times. The entire time Abibi watched him, she became more curious. Who was this man? Why was he watching the crowd so carefully?

As the auction started, Abibi moved to the back of the space. On her professor's salary, she didn't have the means to purchase any of the art. That's not why she was there. She liked to attend art auctions to not only see art that she would never see in a museum, but to make contacts in the industry. One never knew when those could become important.

DR. ABIBI ROUX was born in Kenya. She was the second daughter of a mom who was an artist and a dad who worked in Kenya's growing technology industry. Compared to most of the people in Kenya, even their small home seemed like a mansion. Early on, Abibi's mom recognized her innate art ability. Some of Abibi's fondest memories were from the hours that she spent outside working on art projects with her mom under a sparsely leafed tree in the shade.

Though not every child in Kenya got a good education, her father's hard work ensured that she was able to go the entire way through high school with no problems. When Abibi was seventeen, her parents sat her down to have a talk. She could still remember the day clearly. Her mother sat with her hands folded on the tablecloth in their small dining room. Her father sat on the other side looking far away. "Abibi," he said, "We love you very much and only want the best for you. We'd like you to consider pursuing your art education in the United States."

At the time, she had been crushed by the idea of leaving her family in Kenya, though she knew what her father had said was true. Six months later, when her father drove her to the airport to send her to the United States, she knew it was a moment that would define her life. It had. After going to art school in Virginia, she had gone on to get her graduate degree and decided to accept a position at the Savannah College of Art and Design. For the first few years, her work was interesting and exciting. She loved the idea of developing new artists. The looks on the student's faces when they discovered they could see a new shape or get a medium to reflect what they were seeing in their heads on canvas took her breath away.

But it wasn't enough.

The hours and the pay simply weren't enough to give her the lifestyle that she desperately wanted. And, she had found no man that could keep her happy for longer than a few months. That was until the night that she was at the art auction in New York City and saw the strange blonde man moving through the crowds. "I haven't seen you at the auctions before," she managed before he walked away again.

"I haven't seen you either," the man said, his comment hanging in the air. "My name is Christopher Lavaud."

Abibi studied him as she would've studied a piece of art or a model for a piece she was creating. "It's nice to meet you, Christopher." As he stood next to her, she realized how large a man he was. Broad shoulders, well over six feet tall with a wide frame. Strength radiated from his body. She imagined that underneath the carefully tailored suit and overcoat that he wore that he had the body of an American football player.

"Do you come to these art auctions often?" he asked.

Abibi nodded. "When I can... I find them inspiring." Truthfully, it was her first one.

A small smile crept across his face. "Really?"

She looked at him, wondering why he had made that comment. "Don't you find them inspiring?"

"Not especially. However, I do find them to be quite profitable."

Abibi could tell he was about to walk away. For some reason, she didn't want him to. He seemed different from the other people that attended the art auctions. He seemed distant, detached. Abibi wondered why. "How is it that you find them to be profitable?"

"How about if we have a drink and I'll tell you?"

Abibi did just that. Had her father known that she had followed a strange man out of an art auction and got into a cab with him to go to a bar somewhere else in New York City, he would've been horrified. But Christopher was so different from any other man she had ever met that she couldn't resist.

The cab pulled up in front of a small dark bar, and she followed him in. The bartender seemed to know Christopher and simply pointed him towards the back of the restaurant. There was a single booth in the corner, sitting empty. Abibi slid in across from Christopher, who put his overcoat off to the side. A skinny waitress came over and brought him a drink without even asking. It looked like scotch or whiskey, but which one it was, Abibi couldn't tell. "What would you like, honey?" Abibi ordered a glass of white wine.

"Tell me about yourself," Christopher said.

Abibi only spent a few minutes answering his question. She told him about Kenya, about how she ended up at art school, how she initially loved the work that she did at SCAD, and how she had gone to the art auction to cultivate new contacts in hopes of furthering her career. In her mind, there was no reason to be deceptive. Many Americans wouldn't have been quite as honest, but she wasn't American, after all.

"What you're saying is very interesting to me," Christopher said.

Abibi noticed for the first time that he had a slight accent. "Where are you from originally?"

"Paris. I studied business there."

"Paris?" Abibi tapped her long, painted fingernails on the bowl of her wine glass. "And you studied business? How did you get interested in the art world?"

"There are a lot of unique opportunities in the art world that can't be found anywhere else."

While Christopher didn't tell her much about his business the first night they had drinks, Abibi learned more over time. As she thought back to that night, Abibi realized that she still didn't know much about what he did, even after two years of working with him.

ABIBI'S first assignment from him came about two months after they had met at the art auction. One day, right after class her phone rang with a number she didn't recognize. "Hello?"

"Abibi."

She recognized the voice immediately. She and Christopher had talked on the phone several times in the last couple of months and had even had other meet ups for drinks. Nothing more, though. Not that she wasn't interested, but he seemed to have business on his mind. "Hello, Christopher."

"I have a favor to ask. I was wondering if you are available for lunch today?"

"Are you in Savannah?"

"Indeed. I'll text you the address."

He said nothing more but a moment later Abibi received a text message with the location for a small, upscale restaurant on the other side of town. He had set the time for one o'clock. Looking at her phone, she realized she had just enough time to make it across town to meet him. How he knew that she'd have time to meet today, she wasn't sure. Maybe he didn't. Maybe it was just a good guess. She took one moment before leaving, pulled a dark red lipstick out of the drawer in her desk and used the mirror hanging on the wall behind her, one with a gilded frame, to check her hair and makeup, dabbing on a fresh coat of color.

Abibi arrived at the restaurant right on time. She hadn't been there before. Morton's Seafood was a restaurant that mostly locals frequented, but it was anything but casual. The tables were covered in starched white tablecloths with long-stemmed glasses that picked up the sunlight streaming through the window. While the waiters and waitresses wore blue t-shirts, jeans and small black aprons, Abibi could tell that they were nothing but a professional crew simply by the way they moved around the restaurant in efficient order.

After an appetizer of raw oysters, Christopher picked up his napkin, wiped his face and rested his elbows on the table. "I asked you here because I have a favor."

In some respects, Abibi was relieved that Christopher was finally getting around to the reason for his phone call. Getting to know him had been nothing short of frustrating. Her stomach started to flutter a little bit, but she refused to let it show. She picked up her napkin, dabbed the corners of her lips, and refolded it in her lap. She did not speak.

"As I told you when we first met, my background is in business. There is a lot of business to be done in the art world." He paused, taking a sip of water, "I have a client, a very wealthy client, that is particularly in love with images that were painted by Rembrandt."

Abibi's mind immediately went to all the information that she had about the famous painter. Born in 1606, the Dutch painter was nothing short of prolific. Her own impression of his work was that he was a master of light and dark, of expression and of movement. Skills like those might not sell with the general public in modern times, but for discerning collectors, Rembrandt's works were astounding and emotive. "That's fascinating. And, what does that have to do with me?"

Christopher froze in space for just a moment, his eyes staring right through her. Abibi didn't know if she should be flattered or frightened. "The favor I have is quite specific. Are you familiar with Rembrandt's worked called 'The Storm on the Sea of Galilee?'"

She was. The image, taken from the Biblical story of the storm that cropped up on the Sea of Galilee depicted the apostles hanging on for dear life on a small boat with a bloated sail. The work was one of Rembrandt's finest masterpieces. Its value was incalculable. "Yes."

"I was wondering if you have a student who might be able to replicate that work for me?" Christopher stopped speaking for a moment as the waiter brought over the main course, seared salmon over spring vegetables for Christopher, and a small salad with asparagus and locally caught shrimp for Abibi. Christopher immediately picked up his fork and took a bite of food, once again staring at her.

Abibi felt uncomfortable and yet curious at the same time. What, exactly, was he asking her to do? Would this be a forgery, or was it just an opportunity for a collector to hang a replica in their home? Abibi took a bite of her salad before answering. She laid the fork down gently on the side of her dish. "Could you tell me a little bit more about the project?" She wanted to see exactly what he would tell her without being prompted or without her asking too specific of a question.

Christopher finished chewing his mouthful of food and put down his fork. "From time to time, I have investors who have their eye on a specific piece of art but are unable to acquire it for one reason or another." He tilted his head to the side, "Sometimes, a piece of art simply isn't available because it is in a museum or held by a church that refuses to sell. Other times, they simply want something to look at for their own home. There are other reasons, of course..."

Abibi instantly wondered what the other reasons could be, but she didn't want to ask. Something in her told her that the less she knew the better it would be. "I am certainly familiar with that piece of art. However, it isn't in my area of expertise to replicate that for you or your client. I do have a few students who might be able to do that work. Can you tell me how soon you might need it and what you are offering in terms of compensation?" It had become evident to Abibi that this favor that Christopher was asking her to do was much more of a business transaction than anything else. The nervous flutter in her stomach had become an excited hum. Maybe this was the way that she would be able to achieve her financial dreams after all.

"Certainly. That's a reasonable question." Christopher took another sip of his water, the melting ice cubes making a quiet clinking noise as they hit the side of the glass. "The overall pay for the project would be one hundred thousand dollars. Generally, I suggest to my brokers that they split the commission with their artist fifty-fifty. After all," he said, bringing the fork up to his mouth with another bite of salmon, "There is a lot of value that the broker brings to the process."

"And, you would consider my role to be one of a broker?" Abibi had stopped eating. The idea that just by finding a student who could paint the replica could earn her fifty thousand dollars had her attention. By the way that Christopher looked at her, Abibi could tell that he knew she was interested. She hoped that she hadn't seemed overly excited. That was never a position of power in a business negotiation. Her father had taught her that.

"Yes, of course." Christopher leaned back in his chair, his broad shoulders landing well outside of the width of the chair back, "The only challenge with this project is that my client is in a bit of a hurry. You see, they are having a gathering at their house in a month's time. The work would need to be complete, dry, varnished, framed and shipped within that time frame."

Abibi did a quick calculation in her head. The work that Christopher was talking about would have to be done in oil. There were quick-dry mediums that you could add to oils in order for them to cure faster, but they compromised the color and texture of the paint on the canvas.

To add to the complication, Rembrandt's work required layer after layer of carefully placed pigments in order to achieve the movement and light contrast that made what he did so remarkable. She turned her head and looked towards the window before answering. The light was streaming in leaving a puddle of brightness on the highly polished floor. Beyond the window, the restaurant had a view of the water. The docks were filled with small and medium-size boats, the kind that someone would use for local river fishing or for a couple taking a sunset cruise. In the distance, she could see one of those small boats cruising slowly. She imagined they might be out trolling for seafood. She looked back at Christopher, "What you are asking is a bit of a challenge, given the timeline and the technical difficulties presented in Rembrandt's works." She paused for a moment judging his reaction. He didn't move. "That said, the level of compensation might make this project a worthwhile effort."

"I'm glad you think so."

For the remainder of their meal, there was little talk except for things like the weather, places to visit in Savannah and the various countries that Christopher had traveled to over his career. Abibi could tell that Christopher didn't want to talk anymore about the project he had proposed.

At the end of the meal, Christopher followed her outside, the sunshine warming her bare shoulders. They stopped for a moment in front of the restaurant. "You are interested in my proposition?" Christopher asked.

Abibi didn't answer for a moment. What was she opening herself up to? Questions coursed through her mind, but her mouth answered before she had a chance to consider much of anything else. "Yes."

Christopher nodded, "Good. Please get it started. I'll be in touch."

ABIBI DROVE BACK to the art school, unable to focus. She drove like a robot, completing all the turns without thinking about exactly where she was going. Before she knew it, she was back in her office, standing by the window, looking out on the quad. A few students were walking by, art materials and portfolios in their hands. Staring outside was something she did regularly. Looking out the window gave her comfort, as though her life was bigger than just the small office that she occupied. After a few moments of consideration, she picked up her phone. She typed a quick text message and waited for a response. Less than a minute later, Hailey Park had responded. She was interested in whatever opportunity Dr. Roux had to offer. Abibi invited her to come to the office immediately.

A few minutes later, Hailey Park knocked on the door.

"Come!" Abibi called.

The hinges on the wooden door that sealed Abibi's office

from the hallway creaked as Hailey pushed the door open. "Dr. Roux? You wanted to see me?"

"Yes, Hailey. Please do come in and sit down." Abibi watched as the college freshman came in and chose a chair near the bookcase, the Buddha just above her. Hailey had taken two classes from Dr. Roux during the year. In both, she was top of her class. She had an excellent eye and technique that could only be God-given. "As I said in my text, I have a unique opportunity for you. I wanted to speak with you about it in person."

Hailey had perched on one of Abibi's leather chairs. She had folded her legs up underneath her, Indian style. She was wearing torn jeans and a tank top. Abibi could see paint stains across the front of her pants. From teaching at the art college, Abibi knew that the students wore their paint, charcoal and other mediums on their clothing like badges of honor. It wasn't uncommon to see students with completely stained hands sitting at a local restaurant or even in the school's cafeteria. The students at the college had no shame about their art. It was one of the things that made Abibi proud to work there.

Abibi had heard from a few of the other students that Hailey was having issues with making ends meet at school since her grandma passed away. Her friends weren't sure if she would be able to continue her classes. Even though there were several thousand students at the art school, the culture was that of a small family. Gossip, tall tales and stories ran wild on a daily basis. "I heard that you might be having some challenges with your tuition."

Hailey's face turned bright red, "I'm not sure how you heard that," she stuttered.

"Come, come. You know that people talk at school. That is no secret." Abibi stood up and resumed her view out of the window. "Hailey, I have to be honest. In my years of teaching art, I have never seen a talent like the one that you have been blessed with." Abibi turned to look at Hailey, wondering how she was receiving her compliment. Hailey wasn't moving, her eyes staring at Abibi, her lips slightly parted. She only pulled on a strand of blond hair that laid on her shoulder.

"Thank you," she whispered.

Abibi could tell that the compliment and the recognition that Hailey was having financial issues made her uncomfortable. Which one caused more discomfort, Abibi didn't know. It didn't matter. Though Abibi didn't particularly care whether Hailey was uncomfortable at that moment, as comfort didn't promote growth in her mind, she did want to move to the subject at hand. "I have a colleague who has approached me about a unique project. If done well, the project may be either extended or new opportunities may be forthcoming." As Abibi said the words, she hoped they were true, for both of their sakes.

Hailey shifted in her seat, refolding her legs. "What kind of project is it? Like an internship?"

Abibi smiled. One thing that never ceased to amaze her was how innocent the students at the school were. They had little understanding of the ways of the world. For that, she was grateful for her upbringing in Kenya, where the conditions were much harsher. Most students in the United States would never know that type of hardship. She, however, was happy about it. It had made her strong. "No, not an internship. It's a paid job."

Hailey wrinkled her brow and leaned forward. "I think I would be interested," she said, sounding unsure. "What does it involve?"

Abibi stepped away from the window, no longer seeing anything on the quad that was worth looking at. She sat in the chair facing Hailey, crossing her long legs at the knee. "This project would involve replicating a famous work of Rembrandt."

"I could do that," Hailey said.

"Before you agree to the project, there are a few things that you need to know. First, the work would have to be of the highest quality. My reputation rides on the work that you do and your ability to deliver the piece at the correct time." Hailey nodded. "In addition, there is a short window for delivering the work. You would have two weeks to complete the entire project."

Hailey turned her head and looked towards the books at the back of Abibi's office. "Which Rembrandt is your client interested in?"

"'The Storm on the Sea of Galilee.'" Abibi waited for a moment, watching Hailey intently. She wondered what the young student thought about trying to re-create such a prominent piece from that period. "Are you familiar with that piece?"

"Yes." Hailey looked at Abibi. "I can do that for sure. How much is the pay? And, how would I pay for materials?"

Abibi waited for a moment, weighing her options, not sure if she wanted to tell Hailey about the full payment that Christopher had offered just yet. Hailey's question about who would pay for the materials was a good one. The canvas, oils, brushes, varnish and other materials needed could cost quite a bit of money, money she was sure Hailey didn't have. "The pay is two thousand dollars," Abibi lied. Though Christopher said that there were one hundred thousand dollars on the table, fifty for Abibi and fifty for Hailey, Abibi didn't want to be stuck paying Hailey for work if Christopher didn't come through with the money. She realized that she would have to ask Christopher about that sooner rather than later. "Let me talk to my contact and get you money for your materials." Abibi stood up and walked to the door. "You will do the project, then?"

Hailey stood up, understanding from Abibi's body language that it was time for her to leave. "Yes."

"Good. I'll be in touch." As Abibi closed the door after Hailey, a sense of relief and dread flooded into her system at the same time. She may have just committed herself to pay a student several thousand dollars for work that she didn't need if Christopher didn't come through. It was money that she had, but money that she didn't want to spend. She quickly penned a text to Christopher, letting him know that she had a student ready to start the project. She asked about paying for materials.

A text from Christopher came back almost immediately, as if he had been sitting right by his cell phone. "If you'll give me your bank account information, I will deposit five thousand dollars in it for materials and coordination to get you started."

Abibi sent him the information, curiosity growing in her stomach. Would he really send her the money right now? She had her answer inside of two minutes. Her phone chimed with a notification from her bank that a deposit had been made. She opened the app and looked. Sure enough, Christopher had added five grand to her account. She sat down in the chair behind her desk swinging it gently from side to side as she thought, considering her next move. After a few minutes, she sent a text to Hailey, asking her to price out the cost for all the materials that she would need in order to finish the project. It was a test to see if Hailey was serious about completing the project.

Abibi didn't have to wait long. An hour later, Abibi received a text from Hailey telling her that she had just emailed a list of materials she would need to finish the project. When Abibi opened the email, she quickly saw that Hailey had been very thorough. Everything from three canvases to multiple types of paint, varnish, thinner and brushes was on the list. In her email, Hailey wrote, "Dr. Roux, I tried to choose materials that I thought were the closest to the types that were used during Rembrandt's time. Although we don't have access to exactly what he used, I think these will give me the best chance of making the painting look realistic. Please let me know your thoughts, Hailey."

The cost to get all the materials together was close to two thousand dollars. Abibi wasn't surprised. Quality art materials, especially oils, could be pricey at best. Many of them contained rare materials such as cadmium and tanzanite, precious materials that had to be mined from the earth. That said, Abibi knew that the things Hailey chose would indeed give her the best chance to make the Rembrandt replica look as original as possible. Abibi paced in her office. Although she trusted Hailey's talent, she didn't know Hailey well enough to know if she could be trusted with several thousand dollars in her pocket.

Abibi sent the list over to the local art supply store and asked them to charge the materials to her account and have it ready in two hours. She received an email back fifteen minutes later letting her know that most of the materials were in stock. The rest would have to be ordered. The good news was that at least Hailey would have enough materials to get started.

THEIR FIRST PROJECT together had gone well. Hailey acted responsibly, kept Abibi in the loop about her progress, and even invited her to come and see the work in progress. Abibi offered Hailey a few critiques, and they were able to get the painting done for Christopher two days early.

After Abibi handed off the project to Christopher, he handed her a bag of cash. In her heart, she knew what that meant, but she couldn't turn down the amount of money that she saw in the bag. It was more than she had ever seen in one place at one time.

The next morning, Abibi drove over to Hailey's dorm and texted her, asking her to come downstairs. Out in the parking lot, away from the prying eyes of many of the students, Abibi handed Hailey her portion of the payment. Christopher had paid the full one hundred thousand dollars, even though he had given them a deposit to cover the materials. As Hailey opened the bag, her face paled. "All of this? I thought the pay was two thousand dollars. This looks like a lot more than that."

Abibi smiled, a lie seeping out between her teeth. "My client heard about your plight and paying for your schooling. He said that talent like yours needed to go to school no matter what happened. He's hoping this will help you to stay here."

A smile finally formed on Hailey's face, "It will! Thank you so much!" As she walked away, Abibi called to her, "One thing, young lady."

"Yes, Dr. Roux?"

"You are taking that to the bank right now, aren't you?"

Hailey's face flushed. "Yes, of course." She turned to walk the other way, toward town where Abibi knew the majority of the banks were.

Abibi smiled, "Let me drive you. You shouldn't be walking through the city with all of that money."

THAT HAD BEEN the only project for about three months. Then one day, out of the blue, Christopher had sent Abibi a text, asking if they could meet again. This time, he wanted to see her at a local park. The weather had cooled a little from their first meeting over the summer. Abibi had a light sweater on over her dress. "It's nice to see you again," she said to Christopher when she saw him.

"It's nice to see you as well. Come, let's sit on this bench."

Abibi waited, wondering what he had to say. Inside, she secretly hoped he had another project for her, the tension growing in her stomach. The money he paid her for the first project had gone to some lovely home improvements and some new clothes. Another cash injection would certainly be welcome.

"I have another project for you, if you're interested."

Abibi nodded. "Certainly. What do you have in mind?"

"The student that you used last time did a wonderful job. My client was quite satisfied. Now, I have another client who is interested in a similar piece. If I send you the specifications, might you be able to get in touch with her to see if she could do the work?"

Abibi nodded.

Christopher stood up, "I'll be in touch."

Their relationship had grown from that point. Christopher would send a cryptic message to Abibi asking to meet. After success on the first four projects, with short turnarounds and the same pay, Christopher sent her instructions on how to use an encrypted chat room in order to pass information back and forth. The fact that they had to use something so cloak and dagger made Abibi a little bit nervous, but the money was so good that she couldn't turn it down. Abibi liked it. Hailey needed it.

THOUGH SHE TRIED to hide it, Hailey's death had shaken Abibi to the core. Not only was she suspicious about the stabbing, but Abibi's golden goose had been taken from her. She had pretended for the last several days that nothing was wrong. In her heart, she knew that wasn't the case. She just wondered how long it would be before trouble came knocking at her door...

15

The whine of the airplane engines seemed to have put Eli to sleep for the majority of the flight to Heathrow. Kat didn't have the same experience. Sitting cramped in the middle seat, she twisted and turned as many ways possible but just couldn't get comfortable. The whispers of people around her didn't help either. Kat was used to a much quieter lifestyle, one that didn't include being stuck on a cramped plane for six hours.

Without much fanfare, the sleek silver wide-bodied jet touched down in England. Kat smelled the familiar odor of jet fuel and coffee mixed together as she walked out onto the concourse. Henry had messaged right before they took off, telling her he'd taken care of getting she and Eli a hotel reservation. Her phone beeped, loading texts from the last several hours. Henry said he'd meet them out front. Jack had sent a picture of the dogs. She missed home.

Memories from her last trip to London flooded through her, remembering how suspicious she had been of Henry when she landed, the questions she had asked and how long it had taken her to warm up to him. In a way, she was glad she was careful.

In another way, she was glad that she already knew him for this case.

"Well, hello love!" Henry said, giving her a big hug. Kat stepped back for a moment before answering. Henry looked exactly the same as when she had seen him the last time, two years before. The same rumpled hair and clothes, the same pale face and warm eyes. "Let me get your luggage."

Henry must have noticed Eli standing behind her, "Well, hello. You must be Eli." Henry stuck out his hand. Eli shook it warmly, bowing his head.

"I am indeed. Eli, Eli Langster."

"It's a pleasure," Henry said. For a moment Kat held her breath, worried that Henry would immediately start interrogating Eli about his past. Kat was grateful when Henry did nothing more than introduce himself and get everyone loaded into the car. There would be plenty of time for questions later.

England didn't look much different than it did the last time she was there. The trees were a little fuller with their summer foliage, and the traffic still drove about three inches from each other's bumpers, making Kat catch her breath every single time they got close to other vehicles. Based on what Kat remembered, it seemed that they were heading back to Henry's office until they took the turn off directly into London. "I thought we'd stop by my new office," Henry said. "After that, I'll take you to the building where the art is being stored for customs."

"How long ago did the flight arrive?" Kat asked.

Henry glanced at his watch as he drove. Other than Eli, Henry was the only person Kat had met in the recent past who still wore an old-style watch. "By my watch," Henry said, "It looks like the plane landed just over ten hours ago."

Kat stared out the window as she thought about what they were about to do. The trees, fields and landscapes turned into clusters of buildings crammed together as they got closer to the city. The blue Scotland Yard sedan Henry drove passed just south of the city and out to the west, beyond the city borders. "The building they use for customs is out past the airport," Henry said. "With the number of items that come in and out of the country, they can't keep everything right at the airport. It would get too busy."

Kat nodded, feeling the effects of jet lag starting to set in. Though it was the afternoon in England, it was still morning in Savannah and even earlier where she lived in California. She could tell that her body was starting to struggle with all the time changes. "Is there a chance we could stop and get some coffee on our way?"

Henry glanced over at her and smiled, "Of course." He lifted his eyes to the rearview mirror to look at Eli, who was sitting calmly in the back. He hadn't said a word since I got into the car. "Eli, would you like a cup of coffee?"

"Actually, I'm a tea drinker," Eli said matter-of-factly.

For the next few minutes, Eli and Henry bonded over their love of tea. They had a spirited discussion on loose tea versus bagged tea. They covered everything from the type of teapot to use to how long to let it steep. They lost Kat when they started talking about whether to use a tea cozy or not. Her mind had drifted elsewhere. She pulled out her phone and sent a quick text to Van, letting him know that she was with Henry and Eli and had landed. A text came back right away, "Glad you are okay. Miss you. Call later." Kat felt concerned. Why did Van want her to call? She sent him a text back, "Everything okay?" A few minutes went by, worry starting to creep up on her. Just as she started to take a deep breath to chase the fear away, her phone beeped. There was an attachment to a text. She opened it. She saw Jack and Van laying on the couch, upside down. She started to laugh. What they were doing up early, she didn't know, but she was so grateful for the joy on their faces.

Henry took them through a drive-through where he bought Kat a large coffee and Eli a large tea. The woman at the window, her hair pulled back severely, and a headset attached to her face, passed a bag of food to Henry, as well as a bottle of water. Henry passed Kat the bag, "Here, thought you might need a little pick me up."

Though she hadn't really been paying attention, she was hungry. Starved, in fact. Eating on an airplane was always a scary proposition, no matter how hard they tried to make the food good. She opened the bag. Inside she saw three wrapped sandwiches. "What are these?"

"A few egg sandwiches," Henry said. "Didn't you hear me order them?"

"No," Kat shook her head. "I'm sorry. I guess I wasn't paying attention."

Kat handed a sandwich back to Eli, and one to Henry. She put the bag down by her feet and took a few bites thinking about the day to come. She hoped that within a few hours they would have more answers about the artwork that had disappeared from Hailey's apartment. Why this seemed like such an important part of the story she didn't know. She just had a hunch. The memory that ran through her head was of seeing Hailey's parents in the parking lot of the police station, her mother so sad and weak from the shock that she could barely stand up. Hailey's father was drawn and tired past his years. The artwork that had been shipped to London might hold the answer to why Hailey had been attacked in the first place. There had to be a bigger story here, she knew it. Images of a little boy stabbing a young woman kept cycling through her head. The question kept rattling through her head: Why would a ten-year-old boy stab a college student?

16

C arson was frustrated. There was no other way to describe how he was feeling. He sat in his office, leaned back in his chair, wondering what to do next. He had virtually no leads on Hailey Park's murder. The facts were simple. Someone had taken a long hunting knife and stabbed Hailey Park in the abdomen on her way home after class. That much he knew to be true. What didn't seem right was that the set of fingerprints they had found on the knife belonged to a child. A young child. There was something so wrong and so devastating about that piece of information that Carson could barely process it.

A flash of Julio's smiling face crossed his mind as he tapped the end of a pen on his desk. While Carson wasn't married, he had nieces and nephews he loved. That was one of the things that made Hailey's murder so upsetting, so personal. Not only did he have a niece that was nearly her age, but Julio, his nephew, was exactly ten. Thinking that Julio could pick up a knife and stab someone was an impossible thought. They'd spent a lot of time together. They'd gone to a couple of baseball games just the two of them and he saw Julio and his sister at frequent family gatherings.

Carson shook his head at no one in particular, trying to get the fog out of his brain. In the hecticness of the last two days, he'd been waiting to hear from the boy's lawyer, but hadn't heard anything. He picked up his phone, looking for the card that Alberto Soza had handed to him when he walked Miles out of the police station. Enough time had passed for them to get their strategy in order. He needed answers, and he needed them now. He dialed the phone and waited.

"Soza, Clark and McGinnis, this is Marlene."

"Marlene, this is Detective Carson Martino from the Savannah Police Department. I'd like to speak to Alberto Soza."

"Certainly. I'm not sure he's in his office. But I can put you through."

Carson felt a wave of frustration move through him. He had followed Beckman around the city as she chased the artwork and didn't focus on interviewing the child whose fingerprints were all over the murder weapon. Rookie mistake. The lawyer had outmaneuvered him. No more. He was glad he saw his mistake before his chief did.

"This is Alberto Soza," a voice on the other end of the line said.

"Mr. Soza, this is Detective Martino from the Savannah Police Department. We met the other day when you took Miles out of the police station?"

"Certainly, Detective. How can I help?"

Carson rolled his eyes, glad that no one could see him make a face. Attorneys were that way. They pretended that they had no idea what he wanted when he called. Alberto knew what Carson wanted. He wanted to interview Miles. "I need to set up a time to speak with your client about the Hailey Park incident." Carson chose his words carefully, knowing that Alberto was the type of lawyer who would rather spend twenty minutes arguing about the use of the word alleged versus actually getting any work done. He didn't have the time or the energy to play games.

"I'm sure you would like to speak to him, Detective. But the problem is, the boy isn't speaking right now."

"Mr. Sosa, I'm sure you can understand that our desire is to get this situation resolved as quickly as possible. I do need to set up a time to meet with the boy."

"Detective, I'm not sure you understand exactly what I'm saying. Since his foster mother took him home, Miles is refusing to speak. He hasn't uttered a word."

Carson stood up and started to pace back and forth behind the desk in his office. Miles wouldn't speak? That didn't make any sense. Young children were prone to use more words than literally anyone else. Carson wondered if this was some new legal tactic to try to prevent him from having access to a potential criminal. "I'm not sure what you're getting at, Mr. Sosa. The reality is that in law enforcement we have the obligation and the right to question suspects. Now, when would you like to set up this appointment?" Carson stopped pacing for just a moment, worried that he had overstepped. The last thing he needed was some fancy attorney getting in the way of his investigation.

"As I said, Detective Martino, we can set up all the appointments you would like, but the boy won't speak." Carson could hear some papers shuffle on the man's desk. "The other issue we have is that he is currently under a psychiatrist's care. I really need to get a release from his doctor before he can be interviewed. You know, we don't want to jeopardize the child's mental well-being."

Carson could feel his face flush with blood as the lawyer came up with reason after reason why he couldn't have access to Miles. Most lawyers he had worked with were at least fairly cooperative, or at least willing to stick to the letter of the law.

This lawyer didn't seem to have any scruples or hesitancy about blocking his investigation. "As you know Mr. Sosa, we have an obligation to interview all pertinent suspects in a case. Your client's fingerprints were found on the murder weapon. I think we should just set up that appointment, unless, of course, you'd prefer that I had our district attorney discuss this with you in front of the judge?" Carson was tired of playing games. Whoever this attorney was, he was trying every possible way to prevent Carson from doing his job. That wasn't going to happen. Carson had spent far too many years dedicated to his work to the exclusion of everything else, to let this case slip by with substandard investigative work. It would do nothing for his career, and he had little else in his life to lean on. He didn't wait for Alberto to answer, "Would it be possible for you to bring Miles to the office at two o'clock this afternoon?"

There was silence on the other end of the line for just a moment. Carson imagined that Alberto was thinking through his options. "Yes, that would be fine. I will present my client to you this afternoon."

Carson muttered a thank you before hanging up. He started pacing behind his desk again, running through the facts of the case in his mind. He knew about Hailey, he knew about the murder weapon — what kind it was and whose fingerprints were on it — he knew the location, he knew why Hailey had been there. What he didn't know was why a child would want to kill someone. That was a mystery.

The next several hours passed quickly, Carson clearing his desk of everything except for Hailey's murder file. He went through the images over and over again, looking for things that he had missed. Near lunchtime, Ginny stopped in his office, "You want me to bring you a sandwich from the deli? Looks like you have a lot going on here."

"That would be great. The regular, please."

Ginny was back with the sandwiches in a half hour. She set

the white butcher paper-wrapped sandwich on Carson's desk. "Need help with anything?" She plopped down in one of the chairs in front of Carson's desk, unwrapping her own sandwich. They had known each other long enough that she didn't ask if he'd mind.

"I don't know, Ginny," Carson shook his head. "I just can't make the facts all work together in this case."

Ginny took a bite of her sandwich and leaned forward, looking at the file that Carson had been staring at, "What's troubling you about it?"

"Pretty much everything." Carson slammed his fist down on the desk, the pens rattling in their cup from the concussion. "It just doesn't make sense. I've got a body, a murder weapon and fingerprints from a child. A child!"

Ginny furrowed her brow as she took another bite of sandwich, "I've never seen you like this before, Carson. What's going on with you?"

Carson sighed and leaned back in his chair. He picked up a bottle of water that Ginny had brought in with his sandwich and twisted it open. He took a drink before answering. "You know my nephew, Julio?"

Ginny nodded.

"He just turned ten. That's the same age as the suspect in this case. I have to be honest, the idea a child that age could commit murder is beyond what I ever thought was possible."

Ginny cocked her head to the side and gave him a half-smile, "Good thing you don't work for any of the big city departments. I'm sure they see lots of crazy stuff like this."

Carson took a bite of his sandwich, realizing how starved he was as soon as he started to chew. Ginny was probably right. While the Savannah Police Department dealt with a lot of tourist and vacation type crimes — car break-ins, lost luggage, the occasional missing child — murder wasn't one of the things that were high on their list. It was, for the most part, a quiet and sleepy town, with families who had lived in the area for years. They just didn't see the type of felony crimes that lots of the other major cities did, at least not until Hailey's murder. "You're right," Carson sighed. "It's not so much the fact that someone died, that's bothering me. It's that both the victim and the accused are so young. Something just isn't right."

"That's why we're here," Ginny said. "We specialize in handling all the stuff that isn't right." She pulled a potato chip out of the bag she had put on the corner of Carson's desk and crunched on it. "Did you make much progress with Kat Beckman?"

"The reporter?" He shook his head, "I think she may have led me on a wild goose chase. I spent the last day following her around the city looking for Hailey's artwork."

"I think she'd appreciate being called a journalist," Ginny smiled. "I did a little research on her. She's the real deal."

"What do you mean?"

"I have a couple of buddies in the FBI. I reached out to them and they reached out to people they know. She's been a big help to them on a couple of cases. Where is she now?"

Carson rolled his eyes, "She should be in London. She's chasing down a shipment of art that some guy at Scotland Yard told her was coming in. She took off with a so-called art expert from here."

"And you weren't impressed, I take it?"

"I just can't see how the missing artwork from Hailey's apartment has anything to do at all with her murder."

Ginny stood up, crumpling the white butcher paper her sandwich had come in into a ball and tossing it in Carson's wastebasket, "I don't know, buddy. When I looked her up, she looked like the real deal. From what my contacts said, she really likes to help law enforcement get their cases solved. She doesn't even usually report on the case itself, usually just some aspect of the case. Doesn't take much glory for the paper."

"My sister said the same thing."

"Is Anita ever wrong?" Ginny walked out of the room.

Kat had left Carson thinking about art for the last twenty-four hours. Now, he had to prepare to interview a murder suspect. Maybe Kat was right. Maybe there was some larger link to Hailey's art. Maybe that was the reason that she had been killed. He shook his head again. The whole thing just didn't make any sense at all.

Carson cleaned his desk, using an antibacterial wipe from the canister that he kept in the drawer. He carefully wiped the area, setting the file for Hailey's murder right in front of him. It was not the time for distractions. He opened it once again, staring at the images. From what he could tell, Hailey hadn't had a chance once she was stabbed. The medical examiner confirmed that. Even if she had been able to reach for her phone, there was no way that help would have gotten there in time to save her. Carson hoped that the location of the wound had just been a lucky guess. Either way, it was still horrifying that a child could commit murder... or even be accused of it.

He knew from his training that stabbings were far more personal than getting shot. What he didn't know was the psychology around child homicide. He frowned, wondering why Miles had used a knife. Why hadn't he used a gun? Certainly, there could be an access issue. Maybe it was just easier for him to grab his foster dad's hunting knife then it would be to get access to a gun? That was certainly possible. But a stabbing required strength and precision in order to be effective. Unless Miles, or whoever did this, knew what they were doing it would've been likely they would have missed. Carson shook his head. There was something more going on here. He just couldn't see it yet.

He looked at his watch, realizing that there were just a few minutes left before Miles and his attorney were due at the office. He stood up, closed the file and walked down the hallway into one of the conference rooms, flipping on the lights. The room wasn't newly decorated, but it had been nicely maintained. Just a few months before, Carson had found a maintenance crew in the building putting a new coat of pale gray paint on the walls. On the wall to the left was a large mirror that led to a viewing room on the other side. In the center of the room was a dark brown Formica table made to look like wood. There were four chairs arranged around the table. Generally, he or one of the other detectives sat on one side and the accused sat on the other. On the table, he put a yellow legal pad and two pens. He highly doubted that Alberto Soza would allow Miles to write out a statement, but he had to try. He looked at his watch. He had about ten minutes before he expected the lawyer to arrive. It was just enough time for him to touch base with his boss.

Carson walked to the back of the police station and rapped on the Chief's door quietly. "Come!"

Carson pushed the door open and stayed in the doorway, "Chief?"

Savannah's Police Department Chief, Joe Jackson, had been on the job for nearly thirty years. Some people in the department wondered why he hadn't retired already. Carson knew why. He loved his job. "Detective. What's going on?"

"Not much, sir. Just wanted to check in on the Hailey Park case."

The Chief waved him into the office. Carson stepped behind one of the two chairs that flanked his desk, resting his hands on the back of the chairs, "I've got the suspect coming in with his attorney in a few minutes. Wanted to give you a heads up in case you want to watch from the observation room."

Joe nodded, "I'm glad you got that scheduled."

"Yeah, the attorney gave me a little bit of a hard time."

Joe shook his head, "Those attorneys...they forget they don't run the legal system." The Chief looked up from the paperwork that he had been staring at when Carson came into the office. "Okay, give me a quick rundown on where we are and what you're thinking."

One thing that Carson loved about Chief Jackson was that he spent more time asking questions than barking out orders. Over the years Carson had worked for the Savannah Police Department, he'd seen many good people get promoted and move on to other departments because of the Chief's professional development strategies for them. Carson probably could have moved on to a bigger department, but he liked working for Chief Jackson. He was straightforward and no-nonsense. It made Carson's life much easier. "What I know for sure is I have a dead art school student, a knife that was used to commit the stabbing, and a child's fingerprints on it."

Chief Jackson leaned back in his chair interlacing his fingers behind his head, "I heard you were running around with a journalist the last day or so."

Carson's face flushed. One of the bad things about working for a small department was that everyone knew what everyone else was doing. "Yes, that's true. She's here on behalf of a paper from California."

"California? That's a long way off."

"I wasn't too sure about her. I'm still not completely sure about her. Ginny said that she's done some good reporting and has heard good things about her from her FBI contacts."

Chief Jackson smiled. "Ginny, she knows everyone, doesn't she?"

"That is the case, sir," Carson moved around to the front of the chair and sat down. "The thing that's frustrating me is that the pieces just don't fit together. I was telling Ginny the same thing just a little while ago. I've got a murder, a suspect, a dead body, a bunch of artwork that's gone missing, and something strange..."

"What's that?" Chief Jackson leaned forward in his chair.

"Well," Carson tilted his head, thinking. "It's two things, actually. First, the attorney for the child in question said he hasn't uttered a word since the incident."

"You think he's using some sort of shock tactic?"

Carson shrugged his shoulders, "I have no idea. That leads me to the second thing. A little while ago I found out that the child in question -- his name is Miles -- his psychiatrist was beaten up pretty badly and dumped in front of the hospital."

"You think those two things are connected?"

"I have no idea..."

17

L ondon's customs building was an unassuming brick warehouse on the west end of town. Located in an industrial area, the structure was likely built after World War II as part of the building fury as England tried to regain its identity. Aside from the sign in front stating that it was a government building, no one would ever know that literally millions of dollars' worth of merchandise was housed there waiting to be released by the government. As Henry pulled up and parked the car, Kat took a good look around.

The building itself was made of brown brick with a grayish mortar that had chipped in more places than not. It was the type of building that needed a good facelift. Kat wondered if the government hadn't put money into it so it wouldn't attract attention. Anything was possible, she thought.

Like most areas of England, right next to the warehouse were other buildings that flanked it on each side, a plumbing warehouse and what looked to be offices for a brewery. Although it occupied a corner, the buildings were positioned so close to each other that there was only enough room for a single car to pass between.

As Kat looked up, she realized the brick walls of the customs building extended up three floors at least. Around the building was nothing but concrete. While buildings in the United States typically had grass and shrubs and landscaping, that just wasn't common in England. Without any greenery, the brick building rose sharply up and away from the concrete sidewalk. Henry slammed the car door and motioned for Kat and Eli to follow. They went around the side of the building, to a metal door painted in a rust color with a small square glass window up high enough that it let light in but not high enough that anyone could look through it. Kat could see wire running between the panes of glass. Over top there was a rectangular metal awning that was flat, suspended by two cables, one at each corner. Next to the door handle was a keypad. Henry typed in a series of numbers and then swiped his ID badge. The door buzzed open as the lock was disengaged remotely.

The transition from the brightness outside into the darkness of the warehouse blinded Kat momentarily. She squinted, trying to make out what was in front of her. The windows of the building, high up in the walls, let down an eerie light. From where she was standing, it looked like they had not been cleaned since the day the building was completed. Given the fact that the customs building simply housed merchandise welcoming it in and then ushering it out, it wouldn't surprise her if that was actually the case.

As she followed Henry, Kat realized the building had a funny smell, the combination of damp shipping containers, raw wood, and what she was sure was some sort of mold. As her eyes adjusted to the light, she realized they were in a small anteroom that had a high cyclone fence just inside the doorway. There was a locked gate in front of them and someone sitting at a desk on the other side.

"You are?" the guard said from the other side of the fence. Kat looked at her closely. She was dressed in a light blue long sleeve shirt with a blue vest over the top. She wore dark pants and even darker work boots, her hair tied so tightly to the back of her neck Kat wasn't sure how she didn't have a headache. Her body was thick, the kind of frame you would expect from a Russian woman, though she spoke with a heavy British accent that made her difficult to understand.

"Henry Nash, Scotland Yard." Henry flipped open his ID badge and showed it to the woman through the fencing. She pulled a set of keys out of her pocket and unlocked the door from her side.

"Come on in," the woman shut the gate behind them, the metal clanging together as the lock reengaged. "Who are your friends?" the woman said, walking back behind her desk. The guard didn't have much of a workstation, Kat realized. An old reclaimed office desk, a set of file drawers, and a chair whose wheels rattled on the floor. It wasn't even a proper office, just some furniture shoved up against the cyclone fence. It seemed kind of strange for a warehouse that kept so many valuables.

"Guests of Scotland Yard," Henry answered, not being terribly specific about who Kat and Eli actually were.

The woman sat down in her chair with a harrumph, "Well, your guests will need to sign in here." She pushed a three-ring binder towards them, the pages open with other signatures listed. She tapped on the page with a ballpoint pen pointing where they needed to sign.

After Henry and Eli signed, Kat took a moment and filled out the line where her information was required. She scanned the lines above to see who else had signed in recently, but it seemed the dates were few and far between. There had been a few visitors the month before, but not many. Kat realized that the guard must sit at her desk day after day with little to do other than to wait for the next person to show up to sign in.

"Do you know what you're looking for?" the woman asked, not getting up.

Henry nodded, "We're looking for a shipment they got here just a few hours ago. Pieces of art."

The woman tapped on the keys of the computer that sat on the corner of her desk. Unlike most offices that had flat screen monitors, her monitor was old and bulky, part of the entirely reclaimed set of furniture and accessories she had for her little makeshift office. "An art shipment?"

Henry nodded again, "Yes, it came in from New York."

The woman squinted and then frowned, "Yes, we did just get a shipment in from New York. Not sure if it's what you are looking for, but it will be back by the receiving dock until we have a chance to process it." She pointed a short, thick finger past them and to the left, "Walk down this aisle to the back of the building until you see the loading dock. What you are looking for should be there." She squinted again, "The manifest reads the last four digits are eight, nine, two, three. Look for those numbers painted on the side of the crates."

The three of them walked off, Kat and Eli following Henry. His work boots didn't make any noise at all on the dusty concrete floors. Kat took a deep breath then, glad for the fresh air after getting off the airplane, even if it was filled with mold and the smell of new wood from the warehouse.

On either side of her enormous metal racks rose like giants out of the floor. They seem to be made of structural steel, the kind industrial spaces would use. From floor to ceiling there were wooden crates and containers stacked, some of them covered in plastic, some of them just raw wood. Kat wondered what was in each one of the crates as they passed by. "Henry, what kind of things come through customs?"

"Well, all sorts of things have to be checked through customs. Everything from items that are purchased overseas to shipments of personal items, furniture and even food — something like olive oil," Henry said, not breaking stride.

While the building from the outside didn't seem to be that

large, walking to the loading dock convinced Kat that it was much bigger than she thought it was, probably at least five hundred thousand square feet. Off in the distance, she could hear beeping, the kind that a forklift would make when backing up. Accessing stored items that were nearly three floors up from the ground would require something that large.

Kat drifted back and walked next to Eli for a moment, "You okay?" Eli hadn't said a word since they got out of the car in front of the customs building.

"Yes, quite," Eli shuffled along as quickly as he could behind Henry. "I don't like to get too involved with government types, if you know what I mean," he said motioning his head towards Henry. "Haven't had good luck with them in the past."

"Henry's a good guy," Kat said. "You don't have anything to worry about."

"I wouldn't be so sure."

Before Kat could ask Eli what he meant, light glowing from up ahead told her they were getting close to the loading dock doors. Instead of crates and boxes being organized neatly on the Industrial sized shelves they had passed, the items that had just been received were simply stacked at the entrance, awaiting search and processing.

To the right of the loading dock doors, there was a work area. Incandescent lights hung from the ceiling, making a quiet buzzing sound and bathing the area in a harsh light. Long worktables were set up end-to-end, with a few customs agents looking inside smaller boxes. Along the back wall, it looked like someone's garage. Tools were hung against the wall in a precise order. Kat guessed those were for opening the crates and accessing their contents. Sitting against the wall between the loading dock doors where the tools were hung was a stack of crates. Eli walked straight over to them, running his finger across the numbers, "Here."

His voice caught Kat's attention, "Eli, did you find something?" Kat was standing, suspended between the work area and the pile of crates. She walked over to him, wondering what he had found.

"I think these are the crates." He pointed to numbers that had been spray-painted on the side in light blue paint. "See? They match the numbers the agent at the front gate gave us."

Henry had come up behind them without Kat realizing, "Indeed. Those are the numbers the person at the gate gave us." Henry strode towards the two agents that were working at the tables. Kat couldn't hear what he said, but she saw him flash his ID and then one of the agents, a blonde woman wearing rubber gloves and inspecting a box filled with small items, walked over to the wall and handed him a crowbar.

"They're going to let us open it," Henry said with a smirk. "I always wanted to open one of these customs crates. It's like treasure hunting. Never know what you might find."

Henry wedged the edge of the crowbar in between the box and the wooden top giving it a little push, the wood creaking as he did. Before he could pull the crowbar out, the woman that had handed him the crowbar walked over. "Excuse me, I didn't ask, but what are you looking for?"

The woman that had approached them was far more pleasant than the guard at the gate, Kat realized. She was white pale, with yellow blonde hair and green eyes. She wore the same uniform as a guard at the gate, but she looked better in it for some reason. Kat wasn't sure why. Henry glanced back at her, setting the crowbar down. "Sorry. I assumed the guard at the gate let you know. We need to check on this shipment that came in from New York. Apparently, there is some art in it that may have been misplaced."

The customs agent, her last name Davis, emblazoned on her vest, nodded, "I see. Well, if you don't mind, I'll stand here while you do this. It'll save me some time anyway."

Henry nodded. "Of course." He picked up the crowbar

again and reinserted it in the top of the crate. Overall, the crate was more than eight feet wide, Kat guessed. It was taller and wider than it was deep, probably only being about four feet in depth. Kat wondered how they could have gotten all of the art in one crate. Thirty pieces wouldn't fit. Before she could ask the question, the customs agent said, "There are two more crates just like this one over there." She pointed to the other side of the loading dock, "We just haven't had time to take a look at them yet. They just got here."

"That's understandable," Henry gave the crate top another push with the crowbar. Cracking and squeaking ensued, the top of the crate pulling away from the wood. Kat could see nails sticking out through the lid. Henry worked his way around the top, loosening it in places. Within a minute or so, the top was free from the base. Kat, Eli, Henry and the customs agent each took a side and lifted the heavy wooden top away from the base, setting it over to the side, leaning it up against the wall.

Kat peered inside. On the top, there was a layer of packing peanuts, the kind that you would see in nearly any type of shipping box. Eli, like a kid in a candy store, started digging through the box for the canvases, shipping peanuts spilling out the corners of the crate and onto the floor. "Here," Eli said, his hands buried below the surface of the shipping peanuts. "I feel something." He looked up at Henry, "Can you give me a hand getting this out?"

The two men lifted a wrapped package out of the crate. From where Kat was standing it was impossible to see what was inside, the plastic wrapped around it in so many layers. "Let's take that over to one of the worktables," the customs agent said. "You'll be able to get a better look at that over there."

The men didn't say anything, simply carrying the rectangular object over to the table. From the way they were moving, it didn't look like it was that heavy, though it was definitely bulky, Kat thought. From a tool chest on the wall, the customs agent, Davis, went and retrieved a box cutter. "You'd better let me do the cutting. If you damage the interior, I'll get into trouble. If I damage it no harm done..." Davis shrugged her shoulders. "It's part of the job."

Kat stood back for a moment watching as Davis cut away the layers of plastic exposing a wooden frame. Even when the plastic was removed, Kat still couldn't see what was inside the crate. It was almost as if there was a crate within a crate. There was a solid sheet of Styrofoam four feet by four feet and maybe an inch in depth that covered whatever laid beneath. Kat held her breath. She hoped that they hadn't traveled the entire way to London only to realize that the shipment Henry had found out about was nothing more than a common customs exchange between an art gallery and a customer. That would be disappointing, not to mention it would leave them with no motivation for Hailey's murder. Kat had to keep reminding herself that that was the reason they had traveled so far to look at what was in the crates. It was all about Hailey. The memory of her parents and the stricken look on their faces passed through Kat's memory. She closed her eyes for a moment and shook her head, trying to dislodge the thought. She needed to focus on what was in front of her. That was the crate.

Henry lifted the thin piece of Styrofoam off the surface of whatever was below. Kat expected to see a painting, but all she saw was brown craft paper, carefully wrapped around an object. She sighed. Davis looked at her, "Always amazing how much packing they put in these crates." She shook her head. "I've worked here for ten years and it seems like each year they come up with new and more bloody difficult ways to pack things."

Kat smiled and immediately turned her attention back to the crate. She watched Henry and Eli wedge their fingers up underneath the covered object and lift it up, carrying it over to the worktable, the harsh light growing dull as it hit the kraft paper.

By the way that Eli moved, Kat could tell he was excited. His small fingers lifted the object, flipped it over and found the seams where the paper had been folded and taped. He carefully started to unfold it. From where Kat was standing, she could see the back supports of the canvas emerge, the wood peeking out from around the edges. Eli pressed his fingers on the edge of each side of the canvas without touching the paint. He quickly, with one movement, flipped the canvas over and laid it down on the table. He stepped back and stared. "Ah, yes," he said, leaning over to look at the painting, his fingers interlaced behind his back.

Kat moved closer to the table, trying not to trip over the packing materials they had left on the ground. The painting that lay before them looked like it was in the spirit of the paintings that Kat had seen at the exhibition hall of the art college. The mood of the painting was dark, with a bright spot of light in the middle of it where a woman, the left side of her face illuminated almost to white, stared back from the canvas. She was leaning slightly forward, a blue coat draped around her shoulders, a red hat perched at a tilt on her head. Eli sucked in his breath, "Oh, my word," he said, stepping back from the painting.

Kat furrowed her brow. Although she recognized that the style was the same as the painting she had seen in the exhibition hall, she didn't understand why Eli was reacting the way he was. She glanced at Henry, who shrugged his shoulders. "What is it, Eli?" Kat tilted her head and looked at him, wondering what made him react so strongly.

"I've never seen anything like this up close before," Eli said. "It's breathtaking." Eli started to move around the three sides of the table that he could access, his body bent over, peering at the painting. "The work is detailed, yet fluid," he whispered.

Kat felt like she had lost him into a different world. She stared at Henry.

Henry took a step back from the table. "I'm sorry, mate. You are going to have to fill us in..."

Eli stopped and stared at both of them. "If what I'm seeing is right, we've got a bigger problem on our hands than I suspected."

18

Carson had just stepped out of the interview room, finished with the setup, when Alberto Sosa, the attorney for Miles Nobesky, arrived. Alberto stuck out his hand, his long fingers looking like they had just received a fresh manicure. "Good to see you, Detective."

Carson took his hand, resentfully, "Thanks very much for making this happen."

"I know how the game works. I realize you are just trying to do your job."

"That's exactly the case," Carson nodded. "As you can imagine, the president of the art college, the mayor, and my chief really want to get this case closed as soon as possible." Carson had no idea how the president of the art college or the mayor felt about the case. It didn't matter to him. It would matter to someone like Alberto. "I've got a room set up over here for us. Where's Miles?"

Alberto shifted his gaze back towards the front door, "He should be here any moment with his foster mom."

"Barb?"

"That's correct. She's had custody of him for about two years. From what I understand, he had a rough start to life." Carson couldn't tell if Alberto was trying to build some sympathy for Miles or not. Knowing what kind of attorney he was, Carson wouldn't have been surprised if Alberto was already playing the sad case game. Unfortunately for Alberto, Carson had been on the job long enough to know that everyone had some sort of tragedy in their life. It didn't matter how happy their life was overall or not. Bad breaks were a fact.

Before Carson could respond to Alberto's comment, he saw a woman and a young boy walking back through the cubicles of the police department. It was Miles and his foster mom. Barb was a short woman, with uncolored hair that desperately needed a touchup, caught in a ponytail behind her back. She had a broad face and small eyes. "Alberto?" she said, "How long is this going to take? I have other kids to take care of." She didn't bother to say hello to Carson.

When Carson had started working as a police officer, the fact that Barb had ignored him would've gotten under his skin. Now he knew better. Over fifteen years he'd seen most of the games, and the new ones that he hadn't seen he could usually sniff out within a few minutes. Playing ignore the detective was an old one, one that wouldn't work with him. "Barb? I'm Detective Carson Martino. Thanks for bringing Miles in."

She nodded without saying anything. She just kept staring at Alberto. Alberto quickly took up the slack in the conversation, "Detective Martino has a room set up for us over here. Would you like to come in with us? Would you prefer if I handled the interview with Miles?"

Barb shook her head and eyed up a chair that was positioned just outside the door. "I'll stay out here. You can handle it," she said brusquely.

Carson wasn't surprised by her reaction. When people were interviewed, they seemed to fall into one of two tracks. Either they clung onto their attorney and glanced at him or her before answering any question at all, or they completely disengaged with their attorney and went off the rails. It looked to Carson like Barb was one that would cling. Was Barb a foster mom for the right reasons? He pushed the thought away. At this point, it didn't matter. That was something for Social Services to figure out. "Let's have a seat in here," he said to Alberto and Miles. "This won't take too long."

Carson followed Alberto and Miles into the room. Miles took the chair that was farthest back on the same side of the table as Alberto. Alberto set his briefcase down on the floor. Carson took the chair on the other side of the table, sitting across from Miles. "Miles, how are you doing today?"

Miles shifted in his seat, looking down at the table. He didn't make eye contact, but he did speak. "Okay, I guess."

Carson stared at him. So much for not speaking, he thought, looking at Alberto and then back at Miles. Alberto shrugged as if he didn't know what to say. Carson turned back to Miles. "So, this is going to be really easy today. I'm going to ask you a few questions, and you just answer them the best you can." Carson shifted in his seat, "Now if your attorney has another question or he doesn't want you to answer, he will let me know that. Okay?"

Miles nodded.

"Great. So, what can you tell me about the day you went to go play basketball in Calhoun Square?"

"A couple of my friends texted and wanted to know if I wanted to go."

"Yes," Carson looked down at his file. "They said they were playing basketball at the other end of the square and you disappeared for a few minutes. Is that true?" Carson watched Miles carefully, looking for any signal to let him know whether Miles was telling him the truth or not.

"I don't know."

"Okay, that's okay." Carson opened his file and pushed a picture of Hailey Park toward Miles. "Do you know this girl?" Carson had been careful to choose a picture of Hailey when she was alive, not one of her bloodied body. He was sure that Alberto would have an objection to that. Carson didn't need any reason for Alberto to pull Miles away from the interview. This might be the only chance that he got.

Miles shook his head, his eyes riveted on his lap.

Carson furrowed his brow, "Miles? Did you look at the picture?"

Alberto shifted in his seat as Miles' eyes flickered up from his lap and rested for a split second on Hailey's image. "I don't know her."

Carson sucked in a breath, getting ready to ask Miles to look again, but Alberto interrupted. "Detective, I think we've established that Miles doesn't know the young lady. Do you have any additional questions?"

Carson nodded. Alberto was clearly a very skilled attorney that wouldn't let him ask again. A ball of anger started to form in Carson's chest, but he kept it under control. Carson slid the picture of Hailey back in his file, closing it, and resting his forearms on the table. He'd been in interviews like this many times before. Attorneys who made a lot of money had no scruples about shutting down an investigation. After all, it was their job to protect their client. Carson still couldn't figure out the connection between Alberto Sosa, and Miles. Clearly, Alberto was being well paid. From the look of the foster mom, there was no way that she was paying the bills. Carson's brain reached for answers. Who was paying the attorney? "I do have another question. Miles, after you played basketball, what's the next thing you remember?"

Miles glanced at Alberto, who gave him a curt nod. "I don't really remember anything until a policeman found me."

Carson looked at Miles, trying to decide if he really didn't remember, or if he was lying. From the look on his face, the relaxed way that his mouth moved, Carson suspected that he actually didn't remember. How that was possible, Carson wasn't sure.

Alberto interrupted Carson's thoughts. "Detective, do you have any other questions for Miles?" Alberto looked at the gold watch on his wrist, "I know Barb said that she has some other things to do today."

Carson sat for just a moment. Trying to hurry through an interview was a common tactic by attorneys. When the police needed to interview you, that's where you needed to be. Carson wouldn't fall prey to his pressure. Carson opened the file, tipping it toward himself, so Miles wouldn't be able to see the pictures of Hailey's body. He pulled out another photo and slid it towards Miles. "Do you recognize this person?"

Miles nodded. "Yes, that's Dr. Kellum."

"And how do you know Dr. Kellum?"

Miles licked his lips, "I go and talk to Dr. Kellum two times a week. I go on Tuesdays and Thursdays."

Carson glanced at Alberto, whose face had stiffened. "What do you do when you go and visit Dr. Kellum?"

Alberto interrupted, "I think we're getting close to treading on patient-doctor confidentiality..."

Carson raised his eyebrows, "Miles, are you okay talking to me about this?"

"No, no, no." Alberto shook his head. "Miles is a minor. He can't give permission to talk about medical treatment. Only Barb can."

Carson paused. He needed to take the next step very carefully. He could go out and ask Barb for her permission to ask questions, but if she said no it would shut down the interview. If he didn't, he might not get the answers he needed. He decided to risk it. "Excuse me for one second," he said standing up. Carson walked to the door of the interview room and pulled it open. "Barb?" Barb was sitting, perched on the chair right outside the interview room, her face buried in her phone. From where Carson was standing it looked like she was on her social media feed. She looked up. "Is it okay if I ask Miles about his sessions with Dr. Kellum?"

Barb nodded. "Yes. Whatever you need so we can get out of here."

Alberto tipped his head as if he had lost a point in a tennis match. "Careful on your questioning, Detective. I won't hesitate to get my client out of here."

Carson nodded. His gamble had paid off. The question was what it would tell him. "So, Miles, what did you and Dr. Kellum do during your sessions?" Carson was hoping by asking what they did during their time together, that Alberto wouldn't object. After all, he wasn't asking what they talked about.

Miles fidgeted in his seat picking at the cuticle of one of his fingernails. "Well, for a while we would play games."

"What kind of games?" Carson asked.

"Card games, mostly. We'd look at people's faces and he'd ask me what I thought."

"Did you like that game?"

Miles nodded. "It was fun."

Carson looked at him, "You said you did that for a while. Did something change?"

"I think Dr. Kellum got tired of playing cards."

"Hmmm. So, what did you do instead?" Carson started to get excited, but he didn't know why.

"He had me lay down on the couch. It felt like I was taking a nap."

"During the whole session?"

Miles nodded.

Just as Carson was about to ask his next question, Alberto's phone beeped. "I'm sorry, but I need to cut this short. I just got an urgent text from a client. As you know, Miles can't speak to you without my presence." Alberto stood up, lifting the brief-case with his left hand. "Come on, Miles," he said, putting his long-fingered hand on the back of Miles's shoulder, "It's time to go now."

Carson stood up, "I'm not done with my questioning."

Alberto paused in the doorway, "I'm sorry, but we are done for today. Please forward any additional questions you have in writing to my office. We will make sure to get the answers back to you." Alberto glanced down at Barb. "Barb? Are you ready to go?"

The three of them left without so much as a goodbye, Alberto's tall, custom suited body, towering over Barb's stout form and Miles' frail figure. Carson watched as they wove their way through the desks and officers that were moving through the police department. He suspected there was something else going on.

Behind him, a door clicked open. The Chief stepped out. He shook his head, "That's quite an attorney that's representing that little boy."

"You can say that again."

The Chief narrowed his eyes at Carson. "What are you thinking?"

Carson shook his head, "At this point, I've got more questions than answers. I'd like to know how a foster mom has the funds to hire an attorney like that guy. She certainly doesn't appear to be the kind of person that can pay five hundred dollars an hour for representation."

Chief Jackson nodded, "I was wondering the same thing."

19

D
r. Oskar Kellum sat gingerly on the side of his hospital bed, trying to listen to the doctor through the wave of pain that was going through his body. "You sustained some pretty serious injuries, but there is nothing that would require you to stay here any longer. You're going to have to take it easy for a while. I'll have the nurse come in and give you the discharge papers." The doctor left without any other comment.

After spending two nights in the hospital, Oskar felt weary. His bones ached, and his eye was still fairly swollen shut. The swelling had gone down enough for the ophthalmologist to determine that his retina hadn't been damaged. Sitting on the edge of the bed, he wondered what to do next, but his mind was so foggy from the cocktail of pain medication and steroids that he could hardly think straight.

The nurse came into his room a few minutes later, her fancy tennis shoes in a range of orange yellows and pinks, making her look more like a medical track star than a nurse. "Okay, Oskar. I have all of your paperwork in order."

Oskar didn't hear much more after that. He stood up out of

bed as soon as the nurse left, collected the bag that held what was left of his belongings — his keys, wallet, phone and the watch that had been his grandfather's, the face of it shattered. He shuffled down the hallway and went to the elevator. Just lifting his arm to press the button for the first floor sent a surge of pain through his body. As the doors opened, he made his way out of the elevator and into an open area, where couples and families were walking together. He imagined they were either going to visit a loved one or friend, or worse, they were going for testing. For a moment he felt their fear.

Oskar pushed the revolving door and felt the warmth of the morning touch his face. Normally, he wasn't a fan of the overly hot summers in Savannah, but he felt different today. The cold, dry air conditioning that ran incessantly in the hospital had left him feeling chilled to the bone. The warm, moist air filled his lungs. He took as deep of a breath as his broken ribs would allow.

Oskar found a bench in front of the hospital and sat down. The nurse had been nice enough to order a cab for him so that he could get home. The police department had arranged to have his car towed to a local repair facility. He would have to deal with that later. He simply didn't have the energy right now.

The cab driver seemed pleasant enough, chatting about the weather and the barbecue that he'd eaten the night before. He was a middle-aged man with a round face. The drone of his voice kept Oskar entertained on the way back to his condo. Once Oskar made his way out of the cab, he left the driver a nice tip. It wasn't his usual custom, but he felt like if nothing else, he had learned that kindness was underrated.

Meowing met him at the door. His cat, Ralph, met him with a large amount of noise. Oskar imagined he was complaining about how he'd been left alone. Luckily, Oskar did know one of the neighbors, a woman named Susan, who had a key to Oskar's condo. With the amount of pain he was in, he only managed to send her a text. She gave Ralph his food and a fresh bowl of water while he was stuck at the hospital. Oskar knew the litter would need to be changed, but the idea of bending over to do anything at that moment simply wasn't going to happen.

Oskar eased his way down onto the couch, staring out the big windows that gave him a small view of the park, and a bigger view of the side of the building next door. He had lived a quiet life until now. He never even been in a scrape in elementary or high school, never late to class, never even gotten a parking ticket. The fact that thugs took him away and beat him left him reeling not just physically, but mentally and emotionally. He sighed, trying to adjust to a comfortable position on the couch. The bag he brought back from the hospital was next to him, resting on the cushions. He poured it out on the couch, a tumble of prescriptions, follow-up appointments, personal items and orange vials filled with medication settling in the cracks. It would all need to be sorted, but now wasn't the time.

Oskar had always loved his work to the exception of everything else. That was until he found gambling. He never had any family to give him a reason to come home at night. The thrill of placing a bet was a stark contrast to the high level of control, quiet and focus that he needed to maintain in order to help his patients, particularly the pediatric ones. His mind drifted to Miles. Oskar wondered what he was doing right now. He had done as he had been trained, but the question was whether the memories would resurface or not. He hadn't told anyone that there was a possibility that Miles could eventually remember what happened and Oskar's part in it. Oskar closed his eyes. The way he was feeling at the moment, none of it mattered.

There was a sharp rap at the door. Oskar turned his head to the right, wondering who it was, contemplating ignoring it, when he heard a voice. "Dr. Kellum, Savannah Police. Open up."

Oskar's eyebrows twisted together. How did the police know he was home already? "One minute, please," he croaked, his voice still hoarse from the dry air in the hospital. Oskar pushed off the couch, trying not to create too much pain in his ribs. No matter which way he moved, he was in pain. There was no avoiding it. He walked over to the door and peered through the peephole. Outside of the door to his condo, he could see two uniformed police officers and a man with dark hair in a suit. They were either all in uniform or had a badge visible. Oskar didn't want to open the door to just anyone. Not after what happened to him.

He turned the knob on the deadbolt, realizing that as soon as the police officers left, he would be calling a locksmith to add more locks to the door. He had never felt so unsafe before. "One minute," he said.

Oskar cracked the door open and peered out. The suited man that was standing on his doorstep was the same one that had met him at the hospital. "I just got home from the hospital. What do you need?"

"Let us in, Dr. Kellum," Carson said.

Oskar pushed the door back with his left hand, feeling an ache run through the side of his body. It would be time for more painkillers soon. "I need to go sit down. Come on in but close the door."

Oskar shuffled back to the couch, using both of his hands to brace himself as he eased himself back onto the cushions. "I'm sorry. I'm in a lot of pain. How can I help?"

"Okay if I sit down?" Carson asked.

Oskar nodded, realizing he didn't have much of a choice. It was probably better to just be polite, answer their questions, and send them on their way. All he wanted to do was sleep.

Carson crossed his left foot over his right knee and leaned back on the couch. "Nice place you have here," he said. "I have some follow-up questions for you."

Oskar shifted from one side to the other, not feeling comfortable no matter how he sat. "Sure, go ahead."

"Tell me again how you ended up at the hospital?"

Oskar pursed his lips together, not sure how much he could say without bringing the wrath of the thugs back down on him. "I'm not sure. I don't remember much. I was driving home and then the next thing I remember was finding myself in the emergency room." He hoped that pleading amnesia would keep the police from asking too many questions, questions he didn't want to answer. The beating ran back through his memory, the feeling of his car lurching as it hit the nail strip, the rough way the men had pulled him out of the car and dragged him into the warehouse. He remembered the first and second punches, but as for the rest of them, he couldn't remember them all. He thought there might be mercy in that.

Carson squinted at Oskar, "You're telling me that after this drastic of a beating, the only thing you remember is driving your car and then ending up in the emergency room?"

Oskar felt a flush of heat go through his face. He hoped he didn't start to sweat. He knew that would be a sure sign to the detective that he was hiding something, even if the detective hadn't already figured it out. "Yes, yes. That's really all that I remember."

"Hmmm. That's really interesting. Here's what I don't understand: we found your wallet on you and no cash was taken. Why do you think you got beaten up? Couldn't have been a mugging, unless they took something that you haven't told us about yet."

Oskar closed his eyes for a moment, trying to deal with a new wave of pain that was surging through his body. He didn't have the energy to fight with the police, but he was worried that if he told them anything the next meeting with them wouldn't be quite so kind. "As I said, Detective, I really don't remember anything. I can't even begin to guess why those thugs beat me up. Maybe they thought they could steal my car."

Carson shook his head. "But they didn't."

Oskar watched for a moment without answering. He saw Carson uncross his leg. He leaned towards Oskar, squinting. Oskar realized the more that he talked, the less plausible his explanations were. "I'm sorry," he said. "I just don't know what to say. If you'll excuse me, I'm really not feeling well."

"Just one other thing that's bothering me, Oskar," Carson said, "How is it that your name came up in another case of mine? Hailey Park? Do you know that name?"

Oskar sucked in a breath. It was clear the detective was on the scent of what had happened but hadn't quite figured it all out yet. If he did, Oskar wasn't sure what the consequences would be. He shivered. He didn't want to think about it. "Detective, I treat many pediatric patients." He wasn't about to admit he knew Hailey's name.

"Here's the thing that I find to be interesting," Carson said slowly. "You and Miles have something in common. He can't seem to remember what happened while he was at Calhoun Park, but I have his fingerprints all over the knife that was used to murder a young art school student. Similarly, you end up getting beaten nearly to death, but can't seem to remember what happened. I'm sensing a pattern here..."

Oskar felt the blood drain from his face. He just hoped he didn't throw up. "I'm sorry, Detective. I don't know what to say."

"Can you tell me anything about the work that you've done with Miles?"

Oskar shook his head, "As you can imagine, I am forbidden to talk about my patients and the work that I do with them unless I have a court order." Oskar swung his legs up onto the couch, one at a time, grimacing in pain. "I'm sorry, Detective. I don't mean to be rude, but I really need to rest. I'm simply not feeling well. Please show yourselves out." A surge of tension ran through Oskar's body. He had never been so forthright with anyone in the past, except patients that were frustrating him. He held his breath, hoping that the detective and the two officers would leave without an argument. He closed his eyes and listened. In a moment, he heard the squeak of the chair that Carson had been sitting on. Oskar fluttered his eyes open.

Carson stood over him, "I certainly hope that you feel better, Dr. Kellum. When you do, we still have a few things that we need to talk about. We'll show ourselves out."

Oskar started to breathe again. He felt trapped, trapped by the pain in his body, the work that he had done with Miles, the fact that the police were on his tail. He had no idea when or if the thugs would return. He turned his head to the side, and closed his eyes, hoping for sleep...

20

I n an old Buick stationed down the block from where Dr. Oskar Kellum lived, a man sat, listening to oldies music and smoking, the tendrils of his exhales curling out the side window. He watched the two police officers and the detective walk out of the front door of Oskar's building. The bug that they had put into Dr. Kellum's condo while he was in the hospital worked like a charm. He had heard everything.

The man picked up the flip phone that was sitting on the vinyl seat next to him, opening it up. He'd only used it one other time, pretty much getting a new phone every couple of days. That was the way they kept things quiet. "The police were at the condo," he said. "What you wanna do?"

"Did he say anything?" the voice on the other end of the line asked.

"Not yet, but it sounded like he was close."

"You think he's a threat?"

"Maybe."

"Take care of it."

"What about the eighty grand he owes us?"

"Will get it off some other schmuck. No shortage of people that like to lose money gambling."

The line went dead. The man turned off the Buick, leaving it parked where it was. He had carefully planned routes over the last couple of days just in case. He pulled a nine-millimeter pistol out of the glove compartment, making sure it was loaded. He pulled gently on the slide, the dull copper color of the bullet casing peeking through when he inched it back. He flipped the safety off. As he got out of the car, the man shoved the gun into the back of his pants. He had put his holster on just in case, so he didn't have to worry about the pistol clattering to the ground and making a scene. That was the best way to get caught.

The man left the Buick and walked half a block to the front door of Oskar's condo and keyed in the code to get the door to buzz open. The team had been watching the condo for long enough that they knew pretty much everything there was to know about the building and the surrounding area. The man used the steps to go up to Oskar's floor, avoiding surveillance cameras that were in the elevators, not that anyone ever looked at the feed. He climbed the three flights of steps, feeling a little winded by the time he got to the door, reminding himself that spending a little bit more time working out might not be a bad thing. "Why did you have to buy a unit on the third floor?" he mumbled to himself.

The man walked down the hallway and went directly to Oskar's door, pulling the key out of his pocket. While Oskar had been in the hospital, another guy had come in, set up a couple of bugs and got the keys to the door. He was a good lock-smith, the kind that didn't ask questions and preferred to be paid in cash.

The man slid the key into the lock, turning it quietly, hoping that the click of the bolt coming away from the frame wouldn't alert Oskar. It probably wouldn't matter even if it did, but the less noise the better. As the man cracked the door open, he could see Oskar had fallen asleep on the couch. He was probably in the same position as when the police left him. There was a half-consumed bottle of water and an orange vial of pills on the coffee table next to where Oskar was laying. It looked like Oskar had taken a bunch of pain pills and then laid back down on the couch just after the police left. The man moved quickly but efficiently, knowing that the more time he spent in Oskar's apartment the worse it would be. He found the two bugs that had been placed in the apartment, pulled them off of the underside of the coffee table and from the top shelf of the bookcase and stuck them in his pocket. No need for the police to find those. Luckily, Oskar hadn't woken up. The man made his way back to where Oskar was sleeping, the wooden floor making a slight creak as he approached. He drew the gun out from his waistband, and without thinking, put it to the side of Oskar's head and pulled the trigger. There was no need to check if he was dead. A shot like that to the head would end him. Adrenaline started to surge through the man, realizing he was now on the clock. He had forgotten to pack his silencer, so it was likely someone else in the condo had heard the gunshot. That gave him about a three-minute window before the police arrived. Unfortunately, the Savannah Police Department didn't have much to do, so their response time was way too quick for his liking.

The man looked around the condo, wondering if there was anything he should take. He frowned for a second, and then realized he had left no fingerprints except for a set on the door going in. On his way out, he stopped and wiped the doorknob clean. He turned down the hall and went back down the three flights of steps, going out the back door of the building, rather than the front door.

Outside, he walked down a side street and cut back through the parking lot of the building next door, getting himself lost amid trash dumpsters and the rise of buildings crushed together. The police would start looking on the main roads, not in the back. By the time they figured out what happened, he would be long gone.

The man walked down the sidewalk, his hands shoved in his pockets, his oversized shirt covering the gun he had just used. On the way back to the office, he'd drive by the waterfront and toss the gun in the water. The bosses preferred it when there was less evidence to be found later. He'd probably chuck the bugs in the water as well. He snorted, realizing that whoever was listening to the apartment was about to get a lot of feedback in their ears when he dumped them. That was their problem.

As he got to the Buick, he heard sirens. He shook his head, mumbling to himself, "They seem to get faster every day." He slammed the door, turned the key in the ignition and heard the engine rumble to life. He pulled out into traffic, making a U-turn to head away from the direction the sirens were coming and toward the waterfront. At the first red light, he sent a quick text. "Done."

"Good," was the response he got. It was time for lunch.

21

Carson's mind was racing. He stopped on the way back to the police station at a local Thai restaurant. He wanted curry. Thoughts of his conversation with Oskar and Miles wound around in the back of his head while he mumbled his order to the woman behind the counter. The pieces still didn't add up.

The minute he got back in his car, the smell of chicken, vegetables and red curry filling it, his phone rang. "Martino," he answered.

"Were you just interviewing Dr. Kellum?" the voice asked.

It was Ginny. "Yep. I'm headed back to the office now. Why?"

"Well, you might as well turn right around and go back the way you came. I think your lunch is going to get cold. Officers just called it in. Looks like Dr. Kellum was shot."

"What? I was just there..." Carson glanced down at the MDT that had been mounted in his work unit. Most of the Savannah Police Department now had mobile computers right in their vehicles. His detective unit was no exception. As he spun the unit around, he glanced at the time on the MDT. Barely thirty minutes had passed since he and the other officers had been at Oskar's apartment. Someone was cleaning up loose ends. The question was who?

"Yeah, I know you were just there," Ginny's voice broke through his thoughts. "We got a call from one of the neighbors, I guess a lady across the hall, said she heard a gunshot."

"How did she know it was from Oskar's apartment?"

"I guess she watched Oskar's cat for the last couple of nights while he was in the hospital." Ginny had an uncanny way of knowing what was going on in nearly every case in the department. "When she heard the shot, I guess she went to the door and peered out. Oskar's door was cracked open. When she looked inside, she saw the blood and called it in."

Carson shook his head. "All right. I'm on my way. Thanks for the call." As soon as he hung up the phone with Ginny, he pounded his fist on the steering wheel. Rage burned inside of him. Who were the people responsible for this? How did they get ahead of him? Carson felt the muscles in his jaw clench and reminded himself that he needed to stay relaxed if he hoped to solve the case. The last thing he needed to do was start grinding his teeth again. He'd done enough damage to his mouth already.

The drive back over to Oskar's condo didn't take long, just about eight minutes. Several Savannah Police Department cruisers were parked in the front, lights flashing. Two officers were standing outside the front door, keeping it open. Carson parked on the opposite side of the street, slipping the cruiser between a pickup truck and a yellow sedan with a bumper sticker that read "GA On My Mind." He nearly got clipped by oncoming traffic when he got out, eliciting a honk from the car horn. "Sorry!" he said, putting his hands up in the air. This case was getting under his skin, that was clear.

He walked across the street, nodding to the two officers that were standing by the door. One of them yelled, "A fresh one, huh?" Carson nodded, not wanting to take the time to stop and talk. Frustration tightened the muscles in his shoulders. He decided to run the three flights of steps instead of taking the elevator to work off the stress.

Carson got to the landing on Oskar's floor and was barely out of breath. The discipline of his workouts took care of his stress, anger and, of course, the department requirements for fitness. He straightened his tie and pushed the door open onto the third floor. He looked to his left and saw a uniformed officer standing outside of Oskar's doorway. "Hey," he said, walking past the officer into the condo.

Once inside, he saw the condo was a hive of activity. There was a woman with dark hair, thick, rimmed glasses, and a dark blue polo shirt taking pictures of Oskar's bloodied body. Carson paused for a moment, trying to remember her name. "You got here fast, Nicole."

She straightened up, resting the camera in her hands. "Yeah, not much going on today until this happened."

Carson nodded. "Notice anything while you were taking pictures?" He put his right hand in his jacket pocket and pulled out a set of blue gloves.

"I'm not a medical examiner, but this looks pretty straight-forward to me. Gunshot wound to the head. Apparently, the killer didn't bother to use a silencer or muffle the noise. The woman across the hall said she could hear it pretty clearly."

Carson glanced that way, "Is she in her condo now?"

As Nicole bent over to take more pictures, she said, "Yeah, I think so. I think an officer is sitting with her. They were waiting for you."

"I'll go over there in a sec. Just want to take a look at this body first." Carson leaned over to look at Oskar. Nicole was right. Even if they had had a trauma surgeon on standby in the hallway, there was no way Oskar could've survived a direct shot to the head. Though the medical examiner would give him a full report on what happened, he always liked to have a little information gathered from looking at the body while it was still at the scene. Oskar wasn't telling him much. From the way it was positioned, it looked like he had been asleep. There was water and a pill bottle on a table nearby.

Carson took a deep breath and scanned Oskar's body. He was laying on his right side, facing the back of the couch. His glasses were on the table by the pill bottle. There was no blanket on him, though one was folded up on the back of the couch. What was left of Oskar's head was resting on two thin pillows. A red stain had seeped into the fabric fibers of the pillow that was closest to his head. There was a small round hole in his left temple just above his left eye. "Gunshot residue," he pointed out the charcoal gray area around the entry wound to Nicole. "Can you get a close-up of that?" Nicole nodded. Carson knew she probably already got the shot, but he would feel better if he saw her do it himself.

Carson turned away from Oskar's cooling body, glancing around the condo. When he had been there earlier, he had only taken in Oskar's belongings in a general sense. Now that Oskar had been murdered, and it was fair to say it was a murder given the circumstances, Carson looked in more detail around the condo.

Oskar seemed to be as much of a neat freak as Carson was. The books on the shelves were lined up, pressed together with bookends, with no dust gathering around their bindings. Decorative items were placed carefully on each surface, but there weren't too many of them, nothing like Eli's antique store, that was for sure. For a moment, Carson's mind drifted to Kat and Eli. He needed to check in with them. He glanced at the time on his cell phone.

Carson walked through Oskar's bedroom and his bathroom, pulling on a pair of blue latex gloves from his pocket. He wandered into a second bedroom that looked like Oskar used it for work. Carson stood behind an old antique desk that was positioned toward the back of the office space. He muttered, "Eli would love this." He carefully opened the drawers trying to figure out what had made Oskar a target. In the top drawer, there was nothing more than a small divider with pencils, pens and a few notepads. The next drawer down held a couple checkbooks and some old photos that Carson thumbed through.

The third drawer had been retrofitted to handle hanging files. Carson sat down on Oskar's desk chair, and pulled the drawer open wide, thumbing through them. In the front of the drawer were notes from the last condo association meeting, a thin folder that look like genealogy information, and a few miscellaneous files for paid bills and documents. Carson was ready to close the drawer when he saw something at the bottom. It wasn't hung up the way the other files were. Carson pushed the files to the side and reached down into the bottom of the drawer and called into the other room, "Hey, Nicole, can you come document this?"

As Nicole snapped a few photos of the bottom of the drawer, Carson held up his hand, "Hold on for a second, would you? I want to pull this file out of here and have you document it." Carson reached down into the bottom and pulled the green file up through the tangle of the rest of the file folders that were hanging. He held it out for Nicole to take a couple of pictures and then opened it up while she took a few more. Establishing where the information came from would be important if they ever hoped to catch Oskar's killer. Carson lifted his head, "Thanks."

Nicole nodded, "No problem. Call if you need more pictures taken."

Carson stared down at the file folder that was in his hands. Why Oskar had chosen an almost fluorescent green for something he was trying to hide, Carson wasn't sure. If it had been him, he would have chosen a color that was as close to the bottom of the drawer as possible, but not everything in a crime made sense. Carson flipped open the file and looked at the sheaf of papers that were stuck inside, laying them on top of Oskar's desk. There wasn't much else there, save for an expensive desktop computer and a few psychiatric trade journals stacked in the corner.

In the file, there appeared to be sheets of paper that logged transactions. It looked like Oskar had torn pages out of an old-fashioned accounting journal, and then carefully trimmed the edge to make them straight. In the left-hand column there were dates, and the rest of the columns followed with numbers. There were no discernible headings, other than he could tell what the dates were. "What were you up to, Oskar?" Carson muttered.

Carson shuffled through the rest of the papers that were in the file. The other pages weren't accounting information. They appeared to be case notes about a particular patient. Each page was dated with information about a session that had happened, but there was no information as to what patient it was about. Carson scanned the pages and saw times, medications, and longhand sentences about what had occurred during the session. Carson frowned and shook his head, wondering what patient the notes referred to. Why were there patient notes at Oskar's house? Shouldn't they be at his office, he wondered? It was interesting to him that there was accounting information in the same file as patient notes. He looked back at the accounting page. Was it possible that Oskar was treating a high-profile client in cash? Carson looked at the page of accounting figures and realized the balance at the end was negative, not positive. That didn't make sense. He was just about to read through the case notes in more detail when Nicole came back into the room. "If you've got a minute, the officer across the hall said the resident is getting antsy and would like to talk to you."

Carson nodded. "Do you have an evidence bag big enough to put this in?"

Nicole reached behind her and pulled out a bag that had been stuck in her back pocket. "Here ya go."

Carson slid the folder in the bag, sealed it, signed and dated it. He would take it back to the office with him after he was done talking to the neighbor. "Can I leave this with you while I go do this interview?"

Nicole nodded and picked up a pen from Oskar's desk, signing her name to keep the chain of custody intact. "Yep. Just come and get me when you're done."

"Thanks." As Carson walked away, he could hear the shutter from Nicole's camera fire. She was taking pictures of the inside of Oskar's office. He shook his head. The amount of detail that the forensics teams had to document was just staggering. Attorneys like Alberto Soza made their life nearly impossible.

Carson pulled off the blue gloves he had been wearing and shoved them back in his jacket pocket. He walked out the door and took a couple of steps across the hallway, tapping on the door. "Savannah Police. Can I come in?"

"Yes," came a weak voice from inside.

Carson turned the knob on the door and gave it a push. Inside, he spotted a small woman sitting next to an officer, the sunlight from a large window covering their backs and shoulders. The officer stood up, "Detective, this is Susan. She knew Oskar and was the one that reported the gunshot."

At the mention of the gunshot, the small woman crumpled into a tiny ball, whimpering. The officer looked at Carson, raised his eyebrows and said, "I'll be just outside the door if you need me."

Carson swallowed, knowing this wasn't going to be an easy interview, "Thanks." He walked over to the couch where the woman was sitting. "Okay if I sit here with you?"

The woman looked up, her eyes wet with tears. She nodded. Carson wanted to get the interview over as quickly as possible. Hysterical people made him nervous. "Susan, my name is Carson. I'm sorry to meet you under the circumstances."

"I'm sorry, too."

It seemed a strange thing to say, but Carson knew that people who were in shock said all sorts of crazy things. He let it slide. "Can you tell me what happened?"

The woman sniffled and wiped her nose with the sleeve of the oversized light pink sweater she was wearing. Carson glanced around and saw a box of tissues behind him. He stood up and brought it to her, offering her one. "Thanks," she said, pulling one out of the box. She paused, wiping her nose. "I'm not sure why I'm so upset," she said. "It's not like I saw anything. I didn't even know Oskar that well, to be honest."

Carson leaned back on the floral couch and waited. He had learned that some interviews he needed to ask questions and other interviews it was better if he stayed silent. It seemed like Susan would do most of the talking on her own if he gave her a second. "It's okay to be upset," he said.

She sniffled again, and uncurled herself from the ball on the couch, "It's nice of you to say that." She dabbed at her eyes and looked at him, "I'm sorry to be so dramatic. How can I help you?"

Carson's tactic to give her a minute to settle down had worked. "Can you tell me a little bit about your relationship with Oskar?"

"There's not much to tell. I didn't really know him. He had given me a key one time because he was expecting a delivery and asked me to let the man and while he was at work. After the delivery, he told me to keep it. I guess he didn't have any family."

Carson nodded. "So, when did you know there was trouble with Oskar?"

"Trouble? Oh, you mean when he was in the hospital?"

"Yes. Can you tell me about that?"

She furrowed her eyebrows, "Yes, it was strange." She shifted in her seat on the couch, "I got a call from a number I didn't recognize, But I decided to pick up anyway. It was a nurse from the hospital, saying that Oskar wanted to talk to me. She put him on the line, and he asked me if I still had the key to his apartment."

"And you told him you did?"

Susan nodded, "Yes. He said he'd been in an accident and asked me if I could feed Ralph and make sure that he had water."

"That was all he told you?"

"Yes. So, I did what he asked. I went into his apartment last night and fed and watered Ralph and came back to my own apartment."

Carson pulled a notebook and pen out of his left jacket pocket and made a few notes. "How about today? What can you tell me about the last few hours?"

Susan's face collapsed. Carson was worried that she would start crying again, but she didn't. "Well, I heard some footsteps in the hall coming and going, but I can't tell you whether they went to Oskar's or not. I was in the back of my condo cleaning a closet. Then I came out to make a cup of tea and I heard a loud bang. It sounded like a firecracker, but I realized that didn't make any sense. I ran to my door but didn't open it. I looked out through the peephole, but I didn't see anything. I waited for a minute and then decided I better call you. The police, I mean."

"So, you didn't see anyone coming or going that you could identify."

She shook her head no. "I just heard footfalls on the floor. You know, this building, it was pretty expensive to buy here, but it wasn't built all that well. The walls and floors are thin."

"So, the gunshot made quite a loud noise, is what you're saying?"

Susan nodded, her eyes misting over with a new set of tears. "I just can't understand why anyone would want to hurt Oskar. Are you sure someone shot him?"

Carson nodded, trying to stay patient with her. Susan was clearly having a hard time processing what had happened right across the hall from her condo. "Yes, unfortunately, that's the case." He stood up, "Is there anything else that you'd like to tell me?"

Susan reached her hand out, grabbing his wrist, her clammy fingers leaving a damp smudge on his skin, "You aren't going to leave me here by myself, are you?"

"You will be fine. The officers will be here for a few more hours. I am sure there is no threat to you. But, if you need anything, call 911 and we will come back out." Carson quickly stepped away from Susan and walked to the door before she could grab him again.

"She didn't know anything?" the officer asked.

Carson shook his head no. "Not really. She just heard some noise. I'll add it to the report, but I don't think it's going to be that helpful."

Out in the hallway, the door to Oskar's condo was open. He looked inside. The medical examiner had arrived. There was a gurney pulled up next to the couch where Oskar was lying. The medical examiner, a gray-haired man who was nearly ready to retire, was standing with his assistant, unfolding a black bag. Carson debated for a moment whether he should go in and talk to him or head back to the station. The cause of death was obvious, so there was no point in talking to the ME. He gave them a wave and headed down the hallway to the stairwell.

Back out in the sunshine, Carson realized what a hot day it had become. He was grateful for the air conditioning in his car, turning it up to high as soon as he got it started. The smell of curry that had been sitting in the hot car for too long was strong, turning his stomach. He'd have to throw out his lunch when he got back to the office. As he drove, questions followed him. The information that was in the file was particularly confusing. He tried to put the pieces together. It had all started with Hailey's murder, which led to Miles, which led to Dr. Kellum, who was now dead. How they were linked, he just wasn't sure. The relationship between Miles and Dr. Kellum was obvious. How the rest of it all fit together was a mystery. A shiver ran down his spine despite the heat. He was worried that if he didn't figure out what was going on, more bodies would fall before he could save them.

22

K at and Henry had spent the better part of an hour unpacking the first crate and laying all the artwork out on the long table in the customs building, watching Eli walk from canvas to canvas staring at each piece individually. Just as they pulled the final canvas out of the first crate, her phone rang. It was Carson.

"Hey, Carson. How are things going?" Kat asked. From the background noise, it sounded like Carson was driving. "Are you in the car?"

"Yup. You and Eli made it to London okay?"

"Yes. We're at the customs building right now."

"Did you find anything?"

Kat started to pace. Out of the corner of her eye, she watched Henry and Eli. Eli was making lap after lap around the canvases that were arranged on the tables. "Well, Eli just started doing his evaluation, but it looks to him like the work that was shipped was Hailey's."

"How can he tell?"

"We talked a little bit about this while we were waiting for our flight. I guess painters approach subjects in a way that makes their work almost like an individual fingerprint. Eli said the part that makes this difficult is that she was copying someone else."

"Keep working on it."

"We will." It sounded to Kat like there was something else Carson wanted to say. There was a tension in the air between them, but she couldn't quite figure out what was going on.

"I wanted to update you on something else that happened since you left."

Kat's heart started to beat a little faster. "What's that?" She could tell by the tone of his voice that something serious had happened.

"Oskar Kellum is dead."

Kat swallowed. "What?"

"Yep. I'm just leaving the scene now. Someone went into his condo and shot him at point-blank range."

Kat tried to catch up with the story, "Wait, when I left, he was still in the hospital?"

The phone connection between the two of them broke up a little bit. "That's right," Carson said. "They kept him in the hospital a couple of nights and discharged him this morning. Poor guy probably wasn't home for more than a couple hours before someone shot him. I was there talking to him just before it happened. They must have gotten to him when I left."

Kat started to pace again, her mind reeling with the information. If someone wanted Oskar dead, why hadn't they killed him when they first grabbed him? "What you're saying is that someone beat him to a pulp, left him at the hospital, and then came back later and finished him off?"

"That's where we seem to be. They did it right after I interviewed him at his condo."

In the background, Kat heard a car door slam. She imagined Carson was probably back at the police station. "Was there any other information? Anything else you can tell us?

"Well, I could give you the line about this being an ongoing investigation, but you already know that. Nothing was taken from his condo that we can see, but the forensics people are still there."

Kat motioned to Henry, waving him over. "Carson, I'm gonna put you on speaker with Henry. He's my contact at Scotland Yard. I think he should hear this."

"Yeah, hi Henry. Carson Martino with Savannah Police. I was just telling Kat that a person of interest in the case we are following up on was just shot."

Kat watched for Henry's reaction. Henry glanced at her and raised his eyebrows, then leaned closer to the phone so they could both speak at the same time. "And who was this gent?"

Carson replied before Kat had a chance. "Interestingly enough, he was the psychiatrist for our prime suspect, who is a ten-year-old boy."

Kat looked at Henry, "We talked to the guy right before I left to come here. He was grabbed by someone and savagely beaten. Broken ribs, swollen eye, a couple of bruised organs. Carson told me they kept him overnight in the hospital and just released him a little while ago. He was shot."

"Sounds like someone is cleaning up loose ends," Henry said.

From behind them, the sound of a dog barking angrily echoed off the walls of the customs building. It was so loud that Kat couldn't hear. "Carson, something is going on. Let me call you back." She hung up without saying goodbye.

Over her right shoulder, she saw what looked to be a police dog charging towards the crate that she, Henry and Eli had just opened. As she walked towards the dog and the handler, the dog went to the crate, sat and started to whine. That wasn't a good sign. The customs officer they had been working with, Davis, walked briskly over to the dog handler. "What's going on here?" she asked.

"I don't know. Bear started to alert. What's in that crate?" the officer said.

"Art."

"What's going on here?" Kat said.

The K-9 officer looked at her. "And you are?"

"Kat Beckman." She pointed to Henry. "I'm here with him." Henry extended his hand to the officer, "Henry Nash, Scotland Yard. Why did your dog alert?"

The officer looked at Henry, "James Kimball, customs. This dog here is Bear. Nice to meet you." James looked at the crate and looked at the canvases laid out on the tables. "I'm not sure what Bear smells. You said this is just filled with art?"

Henry nodded. "Yes. The shipment just came in from New York. These two..." he bobbed his head towards Kat and Eli, "...came the entire way across the pond to take a look at what was shipped. They are following up on an investigation back in the States."

Kat took a deep breath, her face curling into a frown. She knew a little bit about military dogs. If Bear was anything like Tyrant, she doubted that Bear would have responded to the crate if there really wasn't something there. Their noses were way too sensitive for them to make a mistake.

Kat looked down at the dog. He was an enormous German Shepherd, probably at least one hundred and fifty pounds. He had thick brown fur and black markings around his face and on his legs. His tail was draped on the floor as he sat next to Kimball, looking up at his handler every few seconds, waiting for a command. "He's a beautiful dog," she said to James. "I don't doubt that he smelled something. The question is what?"

James looked down at Bear, "I don't know. I can have him look again so maybe we can figure it out."

Henry nodded, "Let's do that."

As James got Bear ready to do a search, Kat saw Henry glance at Eli. He looked like a deer in headlights. "You nervous about something, Eli?" Henry chided. "You just keep looking at those canvases, okay?"

Eli nodded, "Yes. Okay. Right."

Kat could tell Eli was nervous, but that wasn't what she was most interested in. Why would a trained customs enforcement dog alert at a crate of artwork? "James, what was Bear trained to find?"

James gathered the leash a little tighter in his hand, "He's been trained to look for drugs, particularly ones in the opioid class. He's also had a little training on explosives, but not much. The way he alerted, though, that was for drugs." He gave a curt nod and a tug to the leash, "Let's see what he finds."

Kat stood back next to Henry as James gave Bear the command to search for drugs. "Suche!"

Most working dogs were trained in commands from another language, usually either Dutch or German. Kat had to learn quite a few commands when she took Tyrant home. The police department in England that gave her the dog insisted that she contact her local police department to make sure that no one got hurt because of Tyrant's training. She wasn't as big as Bear, but working dogs were dangerous in the wrong hands, nonetheless. Kat had spent some time with the Sauk Valley Police Department's K9 trainer. He was a small man, with a soft face and thin limbs, but Kat liked him immediately. Tyrant did, too. The trainer had put Tyrant through her paces and then taught Kat what to do if she responded to something. "She's a good dog," he said when he handed the leash back to her. "Just make sure you give her a lot of exercise and run her through her commands at least twice a week. If you need anything, or she becomes difficult, let me know." The man had looked at Kat sternly, "Don't take any chances. It's better for you to call me sooner rather than later if you need help."

Kat thought about her time with the K-9 trainer as she watched James work with Bear. Using a K-9 wasn't as simple as it seemed. A lot of people thought you just let go of the leash and let them run. That wasn't the case. Ultimately, it was the responsibility of the officer or the owner to make sure that the dog was doing what it was supposed to do.

James walked Bear in a circle away from the crate that he had alerted on. Kat remembered from her brief training that James was getting ready to reapproach the object to see if Bear would alert again. James turned back towards the crate repeating the search command. Before Kat could blink, Bear had started to pull on the leather leash James had wrapped around his hand. Barking echoed off the walls of the building. James followed, taking stilted steps towards the crate as Bear pulled him along. Bear stuck his head down in the packing peanuts and started to whine. Kat and Henry moved forward at exactly the same time, heading towards the crate. James pulled Bear back just as they got there.

Kat knelt down on the concrete floor, using her hands to dig through the crate. Henry tapped her on the shoulder. "Here, use these," he said, handing her a pair of gloves.

Kat pulled on the blue latex gloves, realizing that Henry was right. There was no telling what could be buried in the crate. If someone had taken the time to break into Hailey's apartment and steal the artwork, they could have easily stashed something else in the crate.

Davis pointed at two other matching crates that were leaning against the wall. "Think we should have a look at those?" she asked.

James and Henry nodded at the same time. James did a quick walk around with Bear who started to bark again. Henry shook his head. "That's strange. What do you suppose he smells in there?"

James shook his head. "I dunno. Did you find anything else in the first crate?"

Kat had moved the packing peanuts to the side exposing

the edges of the crate. She couldn't find anything else that had been shipped in the box. Davis walked over to her, pulling two enormous tote bins. "Here, let's put the packing peanuts in these totes so we can have a better look at the inside of the crate."

Kat nodded and started moving handfuls of the peanuts into the totes. Davis walked away, toward the wall of tools that was laid out behind the inspection tables where Eli was still peering at the paintings. She pulled two snow shovels off the wall and walked back. "These come in handy for situations like this."

"This happens often?" Kat asked.

Davis nodded. "More than you might think. People put weird things in their shipping crates, not realizing that we do a full inspection on pretty much everything that comes in and out of this building. We must protect the Kingdom," she smiled.

Kat smiled back. The people in England were still quite captivated by the monarchy and what that meant. It seemed they were much more likely to listen to the Queen and her opinions many times than the Prime Minister. Kat wondered if it had always been that way. "What kind of things do people try to pack in these crates?"

Davis shoveled a pile of peanuts into one of the totes and shook her head. "You'd be surprised. The strangest thing I ever found was a bag filled with amputated human hands. It was quite disgusting."

"What? Why would someone ship hands?" Kat's mind ran on ahead of her trying to figure out how amputated body parts would end up in a crate.

"The short part of the story? The hands were supposed to be shipped as part of a medical transport but got misplaced. They were going to a medical school for use by students in the anatomy labs. It was truly awful," Davis shivered. "That's not something I'm going to forget ever."

Kat glanced over at Henry and James. They were looking at the other two crates that were part of the art shipment. Henry had a long crowbar in his hands and was working on taking the top off of the second crate. James had put Bear in a down position out of the way. The creak of the crowbar pulling the nails out of the edges of the crate could be heard bouncing off of the hard walls and ceiling. It sounded like nails on a chalkboard as the metal scraped against the wood. As soon the men lifted the wooden top off of the box, Bear started to whimper again. James frowned and then looked at the second and third crates, "This is a complete mystery. Why he is fussing, I have no idea."

While Henry and the agents were working on the crates, Kat decided to go check on Eli. She had found nothing inside of the crate other than the artwork, sheets of Styrofoam, packing materials and peanuts. "How are things going, Eli?"

Eli straightened up from the hunched-over position he had taken over each canvas, "Honestly, this would be much easier if we had easels, but at least the light is good."

Kat looked at the paintings that were spread out on the tables. Some of them were larger than others and although they looked to be from a similar time, the style of each one seemed to be a little bit different. "Are you thinking these belonged to Hailey?"

Eli nodded, "I believe so. Several of these look identical to the ones I spotted in her apartment a few days ago." He picked up one of the canvases and turned it over, looking at the back, his fingers lightly pressing on the side of the canvas without wrapping his fingers around it. "You'd never know that this was a replica."

Kat furrowed her brow. She hadn't noticed when they looked at the artwork while it was in Hailey's apartment that the back of the work had been altered as well as the front. It looked as though someone had used some sort of solution to age the canvas so that even from the back it would be difficult to tell if it was an original or not. "I don't understand," she said. "I mean, these look like the pieces of art we saw at Hailey's, but I would never know whether this was an original or not."

Eli smiled. "I will tell you that whoever trained Hailey did an excellent job. I'm not sure who taught her to age the canvas but is done quite masterfully. It's a shame that she's no longer with us." He set the canvas back down on the table and pointed. "See the brushwork and the thin layers of paint? Exceptional..."

Kat nodded. The only thing she had to compare it to was some of the work she had seen in art museums over the years. While Eli continued to look at the canvases, Kat took a deep breath. Her head was swirling. So many things had gone on over the last couple of days. From the time she arrived in Savannah, she hadn't stopped moving. Now, she was in London, with missing artwork, a dead psychiatrist, and a dog that was alerting on drugs that didn't seem to be there.

Kat lifted her head and looked around. Eli was still studying the canvases, looking for what, she didn't know. Henry and James were digging through another one of the crates, unloading more pieces of artwork. She watched Eli scurry across the floor from the tables to where Henry and James were stacking more canvases along the wall. "Careful," she could hear him say, "We don't want to damage these pieces."

Kat chewed her lip, watching the artwork get unloaded, Eli supervising. She still couldn't quite wrap her brain around what was going on. Why would someone steal student artwork out of an apartment if it weren't valuable? And, if they were trying to hide drugs, why would they spend the money to ship so many pieces of art? Not to mention, where were the drugs? Kat shoved her hands in her pockets, frustration filling her. There were no drugs. They had searched the boxes from top to bottom, scooping out every single one of the packing peanuts. There was nothing there.

Kat walked over to Eli. "Hey, does this artwork look like Hailey's, too?"

"Most definitely. It looks like they shipped all the artwork that was in her apartment." He tilted his head, "it'll take me a little time to verify this, but that's what I would guess."

Henry stepped off to the side and joined Kat, brushing his hands off on his pants. "What do you make of this?" he asked her.

"I'm not sure."

"The fact that the drug dog alerted on the art is interesting, don't you think?"

Henry had a way of making something exciting sound completely boring. "Interesting?" Kat said, "Perplexing is probably the word I would use. Henry, nothing about this case fits together."

"Really? I think it fits together quite nicely."

"What?" Kat felt a small twinge of anger run through her shoulders. What was Henry trying to say? She knew they had butted heads the last time that she was in London, but how was it that he thought he knew everything that was going on?

Henry raised his eyebrows, "It's quite brilliant if you ask me."

Kat shrugged, "All right, what's your theory?"

"The art forgery business is an enormous one. My guess? Someone saw Hailey's talent and decided to leverage it for their own good. How the drugs fit in, I'm not sure yet."

"We didn't find anything in the crates."

"I know that."

"So, why do you think drugs are even part of the equation here?"

"Bear smelled them. I have yet to meet a K-9 that is wrong."

Kat's mind drifted to home. Her heart ached for her dogs, Van and Jack. She was on a wild goose chase as far as she could tell because Van wanted to get some sort of a story out of this.

She wasn't sure that was a possibility no matter what Henry said. A little flare of annoyance ignited in her. It was Van's fault that she was here. That was the challenge when you worked for your husband, she supposed. She pushed the thought aside, "You think this is all about art forgery?"

Henry looked confused for a minute, "You don't know how big of a business art forgery is?"

Kat shook her head no. She'd been learning on the job. She looked back at Henry, "Wouldn't someone know that these were student pieces of art?"

Henry shook his head no. "Not necessarily. And if they didn't figure it out, each piece could be worth hundreds of millions... "

23

C hristopher Lavaud leaned back in the chair. He'd arrived in New York having finished his work in Savannah.

He sat in his suite at the St. Regis Hotel. There were times that he chose to stay at smaller, less opulent hotels, but after the last few days, he felt he deserved a higher level of treatment. When he called the hotel, he spoke directly to the manager, someone he had known for ten years. Without any discussion, the hotel had opened up their finest penthouse for him and had it ready when he arrived, a limo moving him from the private airport to downtown, the driver not speaking a word. That was the way Christopher liked it.

He gave a generous tip to the driver and bag man. He knew they would unload his luggage and get it up to his room. The manager, a small man with round glasses, met him in the lobby. "Lovely to see you again, Mr. Lavaud. Here's your room key. Don't hesitate to let me know if you need anything."

Christopher nodded and walked off. He went directly to the elevator, pressed the button labeled PH, and inserted his key card. The doors closed as the mechanism recognized the permission to go to the penthouse level, a quiet whirring carrying him up to the fourteenth floor.

Christopher got off the elevator, quietly padding down the hallway, the thick carpet cushioning his every step. The doors to the penthouse were at the end of the hallway. He inserted his card in the key slot and heard the door click as it unlocked. He pushed the door open and quickly closed it behind him, in case there were any peering eyes from the other rooms. He hadn't heard any of the doors creak open as he passed, but you could never be too careful.

He had barely set his wallet down on the top of an antique chest that was right by the door when a soft knock came. Christopher cracked the door, the bellman outside. He only nodded and handed the man another generous tip, quickly closing the door behind him. Christopher was in no mood for visitors.

The St. Regis was one of the oldest and most traditional hotels in New York City. Positioned by Central Park, it was easy to access some of the most notable places in the city just by walking. But that wasn't why Christopher was in New York. He shook his head and glanced around the penthouse.

The hotel manager had done his job. The penthouse was beautiful, even opulent. A mix of dark and light furniture contrasted with the white walls. Lemon yellow furniture filled the center of the suite, a large couch with loose pillows accented by a claw-footed wooden table that faced a fireplace. Floral rugs dotted the carpeted floors. Just past the couch was a large bank of windows that overlooked the shopping area below. Christopher slid the door open onto the patio and looked down. He could see clusters of people walking up and down the sidewalks going in and out of some of the boutique shops that flanked the St. Regis. To his left, he could see a large green open space. Though he couldn't see it, he could smell the scent of the river water, the moisture heavy in the air. He walked back into the suite, sliding the glass door closed behind him. If it had been a little warmer, he probably would have left the door open to get some fresh air after being on the plane, but it was just too cool.

Looking around the suite, Christopher walked back past the couch and to his left, down a short hallway. The unit had two bedrooms and two full bathrooms. It was more like an apartment than it was a hotel room. He cracked the door to the first room, seeing a queen bed, covered in a floral that looks to match the rug that was by the couch. Across the hall, there was a full bathroom, marble from floor to ceiling. He walked down the hall and as it ended, he entered the master suite. The master suite had a king-sized bed covered in a down comforter with six pillows stacked three deep on each side. A small settee had been placed at the foot of the bed, probably to allow people to keep their luggage close by. There was a chair with a footstool positioned diagonally in the corner right next to a door that opened to an enormous closet. Christopher wasn't staying long enough to fill the closet, but he appreciated the design. The other door inside the master suite led to the master bathroom. Covered in matching marble from the first bathroom, there was an antique tub, a two-person shower with rain effects and a two-person sink. Thick navy-blue towels were hung from hooks nearby along with two white robes.

He walked back out of the master suite and back down the hallway to the living room area. On the opposite side from the bedrooms, there was a full kitchen, a six-person table, and a desk that was built into the wall. Christopher opened the refrigerator door and pulled out a bottle of sparkling water. He cracked the top and took a long drink. It always amazed him how dehydrated he was after spending just a few hours on a plane, no matter how much he drank while he was in the air.

He took the green bottle with him and sat on the couch, staring outside. Most of the time, he enjoyed traveling. It was a big part of his life. Having been raised in Paris, moving throughout Europe wasn't any bigger deal to him than it was for someone in the United States moving from state to state. He enjoyed the changes in culture, the language differences, of which he spoke seven, and the experiences, from the most mundane to the exotic. But this wasn't a trip where he would get to enjoy any of his interests.

Things had been going well with his art acquisitions until the last few weeks. He sighed, kicking his loafers off and leaving them on the floor. The source that the art professor in Savannah had found for him had been doing great work. All of his customers seemed to be happy with what they had received. If they were happy, he was happy. But then, things changed. The arrangement that he had with his importer got complicated and the girl became demanding. Christopher glanced down at his hand, realizing that he was clenching his fist. He didn't like complicated deals. In his experience, they generally went bad.

He stood up and started to pace, walking laps back and forth between the couch and the kitchen before deciding to open the door out onto the patio. He walked outside and looked down again. Fourteen floors were high enough up that it gave him a good view, but it didn't change his circumstances.

Every now and again, Christopher needed to change suppliers. He was constantly developing new contacts in the art world. What he had found about people in art is they either wanted money or fame or both. Appealing to their baser needs generally got him what he wanted. Unfortunately, his main client was giving him a bit of a hard time and he still hadn't figured out how to completely remove himself from the situation. Eliminating the artist and the psychiatrist had been his first step. Those were solid business decisions. His mind wandered to the boy who had committed the stabbing. Would he talk? Christopher guessed that he wouldn't. The psychiatrist had told him that the child was badly scarred from the way he'd been raised. And even if he did, who would believe him? The worst that would happen to him is he'd end up in a psychiatric hospital for children. That was probably not the worst outcome for the kid.

Getting rid of the psychiatrist had been an unforeseen issue. He had hoped that a beating would keep him quiet but based on his behavior when the police had arrived at his condo, Christopher knew that it was only a matter of time before Oskar decided to tell all. Not that there was a lot to tell. The local bookie he had cultivated didn't have Christopher's name or identity. He'd received instructions from an encrypted chat service that Christopher liked to use and the deposits into a Cayman Islands bank account that would keep him quiet. The money he earned for taking care of the psychiatrist was well more than Oskar owed him and completely covered the risk for him and his team.

Christopher shook his head. His team. Who was he kidding? The local bookie he worked with in Savannah was nothing more than a two-bit criminal with a couple of thugs on his payroll. Christopher had bigger concerns.

The people that Christopher worked with were powerful and influential. Some more than others. Some were downright dangerous. They were people of means. Some decisions they took to better their lives were shady at best. Christopher knew, if he was honest, that he fell into the same camp, but he knew that there was more in it for him than just the money. He enjoyed the strategy and the game. He put both hands on the smooth round metal railing that surrounded the patio and leaned against it. The deals he put together were much like chess matches. In order to win, he needed to be several steps ahead of his opponent. In this case, his opponent had gotten ahead of him. The question was, how would he get the upper hand again? He'd need it if he hoped to stay alive...

24

After spending hours at the customs building, Henry finally took Kat and Eli back to the hotel. "We will revisit this in the morning," he said. "There's no point in standing there all night long while they try to figure out the problem. A new shift of agents will take over while you two get some rest."

As much as Kat wanted to stay to help figure out why the drug dog had alerted on the crates, she was so tired she wasn't thinking clearly. Once back at the hotel, Kat gave Eli a quick wave as he headed up to his room. She felt restless. A walk and some fresh air would help. The long plane ride and the hours spent in the customs building had drained her.

The area around the hotel had clean sidewalks, trendy restaurants and small boutiques one after the other along the roadway. As Kat started to walk, she realized how narrow the streets were. It was nothing like in the United States, where cars seem to have more room to maneuver. As she walked, she noticed that the cars were parked end-to-end on both sides of the street, hardly giving any room for traffic to pass through.

Somehow, it still did. She passed a restaurant and then a book-store, watching the people as she walked.

Darkness had descended on London, the tall buildings arching up and away from the streets. Streetlights cast a dim glow over the sidewalks, the stores and restaurants that remained open pressing light out from inside of them. As she walked, a man and a woman, their arms linked, passed her. A mom with two young kids holding each of their hands walked by as well. Even though the night was cool, there seemed to be many people out and about. Kat stopped into a souvenir shop that was still open and browsed for a moment, passing t-shirts and tiny replicas of London's famed double-decker buses. She picked up a t-shirt, some candy and a toy for Jack and Van and quickly paid for them, heading back out of the store, continuing her walk.

As Kat crossed the street, she caught something out of the corner of her eye. She quickened her steps and then decided to stop in front of a furniture store that was closed, pretending to peer in the window. It was a basic counterintelligence move that she learned along the way. She glanced over her shoulder and spotted a man wearing a black hoodie and a pair of jeans across the street. He was pretending to look at his phone, but Kat wasn't sure. A tingle crawled up her spine. She turned and walked back toward the hotel, hoping to be able to get back inside the lobby before the man could get to her. As she turned, she saw movement. The man had crossed the street and was coming towards her. Kat spun, her heart tightening in her chest, and started walking the other way as quickly as possible. She didn't know what to do. She was going in the opposite direction of the hotel and had no idea where she was. Without thinking, she stepped out into traffic, almost getting hit by a car, the angry driver laying on the horn. "Sorry, sorry!" she said as she trotted the rest of the way across the street.

At least she was on the same side of the street as the hotel.

She glanced back across the street and saw the man weave his way through traffic, moving gracefully. Kat knew she'd never be able to outrun him. She scanned the crowd in front of her, hoping to see a police officer or someone that would help. The few people that had been on the street had all disappeared. Kat was alone. Terror gripped her. Who was this person? Why was he following her?

She turned away and walked faster. As far she could tell, she was probably at least five blocks down from the hotel. Even if she ran, she knew she'd never be faster than the man that was following her.

Kat dodged around a couple walking the other way, her eyes scanning the street. She wanted to turn around and look to see where the man was, but she kept going, afraid to see how close he was.

At the next corner, Kat darted to her right, taking a side street. She started running, hoping she'd be able to dodge into an alleyway before the man found her. Off to her left, she found one. She ran, the smell of rotten trash and urine hitting her nostrils. She didn't have time to think about the smell. There was a large dumpster, black with a green lid shoved up against the side of the alley. She darted behind it, crouching down to see if the man would find her. Kat's heart was pounding in her chest and her hands were shaking. She glanced behind her and saw that the alley ended in a brick wall. She was trapped. If the man found her, there was no way out.

Kat peered around the edge of the dumpster. A long black shadow crossed the edge of the alleyway from the street where she had come from. A figure emerged from the corner, staring in her direction. She shivered. She didn't want to look, but she didn't have a choice. She needed to know if he found her. Her leg started to cramp from squatting down and she slid it on the street, her shoe catching a piece of gravel, the grating sound echoing off the brick walls that surrounded her. Her eyes grew wide as the man looked right at her.

Kat couldn't tell if the man had seen her or had just heard the noise. She hoped for a moment that he chalked the noise up to a stray alley cat. A moment passed and then he started walking toward her. The breath caught in Kat's chest. There was nowhere to go. She looked behind her and saw a screen door that was propped open — she hadn't seen it before. It was about twenty feet from where she was sitting, the light coming out from inside what looked to be a restaurant.

She glanced back down the alleyway, the man steadily approaching. Kat knew she couldn't just wait for him to come around the back of the dumpster. She had no idea who he was or what he wanted, but it was pretty clear it had something to do with her trip to London. Kat had to move, and she had to move now if she hoped to survive. She stood up and sprinted, the cramp in her leg screaming for relief, toward the open door. She didn't stop to look, but she heard heavy footsteps following her. She got to the edge of the door and yanked it open turning quickly inside the restaurant.

The bright lights from the kitchen shocked her eyes as she maneuvered between tables and kitchen equipment, running as quickly as she could. Someone yelled at her, "What are you doing here? Get out!" Kat kept moving, feeling the presence of the man behind her. She ran to a dark space between the seating area and the kitchen and paused for a moment. She leaned up against the wall and glanced to her right, towards the back of the restaurant. As she did, she saw the man coming at her. She had no time to wait. He grabbed for her arm, catching the sleeve of her jacket. Kat groaned and wrestled free. For a moment, she felt his hot breath on her face. She charged out of the front of the restaurant, dodging tables and people. As she exploded outside at a full run, the door to the restaurant slammed against the wall like a crack of thunder. Kat glanced up and down the street and saw a cab sitting right in front of the restaurant. She opened the door and jumped in and locked the doors quickly. "Drive!"

The startled cabbie threw the vehicle into gear and sped off into traffic.

Kat leaned back on the seat, trying to catch her breath, "Sorry about that."

The cabbie, a middle-aged man wearing a gray flat cap with a brim looked back at her, "That was the most excitement I've had all bloody day. Are you all right? Where to, missy?"

Kat gave him the address to the hotel, hoping that the man that had chased her didn't know where she was staying. If he had found her on the street, he probably did, but she didn't really have any other choice. There was nowhere else to go. As she sat in the cab, she weighed her options. She couldn't think straight. The adrenaline was still running through her system, her heart pounding. She licked her lips, feeling how dry they were from the running. She'd decide what to do when she got back to the hotel.

Kat's breathing started to slow as the cab pulled up in front, the lights from the entry seeming friendly and safe. She glanced both in front of the cab and behind the cab to make sure that the man hadn't somehow beat her back to the hotel. The streets were deserted. She got out of the cab and handed the driver some money. The driver shook his head, "The fare has already been paid."

Kat frowned, "I'm sorry. I don't understand."

A thin smile crossed the driver's lips, "Your investigation is raising eyebrows. It might be time for you to go back to the United States. Stay out of business that has nothing to do with you."

As the cab sped off, Kat stood on the street, stunned. What had just happened? Questions rolled through her head as fear took over. The driver could have taken her anywhere, but he didn't. He took her back to the hotel. Kat walked into the lobby, numb and terrified. She sat down on one of the upholstered chairs, putting the bag of trinkets she had bought on her lap and hugging it close. Her heart was nearly beating out of her chest. She picked up her phone and texted Henry. It rang back right away.

"Kat, are you okay?"

"I think so," Kat said. "I don't know what just happened. I went to take a walk and there was a man following me. I ran through a restaurant, got in a cab and that man must have known the other man." She knew that what she was saying barely made sense.

"Where are you now?" The question from Henry sounded more like a demand than a request.

"I'm sitting in the hotel lobby."

"Good. Stay there. I've got police on the way. I will be there shortly. Don't move and don't go to your room."

Kat nodded, "Okay. I'll stay here."

As she ended the call, she noticed her hands were shaking. She set the phone down in her lap for a moment, and then picked it up again, calling Van.

"Hi, honey."

"Van..." she muttered.

"Kat? What's wrong?"

"I, I was just followed. I barely made it back to the hotel. Someone tried to grab me." Kat stopped, not sure what else to say. Her heart was still pounding in her chest, the fear surging through her body.

"What? What do you mean?" Van's tone had taken a serious turn.

"I got back to the hotel and decided I wanted to take a walk. It's a well-lit street with restaurants and shops. I just wanted to clear my head and then some guy, he started following me."

"Are you sure it wasn't a coincidence?"

"No! I ran down an alleyway and hid behind a dumpster. He found me there and chased me into a restaurant. I barely got away, or at least I thought I did."

There was a pause. "What does that mean?"

Kat could barely speak as she thought through what had just happened to her. "He nearly had me between the kitchen and the dining room. He grabbed ahold of my sleeve, but I wrestled away. I ran out the front door. There was a cab sitting right there. I jumped in. I thought it was safe."

"What happened when you got in the cab?"

"I thought it was safe. I really thought I was. He drove me the whole way to the hotel and then when I got out of the car, he told me the fare had already been paid." Kat looked up from her phone and saw that two police officers had just walked into the lobby. "Van, I have to go. The police are here."

"Wait. What did the cab driver say to you?"

"He told me to stop nosing around in their business and that I should go home."

There was silence on the other end of the line. Van didn't respond to what she had just said. "Have you called Henry?"

"Yes. He's on his way."

"Good. Do exactly what Henry says to do, okay Kat?"

As Kat tried to answer him, the words catching in her chest, tears started rolling down her cheeks. "Yes," she whispered.

"I love you. Be careful."

She put down the phone as the police officers approached her, "Are you Kat Beckman?" one of them asked. She nodded. "We were told to stay with you until Henry Nash arrives." Kat nodded again.

Kat sat quietly, trying to suffocate the terror in her chest. She watched as one of the police officers, a tall man with thin limbs, went and stood by the entry door, the other, a woman with blonde hair in a ponytail, sat right next to her scanning the entrances. Apparently, Henry had called the police department and let them know what was going on. The police officer that sat next to her looked at her and said, "Can I get you anything?"

Kat looked at her and said, "Maybe some tissues?" Admitting that she needed something as simple as a tissue made Kat cry even more. She hated being that weak. There was no reason to cry, she told herself. She was okay. She had gotten away. But there was part of her that didn't believe she was okay. Like many of the other investigations she had been on, things went from fine to dicey fast. This seemed like one of those moments.

Kat blew her nose and dabbed at her eyes, as Henry charged in through the front door. "Kat! Are you okay?"

She stood up and he put his hands on each of her arms. "Yes, I'm okay."

Henry dropped his hands and looked at the two officers, "Any movement?"

The woman sitting by Kat shook her head no. "We haven't seen anything since we got here, but it's only been a few minutes."

Henry nodded. "Thanks for getting over here so quickly. We can't risk losing this one." He smiled at Kat.

The words hit Kat like a ton of bricks even though she realized it was nothing but a simple sentiment. She doubled over, crying.

"Kat? Love? Are you okay?" Henry bent down to be on her level.

"It's just, it's just..." Kat sat up. "It's just that every time I get on one of these big investigations, I end up being the target." She stared at Henry, "I was so scared. I thought they were going to get me."

He put his arm around her shoulder. "You are safe now. We're going to go upstairs together and clear out your hotel room. You are going to come and stay with me for the rest of the trip."

"What about Eli? If I'm not safe, he isn't safe either."

Henry nodded, "You may be right about that. We'll collect Eli on our way out." Henry looked at Kat, "Do you happen to know what his room number is?"

Kat nodded and pulled up the information on her phone. "He's on the sixth floor. Room 606."

Henry looked at the two officers. "Okay, you," Henry nodded at the male officer, "Go up and check on Eli in room 606. Tell him I will be right there." Henry looked at the female officer, "You, come with us. I want back up in case someone has gotten into Kat's room."

The four of them, Henry, Kat and the two officers, walked to the elevator together. As they got on, Henry looked at the bag she was carrying. "You went out for a bit of shopping, huh?"

Kat nodded. She tried to smile, "I won't be making that mistake again."

"Now, now..." Henry said, "We are generally very friendly here in London. The blokes you ran into must've been troublemakers."

Joking around with Henry made Kat feel better, "As I remember, this isn't the first time I've run into bad guys in London. You are developing quite a reputation."

The elevator beeped as it got to the sixth floor. The male officer got out without looking back. The elevator doors slid closed. Kat punched the button for the eighth floor where her room was. The elevator gave a quiet beep as it stopped. Henry stepped out first, "Now, I want you to hang back while we get your room open. I want to clear it before you walk in."

Kat nodded. After what had just happened, she had no interest in going into her room by herself. She'd had quite enough excitement for one day. She watched from outside in the hallway as Henry and the other officer went into her room first. In less than a minute, Henry called for her. "Kat?"

Kat stepped into the doorway. "Everything okay?"

Henry nodded. "Seems to be." He took one more look in the bathroom, nodded, then said, "Take a few minutes and get your stuff packed. We will check you out on the way."

Since Kat had come from New York City to Savannah and then to London, she had a few more things to pack than she would have liked. Henry plopped down on a chair that was in the corner of the room, crossing his legs, watching her pack. He had told the other officer to stand outside of Kat's door until they were ready to leave. Kat quickly pulled her clothes off the hangers and stuffed them into the suitcase. There would be time for folding later. As she went into the bathroom to gather her toiletries, Henry called out, "So, what do you make of what the thugs said to you?"

A chill ran down her spine. Kat had been trying not to think about what was going on. She sighed and pushed her toothbrush into her carry case, "I'm not sure. My head is still reeling. First Hailey, then Oskar and now this? I think we've tripped into a bigger hole than we were anticipating."

"I think you could say that fairly." Henry scratched his ankle and then put his feet back on the floor, "You ready?"

Kat rolled her suitcase toward the door, slinging her backpack over her shoulders. "I think so. Let me look around one more time before we go."

Kat walked through the room making sure she hadn't left anything behind when she spotted her laptop charger, "I'll need this."

Henry nodded, "Good job. Now let's get going."

As soon as they opened the door, the officer stationed in the hallway turned towards them. "Everything okay?" she asked.

Henry nodded, "Yes. Let's go down and collect Eli."

The three of them rode the elevator back down to the sixth floor. When they got out of the hallway Kat glanced left and right, trying to determine where Eli's room was. She saw the tall police officer stationed down to their left. When they got to Eli's door, Henry looked at the police officer. "Any trouble?"

"No, sir," the officer said. "Eli, that's the man's name, is it? He was a little surprised to see me, but he's packing."

Henry nodded. "That figures." Henry knocked on the door, "Eli? It's Henry. Open the door, please."

Kat heard some scuffling behind the door and the metal of the locks scraping against each other. She shook her head. Even with a police officer standing outside the door, Eli had apparently bolted every one of the locks the hotel had made available to him.

"Oh, Kat! Are you okay?"

Kat looked at the police officer. His face flushed. "Sorry, ma'am. I had to tell him what was going on to get him to cooperate."

Kat closed her eyes and shook her head. He was nothing if not suspicious, "Yes, Eli. I'm okay."

Henry stepped in front of the door. "No time for chitter chat, Eli. We need to get you and Kat out of this hotel. The two of you are going to come bunk with me until we get this straightened out."

Eli nodded, "Yes, yes. I'm all packed. Ready to go when you are, sir."

Kat wasn't sure if the "sir" was a bit of sarcasm on Eli's part, but if it was, she could hardly blame him. A lot had happened since they had arrived in London.

Henry took the comment in stride. "Good man. Now, let's get moving."

It didn't take long for the four of them to go down in the elevator and check out at the front desk. The clerk tried to give them a hard time, saying that their stay had been guaranteed for another four days. Henry glared at the young man and said, "Do you really want to make an issue out of this? We could go down to Scotland Yard and have a chat if you'd like about interfering in government business."

The clerk's eyes bulged out of his head, "No, sir. Of course not. Enjoy your stay in London."

The police cruiser that the two officers had arrived in and Henry's Scotland Yard vehicle were parked right in front of the hotel. The officers helped Kat and Eli load their luggage into Henry's car. Henry slammed the lid on the trunk. "I've already called your sergeant," he said. "He gave the approval for you to follow me back to my house. I'd like you to help me clear it before I bring Kat and Eli in, okay?"

The female officer nodded, her ponytail bouncing, "Of course, sir. More than happy to help Scotland Yard."

Eli and Henry got in the front of Henry's car, with Kat sliding in the back. Kat tried to settle in the backseat, her backpack sitting next to her. As Kat unzipped the front pocket of her backpack, looking for gum, she glanced up, just in time to see a cab sitting across from the hotel, the same kind of cab that had brought her to the hotel in the first place. A shiver ran up her spine...

25

After the cabbie had dropped at the front door of the hotel, he circled the block and took up a parking space directly across from the main entrance. David Walther had been the backup on this operation. His partner, a guy named Sam, or something like that, was told to grab Kat on the street and warn her. Their bosses thought that would be more intimidating, more effective. But Sam, or whatever his name was, couldn't get the job done and Kat got away.

David heard the back door of the cab click open and then closed. Sam slid into the backseat. "Man, I almost had that bloody girl. She got away from me at the last second."

David shook his head. "That's why the boss sent me as a backup." He glanced into the back seat using the rearview mirror. "Making sure she got the message was the most important job of the night. You almost screwed it up." David wanted to make sure that Sam got the message. In his line of work, which ranged from slightly shady to completely illegal, David knew there was value in getting the job done right the first time. If you didn't, it could cost you your life.

"I'm sorry. She was slippery, that one."

"She's a journalist. And half your size. You should have been able to deliver the message with no problem." David rubbed his hand across his unshaven face, the whiskers pulling against his skin, "I'm not going to tell the bosses, but don't let it happen again."

Sam didn't say anything. Quiet settled over the cab as the two men slid down in the seats to watch the front entrance of the hotel. Before David pulled away from the front entrance of the hotel where he dropped Kat off, he watched her walk in. Unless she had slipped out of the back entrance, which he decided was highly unlikely, she was still in there.

A couple of minutes passed. David watched the traffic going up and down the street, wondering what would happen next. Out of the corner of his eye, he saw a police cruiser pull up and park right at the entrance. A tall man and a shorter woman stepped out of the car and headed straight for the lobby. "Dollars to doughnuts, they are there to help Kat," he mumbled.

Sam's eyes were closed, his arms folded across his chest. He was slumped down in the back seat of the cab. "What did you say?"

"Coppers just arrived. How much do you want to bet they are there for our journalist?"

"I thought you said our only job tonight was to get the message to her? I didn't realize we were going to be sitting here watching."

"Yeah, well unlike you, I like to make sure the job gets finished." David picked up his phone and made a quick call.

A woman's voice picked up. "Yes?"

"Ma'am, the message has been delivered."

There was a pause, "Thank you."

"One more thing. The police have just arrived at the hotel."

"To be expected. Keep me posted."

The call ended before David could say anything else. He knew that phone conversations were kept to a minimum for good reason. There was more and more listening technology that allowed everyone from the government to the police to their enemies to listen to what they were doing. His boss was shrewd. She had them change out their phones every week whether they were working on a job or not.

David tried to stretch in his seat as much as he could. He couldn't figure out how cabbies managed to sit on the uncomfortable upholstery that fitted out the cab. Maybe it was just this cab, but it seemed that the springs were sticking up right through the seats, poking into his backside. A dull ache was running from his back down his legs. After he got paid, he'd call up that cute massage therapist, Carrie, and schedule a time. He needed a little rest and relaxation.

Not that the bosses treated him badly. In fact, working for this family had been the best job of his career. They were fair, slow to make decisions, and hired the best people they could find.

David had gone up in the foster system in England. He got moved from family to family with astounding regularity, sometimes even before he'd had a chance to unpack his bag. The families did the best they could, but David just wasn't the school type. He had a lot more in common with the kids that hung out on the streets and on the corners. Once he became a teenager, he began running with a couple of other boys who worked for a money-laundering front. He didn't do any more than run a few errands, but he did get to watch and see what the life was like. Now, thirty years later, he had stashed away enough money in an offshore account that he could literally go anywhere he wanted to. And, he was nothing more than a low-level member of the organization. He shook his head. It was hard to imagine how much money the bosses probably had. It had to be hundreds of millions of dollars, even billions. David only knew about one small portion of their business, and nothing more, but he knew there was more to it.

One day, David had been walking through one of the warehouses that the family owned and had heard a couple of the brothers talking about interests they had in Las Vegas, Milan, and Moscow. David paused for one second, listening, and then realized he better keep moving. He didn't want anyone to know that he had heard anything at all. His mind started to race. He only knew about their interests in England, and then even those were only the ones that were in the London area. If the brothers were talking about other cities around the world, the family business was much bigger than he thought it was.

Out of the corner of his eye, David saw something else approach the hotel. A blue sedan, four doors, an older model, pulled right up to the front entrance and stopped, completely ignoring the valet. He saw a man with black hair wearing a navy-blue windbreaker with yellow letters emblazoned on the back. The letters read CTC. "Scotland Yard," he mumbled.

"What did you say?" Sam asked.

David shook his head. Sam was useless, "Go back to sleep. It was nothing."

"Okay, let me know if you need anything. Other than that, I'm gonna take a nap."

David didn't say anything. It was no use. Any words he would have said to Sam would have been a waste of his breath. David watched as the man walked in the front door of the hotel, wondering who he was and how he was linked to Kat Beckman. When he had gotten the orders to deliver a message, he hadn't been told anything about earlier surveillance. He guessed that the bosses already knew about this fellow from the CTC. He couldn't be sure though, so he pulled out his phone and snapped a quick picture before the man disappeared into the hotel. "Now, what are you up to?" he whispered to no one in particular.

David didn't have to wait long for his answer. A few minutes later, the two police officers, Kat, the man with the CTC jacket, and a small gray-haired man with a wiry beard left the hotel. David picked up his phone, "Ma'am?"

"Yes?" The voice responded without any emotion.

"We've had a development. They are leaving with Scotland Yard." It was hard to describe a situation when you really weren't supposed to use the phone for long.

"Follow them." The line went dead.

26

A sense of relief flooded over Kat once they pulled away from the hotel. She was with Henry. She glanced behind her. No cab. Just knowing that she was with a group of other people who could protect her helped the fear to subside. She picked up her phone and texted Van. "I'm with Henry. We are all moving to his house."

A text came back right away. "All of you?"

Kat tapped lightly on her phone sending a reply. "Yes. Me, Henry, Eli."

"Okay."

Kat leaned back against the upholstered seat in Henry's car, taking deep breaths. She couldn't afford to get overly excited. Not now. Not after she'd finally gotten control of the PTSD that had haunted her for years after her time in Afghanistan. Just thinking about it brought back some of the images from that day -- the smell of the Humvee, the sound of the explosion, the feeling of the heavy transport rocking and tipping on its side, the searing pain in her wrist and TJ's strong hands as he pulled her out and to safety. That one experience had created a hairpin turn in her life. She ended up in a military hospital healing, at least physically. The mental part had taken much longer, more than a decade. Even now, she wasn't sure she was fully healed. She might not ever be.

Kat pushed those memories away. "Henry?" She saw him glance into the rearview mirror.

"Kat?"

She took a deep breath and closed her eyes for a moment, "Just as we left the hotel, I spotted a cab sitting across the street."

"That's pretty common for a hotel, Kat."

"That's not what I mean, Henry. I think it might've been the same cab that dropped me off."

"Kat, the cabs all look the same in England. Are you sure?"

Kat thought for a second. Was she sure? Henry was right, the cabs did all look the same. It was dark, and the cab had been parked in a shadow. She shook her head slightly, pursing her lips. She couldn't be sure. Henry was right. There was no way to know if it was the same cab or not. "I don't know. I thought it was, but maybe I was wrong."

Eli turned halfway around, "Are you okay, Kat? That had to be quite the scare."

"Yes," she sighed. "I'm fine. I'm just glad to get out of that hotel."

Henry glanced once again in the rearview mirror. "You don't have good luck in hotels, do you?" He had a half-smile on his face.

Kat wasn't sure she appreciated the reminder. The last time she had worked with Henry, they had ended up going back to the States on a military transport. An assassin who was linked to a terrorist organization got into Kat's room and nearly strangled her with a garrote. Only Tyrant, the police dog that had belonged to Henry's ex-wife, had saved her. Without Tyrant, she'd be dead. Kat didn't say anything.

"Too soon, Kat?" Henry said. "I didn't mean to upset you."

Kat was upset, but she wasn't going to let Henry know that. The car bumped over a set of railroad tracks and then made a sharp turn down a side street. The rows of houses were glued together like townhomes were back home. Henry slowed the car and then made a sharp left turn between parked cars onto a narrow driveway. He pulled into the back and parked. The police cruiser parked behind them and blocked the driveway. "We're here. Home sweet home."

As the three of them got out of the car, the two police officers joined them. Kat walked to the back of Henry's car and lifted her suitcase out, setting it down on the driveway. She watched as Eli leaned over and lifted his suitcase out. It was the old-fashioned kind, one from before most suitcases had added wheels and handles that allowed them to be pulled. Eli's was burgundy, a flat rectangle with thick straps crossing over the zipper.

"Here, Eli. Let me get that for you." Henry reached over and took Eli's suitcase and walked to the back door. The police officers were in tow, "All right, you two. I'm going to unlock this and get the lights on. One of you stay here with Kat and Eli and the other one can come inside with me and clear the house. I just want to make sure there aren't any surprises."

The female officer followed Henry into the house. The male officer stood with Kat and Eli. A moment later, Kat heard Henry's voice call from the inside of the house, "All right! We're clear."

Kat tugged on the handle of her bag, tilting it over, the wheels clattering just a little bit on Henry's cobblestone driveway. As she gave it a pull forward, she glanced to her right, just beyond where the police car was parked. A black cab, just like the one that had driven to the hotel, passed by. She sucked in her breath, noticing the driver had a flat cap just like the driver that had warned her to stay away, "Henry!"

Henry darted out of the house, his hair flopping across his forehead. "What's wrong?"

"The cab! I think the cab followed us. They just passed."

"Are you sure? Are you quite sure?"

With all the trauma Kat had experienced, she had a hard time trusting her own instincts. He was right, she couldn't be sure. There were a million black cabs in the London area and just because the driver had on a flat cap didn't mean it was the same person. But for some reason, she thought it was him. A cold sweat collected on the back of her neck. Her gut told her they had been followed. But why? Who would be so threatened by them looking at the artwork that had been shipped? Questions flooded her mind. She felt a lump form in her throat. She swallowed hard as she walked into Henry's house.

Though it looked small from the outside, Henry's house was quite spacious. She went up three steps into a kitchen area that was connected to the family room and a dinette. There was a stack of magazines on the kitchen counter, a plate and a cup that looked like it had been from breakfast. While the house certainly wasn't clean and neat, it was homey. Just being there made her feel better.

"Well, welcome," Henry said. "It isn't much, but it's home. I've got two bedrooms upstairs. Kat, you and Eli can each take one of those..."

Kat interrupted. "If it's all the same with you, I'd rather sleep on the couch. I'd feel more comfortable there." Henry didn't ask her why. She was glad for that because she wasn't sure she could have explained it.

Eli sighed, "I'll take my things upstairs."

Henry raised his eyebrows, "And after you do, come back downstairs. I'm going to make a pot of tea."

Eli offered a weak smile, "I could use a one after all the excitement."

Kat pushed her suitcase into the corner of the room next to

a bookcase and another pile of magazines. Kat had never seen a house with so many. "Henry? What's with all the magazines?"

"Oh, that." Henry tilted his head. "I like to collect things. I read magazines about antiques and other objects. It's become quite the obsession."

"I can tell," she said. "What kind of things do you like to collect?"

"Old toy trains, cars, tools. You know, guy things."

Kat nodded but didn't say anything. It made sense given Henry's life. He was single and divorced, with no one to really care for. Even the dog that he had shared a life with now lived at Kat's house. With the number of hours Kat guessed he worked, collecting things made sense. They didn't require any care or time that he couldn't give. Kat glanced around the rest of the house. It was nicely decorated, though worn. The couch was a beige plaid, suspended over a red and green Oriental style carpet. A wide wooden coffee table sat in the middle flanked by two armchairs. A large-screen television was mounted on the wall. Kat could imagine Henry, after a long day at work, putting his feet up on the table and watching soccer, or as he would call it, football.

She heard rattling from the kitchen. The water started to run. As she glanced up, she saw Henry putting water into an electric kettle. Out of the cabinet, he pulled three mismatched mugs, a few packets of sugar and some bags of tea. "You are still using your electric kettle?"

Henry looked up at her, "And how would you suggest that I heat up water for tea?"

"How about the microwave?"

He frowned, "Are you crazy? That would make the tea foul!"

Kat smiled. Teasing Henry always lightened her mood. The last time she was in London they had gotten into a few scuffles, but by the end of it, she had developed a great respect for

Henry and for the work that he did. She hoped he felt the same about her. "Henry?"

"Yes, love?"

"Where's the bathroom?"

Henry didn't say anything, he just pointed on the other side of the kitchen. Kat walked over, stopping to notice some pictures that were hung on the wall, pictures of his ex-wife Bev, their dog, and Henry standing on the edge of what looked to be the Grand Canyon. "Did you go to the Grand Canyon, Henry?"

"Yeah. I went about ten years ago. Hiked part of the southern rim. It's quite magnificent."

Kat nodded and headed into the bathroom. As she closed the door behind her, she flipped on the light switch, noticing the yellow-flowered wallpaper. She guessed that it had been put up by whoever had owned the house before Henry had bought it. It certainly wasn't Henry's style, but it was Henry's style to just leave it up. She stood at the sink for a moment and splashed water on her face. It had been a long day. From the other room, she could hear the tea kettle whistle. She took a deep breath, holding a soft cloth to her face. She knew they didn't have all the information they needed in order to solve Hailey's murder. Her mind drifted to Carson Martino. She wondered if he had come up with any other leads or if he felt as frustrated as she did. Only time would tell whether they could solve the murder or not. What she knew now was there was a threat against them and they needed a break before something terrible happened.

27

By the time Carson got back to the office, it was mid-afternoon, the sun hanging high over a steamy Savannah summer day. Carson decided to stop back at the police station after picking up a new lunch. He parked the unmarked cruiser in his usual spot, tossing the curry he had ordered in the closest trash bin. He left the windows cracked on the sedan. Whoever drove it next probably wouldn't want to smell spoiled curry during their shift.

He rubbed his neck as he walked into the police station, trying to massage some of the tension out of the muscles. His head was pounding, probably from gritting his teeth. This case just might be the death of him, he thought. He felt like he was running in circles. He needed to somehow connect the parts they had found, but he had no idea how.

"How's your day going?" Ginny stood in the doorway of his office, her hand resting on the doorframe.

Carson set a brown bag down on his desk, pulled his chair out and sat down, shaking his head. "Not good."

"What did you get for your second lunch?" Ginny said, sitting at his desk again.

"Burger."

"Had to trash the curry?" Ginny grinned. Police officers were used to eating partial meals or no meals at all, depending on when calls came in. Emergencies didn't wait for meals.

Carson flattened the brown bag, setting a burger and fries on top of it. "Yep. The car smelled horrible by the time I got back to it." Carson picked up a french fry and put it in his mouth, chewing slowly. He looked at Ginny. No matter what happened around the department, she always seemed to be in a good mood, flitting from office to office. There were two kinds of police officers, Carson knew, those who wore the job as though the badge was pinned to their skin and those who hung on to it loosely. He was part of the former. Ginny was part of the latter. There were days he wished that he could let go of the things that he saw and the things he had to do, but that just wasn't the case. It wasn't his personality.

"How's the case going?" Ginny asked, reaching over and taking one of his french fries.

Carson tried not to be annoyed that she was eating his lunch. It was just Ginny, he told himself, "There are too many moving pieces," he sighed. "This case isn't linear at all."

Ginny reached for another french fry, staring at it for a moment before shoving it in her mouth. "What do you mean?"

Carson shook his head, setting down his burger and wiping his fingers on a brown napkin. He leaned back in his chair, taking a sip of the iced tea that he ordered with his lunch. "This has me running in circles. The cases where it's a simple line between the inciting event and the crime are much easier to solve."

"Can't see the connections yet?" Ginny said.

Carson shook his head. The more he talked about it the more frustrated he got, "No. It's driving me crazy." He stood up from the desk and started pacing, his lunch getting cold. He didn't care. "So, I've got a college art student who gets stabbed by a ten-year-old, that I can't interview thoroughly because he's got a high-priced attorney that his foster mom couldn't possibly afford. Add to that a psychiatrist who was beaten and dumped in front of the hospital who then ends up getting shot. Add to that a pile of miscellaneous art that gets stolen from the art student's apartment, which is too nice for her to be able to afford and ends up in England." He sighed, staring at the back wall of his office.

"Yep. That's a lot," Ginny said, crossing her legs and brushing her hands off on her pants. "What happened to the journalist that was trailing you?"

"She and an art expert went to London to go intercept the shipment."

"And she found the missing artwork?"

Carson nodded. "Yep. According to the art expert, it's exactly the same work that was sitting in Hailey's apartment before it was stolen."

Ginny stood up. "Well, I'm no detective, but it seems to me that everything connects to those pieces of art. If you figure out that part of the story, you'll figure out the rest of it."

Ginny gave Carson a smile as she walked out of the office. Her comment hung in the air. Carson sat back down at his desk, wondering if she was right. Maybe the murder was less about Hailey than it was about the art. He looked at his cell phone. With the time difference, it was night in London. He paused for a moment, wondering if it was too late to call. He decided to call anyway.

"Hello?"

"Kat? It's Carson."

"Carson. Is everything okay?"

"Yes. I'm sorry for calling so late. I just wanted to check in to see if you'd found anything new."

"I wasn't asleep anyway. I'm at Henry's now. We had a bit of an incident tonight."

The hair on the back of Carson's neck started to prickle. "What do you mean?"

"I'm gonna put you on speaker so you can talk to Eli and Henry, too. Hold on for a moment."

Carson could hear Kat call for Eli and Henry and some scuffling as she set the phone on speaker. It sounded like she set it down on a counter or a table.

"Carson? Can you hear me?"

"Yes." There was a little bit of static on the line, but for the most part, Carson could hear Kat clearly. "You said there was an incident tonight?"

"Yes," Kat sighed. "After I got dropped off at the hotel, I decided to go take a walk and do a little shopping. I needed to clear my head. Someone followed me and chased me down an alleyway. They nearly got me in a restaurant. And I thought I got away..."

Henry's voice came on the phone. "Carson? Henry here. Let me give you the recap. Kat's a little upset. Apparently, Kat took a brief tour of about five blocks of the street area near the hotel. It's well populated, generally. Lots of shops and restaurants. Someone decided to follow Kat, chased her down an alleyway and in through an Asian restaurant. She jumped into a cab in front of the restaurant, but it seems that it was a follow car. The car took her back to the hotel unharmed, but with a stern warning."

Carson's stomach turned as a wave of nausea hit him. What had Kat gotten herself into? For that matter, what had they all gotten themselves involved in? The feeling in Carson's stomach turned to anger. Who had threatened Kat? What did they want? "What did they say?"

Kat stammered, "They basically told me to stop nosing around in their business and to go home." There was a pause. "I want to go back to my life, I really do, but I know we're onto something."

Henry came on the line, "As soon as Kat called, I sent the police to the hotel and met them there. I've now moved Kat and Eli over to my house. They'll stay with me until they get back on a plane to the United States."

Carson nodded, "That sounds like a good plan." Before Carson could ask another question, he heard a phone ringing in the background.

"Hold on. That's mine ringing," Henry said.

"Eli? Are you there?" Carson asked.

"Indeed. I'm here, Detective Martino."

"Tell me, what have you found with the artwork?"

"Well..." Eli cleared his throat. "The work that we unpacked was clearly Hailey's. It was meticulously done. Without an expert eye, it would be hard to know whether the canvases were real or fake."

"What you're saying is they are forgeries?"

Eli coughed a little bit in the background. "Well, that depends on how you define forgeries. Many art professors assign their students to copy historic works of art. It's one of the best ways for them to learn. Now, if those are done just for homework, that's one thing. If they are done to be sold on the open market without noting that they are done after a famous work of art, well, that's another thing..."

"What you're saying is they were done to be sold?"

"Now, now, I don't know the intentions of the people who took them from Miss Park's apartment. I don't want to speculate on that."

Carson smirked to himself. Eli was a slippery one. Carson heard Henry in the background, talking loudly. "Okay, we will be right there."

Carson wished he could see what was going on at Henry's house. "Henry? What's going on?"

"I just had a call from the customs agents that checked the

artwork. Remember how we told you that the drug dog sounded off?"

"Yes."

"Well, apparently they did smuggle drugs in. The agent didn't want to get into details on the phone. I'm taking Eli and Kat with me back to the warehouse now."

Carson's breath caught in his chest. Another layer to the story had just emerged. "Okay, let me know when you hear something." The call ended. Carson leaned back in his desk chair, his mind stumbling over questions rattling in his brain. He pulled the file out from the papers on his desk. And opened it. It would be a long night...

28

K at and Eli got back into Henry's Scotland Yard sedan after the call from the customs officer. Kat gripped the back of the seat in front of her while Henry backed out and into traffic. The roads were so narrow in England, she wasn't sure she would ever get used to it. Henry had offered her and Eli each a bottle of water on the way out the door. She had gratefully accepted it, twisting the cap off while they were on their way and taking a long drink.

A reminder crossed her phone. "Schedule pediatrician's visit." She shook her head. It seemed like forever since she had been home. Her heart reached for Van and Jack, their dogs, and their quiet house in California. She knew she would be back there soon, or at least she hoped. She swallowed hard, a lump forming in her throat. She needed to stop thinking about what had happened and focus on where they were going. "Henry? Tell me again what the officer said?"

Henry glanced in the rearview mirror. Kat hoped he didn't notice how pale she was, or at least how pale she felt. "The officer didn't say much. Just that they had found the source of why the drug dog had alerted."

Kat thought back to earlier that day when Bear had responded to the open crates so loudly. The barking had echoed off the walls of the large warehouse. Kat wondered if he was still there now, "What do you think they found?" Henry shook his head slowly. "Honestly, I have no idea. The drug shippers have become more and more creative over time. Really, some of the ways they try to sneak drugs in are quite brilliant."

Kat leaned back. The upholstery in Henry's car had a slight sour smell to it. She started to think about why the car smelled funny but then decided not to. Some things were better left unconsidered. Her mind drifted back to the customs warehouse, the tall brick walls, the cavernous echoing of their footsteps. The news that the customs agents figured out the source of the drugs and that it was enough to pull Henry out of his house late at night piqued Kat's curiosity.

The drive to the customs warehouse wouldn't take more than about twenty minutes. She turned her head to look out the window, listening as Henry and Eli chatted about practically nothing. Most of the homes were dark or only had a single light on. Kat imagined families inside, watching television together, or parents tucking their kids into bed telling them stories to get them to sleep. Kat cracked the window a little bit allowing some fresh air to circulate through the back seat. England smelled surprisingly just like home. She furrowed her eyebrows, wondering why she had expected it to smell differently. She was tired. That was a fact.

As they got into the more industrial area where the customs building was located, the parked cars flanking either side of the street thinned out. The road widened, and there was little traffic. The residential homes dropped off, more and more commercial buildings lining the streets. Kat could see office buildings and small manufacturing firms, their brick façades telling the story of the fact that they had been built in the economic boom that happened after World War II. Kat had read that somewhere after her first trip to England.

What most Americans didn't understand was that much of England had been flattened by the air raids of the Nazis during the war. There were still frequent reports on the news about World War II, memorials and celebrations of their victory. The first time that Kat went to London, it was hard to understand, though she didn't have much time to talk to Henry about it. England was much more historically focused, unlike the United States, which was much more future-focused. Kat wondered if a devastating event hit the United States if that would change the way that Americans looked at the nation. That was a question she didn't know the answer to.

As Henry's car bumped up the side of the curb, Kat stared ahead of the car, realizing they were at the customs warehouse again. Henry pulled the sedan into an unoccupied spot in the lot. There were no other cars there. The three of them got out and walked to the front door, Henry keying in the code on the pad.

Inside, there was a soft glow of lights. They gave the building an eerie feeling, as though ghosts might appear between the crates stacked from floor to ceiling. A young man stood at the gate, opening it the minute the three of them walked into the building. It was a vastly different experience than the one they had earlier in the day.

Kat followed Henry and Eli down the long space between the stacked crates toward the back of the building. She half expected to see the same agents that she'd seen earlier in the day, but when they arrived near the loading dock, she could see a much larger team. There were probably ten or fifteen agents working on the three crates. She glanced around her. The crates had all been dismantled and spread across the floor. They had been stripped down to bare wood. In front of each crate was a pile of the packing materials, the plastic, Styrofoam sheets, shipping peanuts and craft paper that had wrapped each individual piece of artwork. There were small yellow numbered cones in front of each pile. A forensic photographer was taking pictures and documenting as the team worked.

A voice broke through the chaos of the agents moving around, "Agent Nash?" A woman approached Henry, wearing the gold bars that signified an officer of the customs unit.

"Yes. Special Agent Henry Nash. I was told to report here."

The woman, just a bit taller than Kat, with black hair slicked back off of her face into a long ponytail, said, "My apologies. Special Agent Nash, thank you for coming. When we changed over the shift, agent Davis said that you had some special interest in this art shipment. That's why I had her call you. Is that correct?"

"That's correct. Let me introduce you to Kat Beckman and Eli Langster. They are guests of Scotland Yard from the United States."

Kat glanced at the woman waiting for her to respond. She wondered for a moment what it meant to be a guest of Scotland Yard.

"I'm Mary Brown, Deputy Chief Investigator of Region Five. I was called in today when the drug dog sounded off and they couldn't find the source of the alert."

The group of them followed Mary as she walked closer to the crates. "As you can see, we have basically torn apart each one of these shipments based on what came inside of the crate. We've made piles of each shipping material and looked at them carefully to determine if there is any drug residue and if so, where it came from."

Based on the way that Mary was moving from pile to pile, Kat could tell that she was excited, as though she had discovered treasure on a deserted island. Kat moved closer to her so that she could hear better, the commotion of everyone working casting a low din in the building.

Mary pointed, "Our first clue came from crate number two. We took swabs of each one of the packing materials and did an analysis on them. While there was only a small amount of drug residue on the plastic and paper that was used to wrap each one of the canvases, we got a hit on the peanuts."

Eli took a step forward, "Was there any drug residue or testing done on the canvases?" Eli looked nervous, Kat thought. She could tell that he didn't want any damage done to the art.

Mary shook her head no, her black ponytail swinging across her back. "No, we ran a simple swab test around the edges, careful not to disturb any of the paint or varnish." She looked at Eli, "Don't worry. We do this all the time." Her face cracked into a smile, softening her features. "There is no evidence of drug contamination on any of the canvases. We believe that the plastic and kraft paper protected them from any contamination."

Mary waved for them to follow her. Kat, Eli and Henry walked behind her as she moved through the back of the warehouse. What Kat hadn't been able to see when she had been in the building before was that there was a large investigation room towards the back of the building, separated from the tiers of crates that were being stored and waiting for inspection, approval and transport.

Mary scanned her badge at the door, the lock clicking open with a soft beep. "We use this isolation room to do testing when we don't want to expose the rest of our customs deliveries to foreign objects or substances."

Kat blinked as she entered the room. Like the customs inspection area, this room was bathed in brilliant light. Powerful fixtures hung from the ceiling preventing any shadow from forming in the room. As her eyes adjusted, she noticed that there were quite a few stations spaced around the area. The room itself was large, with rows of laboratory equipment and other scientific pieces of equipment she couldn't name.

There were three people working in the lab even though it would have been what they considered the graveyard shift. Each one of them was wearing a white lab coat, safety glasses and gloves. Mary led them forward around the end of a long table that housed what looked to be awfully expensive laboratory equipment to a man who had his arms inside of a Plexiglas box. Kat stared at it for a moment. The man was wearing thick beige rubber safety gloves that had been permanently attached to the inside of the box. As he pulled his hands out, the gloves fell limp and drooped. "Well, hello!" the man said, turning toward them.

Mary nodded, "Please meet William. He's one of our Chief Investigators." The group nodded and waved. Mary continued, "William, this gentleman is with Scotland Yard, and these are his guests. They came here to track down the shipment of art that you have been examining."

William stood up, his diminutive figure not much taller than the Plexiglas box on the table. He took off his safety glasses. He was several inches shorter than Kat, which put him at not any taller than five feet. Everything about him was small. His hands, his features, the width of his body. The white lab coat hung on him like he was simply a hanger for it. "This has been interesting, very interesting."

Henry cocked his head to the side, "I'm sorry?"

"Right, right. When I get excited, I tend to start in the middle of the story, not the beginning." William took a deep breath and pushed up the round frame glasses that sat on his nose. "Mary called me late this afternoon, just after you had left the building, I believe." Mary nodded. William cleared his throat, "She explained that the drug dog had alerted on your art shipment, but they couldn't figure out where the drugs were."

Kat looked at him. "It isn't our art. We are tracking it because of a murder investigation back in the States."

William's eyes got wide, "Well, that does make for an interesting story." He swallowed, his Adam's apple bobbing up and down in his thin neck. "So, when Mary called me, she asked me to come in and see if I could figure out why one of our drug dogs alerted on the shipment." A small smile crept onto one side of his face. "I love those drug dogs. Bear is my favorite. I brought him some organic treats because he's such a good boy."

Mary raised her eyebrows and looked at William, "The story, William?"

"Yes, yes. I'm sorry. Let me get back to it. Anyway, after I fed Bear a few treats, I decided to do a full observation of everything that had come in the crates. I reran swabs on all the packing materials and came up with the same conclusions that the first set of our technicians did. Now, one thing to know is that the tests that I use are far more sophisticated than the field test kits that are customs agents have. That's why I'm here," he shrugged. "At any rate, when I had done the full round of tests, I came to the same conclusion. The only place there seemed to be any drug residue was the Styrofoam packing peanuts." William walked over to a line of equipment that was near the Plexiglas box that he had been working in. "I ran a full set of tests on a sample of the packing peanuts. Actually, three samples, to be accurate. I pulled one from each crate." He pointed to a line of equipment on one of the stainless-steel laboratory tables. "As I did the initial testing, I saw that the test results are coming back positive for fentanyl, carfentanil, to be precise."

Kat frowned. "Isn't carfentanil the more powerful derivative of fentanyl?" she asked.

William beamed, as though Kat had just become the star student in his little class. "Exactly! That's when I moved the testing over to this beauty." He walked back over to the Plexiglas box and tapped the top of it like he was petting a dog. "Anytime we are dealing with the opioids, particularly fentanyl, we use this isolation chamber. It allows us to do research without risking exposure. Carfentanil is lethal."

Kat could tell by looking at Henry that he was getting impatient. "Okay. So, what you are saying is that the only thing that tested positive for drugs was the packing peanuts. What else did you find?"

"Well, we are just at the beginning of the story!" William said.

Kat glanced at Mary, who shook her head slightly. Kat guessed that William rarely got visitors and so having an audience tonight would make his year, "William, I have to confess, I'm a journalist, not a scientist. Could you give us a simple explanation so I can understand what you're saying?"

"Oh, how wonderful! I had no idea. Come here, come here. The best thing to do is to show you." William sat down on the stool that was in front of the Plexiglas box. He inserted his hands back into the long rubber gloves that were mounted into the side of the box, his small fingers filling out the rubber, moving toward a pile of peanuts that were already inside the enclosure. "I decided to take a better look at the peanuts, to get an idea of what we are dealing with." William held up a peanut using one of the rubber gloves, a scalpel in his other hand. "The only thing about using this isolation chamber is that I have to anticipate every tool I could need before I put materials in the box and seal it. If I unseal the box while I'm working to get another tool, I have to start all over again." He shook his head. "So, luckily I had grabbed a surgical toolkit before I started the examination. Watch this."

William took one of the peanuts and laid it on the work surface inside the box. Using the scalpel, he sliced it from end to end, opening it like it was an exceedingly small submarine sandwich. As soon as he sliced it open, Kat could see that the inside of the peanut was actually hollow. White powder came pouring out.

Kat leaned forward, "What is that?"

"That, my dear, is the more powerful cousin of fentanyl. It's carfentanil."

Silence covered the room for a moment. Kat knew that carfentanil was the much more potent big brother to fentanyl that was sold on the streets. There had been cases of police officers in the United States who had approached an abandoned car only to be overwhelmed by the drug the minute they opened the door. "So, what you are saying is that someone is shipping carfentanil inside of packing peanuts?"

Before William could answer, Henry said, "How many packing peanuts have drugs inside of them?"

"One question at a time. Yes, Kat, someone has taken a lot of care to get the drugs inside of the packing peanuts. And yes, Henry, all of them to date. The total number could be in the thousands."

Kat realized that if someone was shipping drugs with the art that changed the equation of what they were chasing substantially. Her mind raced back to the process they must have used to get the drugs inside of the peanuts. "William, how would they have gotten the powder inside of these packing peanuts?"

William sighed, "That part, I haven't exactly figured out yet. I am guessing they injected it."

Mary said, "Aren't packing peanuts usually solid?"

William nodded. "Indeed. They generally are. My theory is that they had this batch specially manufactured for them." He pointed inside the Plexiglas box. "Take a look at this." With gloved hands, he tapped out all the powder that was inside of the single peanut that he had cut in half. "Do you see how there is a hollow section in the center?" Everyone in the group nodded. "What I haven't determined yet is if they were manufactured this way or if somehow the powder was heated to make the inside of the Styrofoam melt as it was injected. That will require additional testing."

Kat leaned forward, staring into the box, trying to see as best she could what William was talking about. William picked up a small brush, much like one that might be used for painting, and dusted the interior of the peanut he had sliced from end to end. "See, the texture of the inside of the peanut looks different than the exterior. I'll have to run some additional tests, but it's possible they melted the interior and injected the drugs." He tilted his head to the side, "This is a new one, for sure. Brilliant plan, really."

Mary led the group out of the investigation room, leaving William with his hands still in the box. As soon as the door closed behind them, the group stopped. Mary looked at Henry, "I'm assuming that Scotland Yard will be following up on this?"

"Yes, of course. I'll get some of our narcotics officers down here shortly."

Mary walked off, the three of them left standing to absorb the information they had heard. Eli had been silent the entire time. Kat looked at him, "Eli, do you have any thoughts? You were awfully quiet."

Eli cleared his throat, "I was just thinking. I was wondering what was more important to the criminals, was it the art or was the art just a way to transport the drugs?"

Kat bit her lip. "That's a good question. Knowing that Hailey's murder has to do with drugs puts a different spin on it, doesn't it, Henry?"

"To the British government, it will. I need to go make a call. Excuse me." Henry walked off. Kat imagined that he was calling his office to get more investigators involved in the case.

Nearby, there were two small crates set off to the side. Kat walked over and sat on one. Eli sat on the other. "We have to figure out how all of this works together," Kat said.

Eli nodded, seeming discouraged. "I just don't understand..."

"What is it that you don't understand?" Kat said.

Eli rubbed his forehead with his short, stocky fingers. "There is no order to what's happening."

Kat understood how he was feeling. She felt the same. Henry walked back to the two of them a moment later. Kat looked up at him from her perch on the crate, "Everything okay?"

Henry nodded. "Yes. There will be some additional officers arriving here shortly. In the meantime, I think we need a new plan."

Kat pulled her phone out of her pocket. "I think we better loop Carson in on this, don't you?" Henry nodded.

Carson answered after the first ring, "Kat? Everything okay?"

"Well, we've had a new wrinkle to the case." Kat went on to tell him about the packing peanuts, the drugs, and the theories that William was working on. The rest of them listened, Kat's phone on speaker.

"That does make things more complicated, doesn't it?" Carson said. "Henry, what's the next step for Scotland Yard?"

Henry leaned over so he could speak into Kat's phone, "Some of the narcotics team members are on their way over. I'll confer with them when they get here, but my assumption is they will open an investigation. The customs investigators will do exactly the same thing. We can't have these drugs on our streets."

"Carson? Any idea how this fits with Hailey's murder?" Kat asked. She could almost hear his head shake as he responded.

"None, but that's what we have to figure out before someone else dies."

29

S tella Rusu sat in her favorite chair by a fire in her living room. She had a cup of tea that warming her hands, the last thing the housekeeper did before she went home for the night.

She stretched her legs out in front of her and then curled them back up underneath the white cashmere afghan that she had pulled across her lap. Though the weather was starting to get warmer, there was still dampness in the air. Typical for London, she thought.

As she took a sip of the bitter tea, her phone chirped. She picked it up, her brows knitting together. Instead of texting, she called. "What happened?" she asked, knowing they were on a secure line that could not be traced.

A male voice answered. It was Bobby, one of her lieutenants. "I'm just getting information about it now, ma'am."

Stella felt the pain of anger surged through her body. She needed to keep it under control so that she could think clearly, "Tell me what you know."

"From what my source and the customs building said, the

drug dog alerted on the packages that were received this morning."

"Why was there a drug dog?" Stella got up and started to pace. Her long blonde hair was piled up on top of her head, her face coated with a thick moisturizer that cost more than she paid her housekeeper for a month of work. She wore an oversized sweater that exposed one of her shoulders and a pair of leggings.

Stella Rusu was used to getting what she wanted when she wanted it. The daughter of billionaire Marcus Rusu, Stella had been given the import-export business to run on her own. Her father, Marcus, had made his mark already, and was in his later years living in a chalet in Switzerland, surrounded by a protective detail and a team of nurses and a hand-selected doctor that stayed with him no matter where he went. Stella had two older brothers, John and Stefan. They were in charge of the majority of her father's business now.

When she was eighteen, her father had sent her to London to go to university. She was a gymnast and graduated with a degree in philosophy. Not that she would have ever used it; the family business was the focus of everything they did.

Every time Stella went to Switzerland to see her father, she came home disappointed. He would greet her warmly, ask her questions about work, and then immediately launch into stories about the old days. He never asked how she was or what was going on in her personal life. Not that she had much of one.

After college, her father had walked her into the main offices of the import business and told her that he wanted her to learn the ropes, to take it over. He would pay her handsomely, more than she could ever hope to make it any other job. She remembered that moment, her feelings swinging back and forth between elation at having part of the family business and sadness knowing that there was no other option for her.

There had been no option for her mother, Christina, either. Stella looked a lot like her mother, blonde and thin. At times, she wondered if she reminded her father of his late wife.

Marcus, her father, had fallen in love with Christina when he watched her dance. She had been a ballerina. They had married quickly and had her oldest brother John just a year after that. Stefan was born two years later, but there was a five-year gap between Stefan and Stella.

Growing up, Stella had noticed that she spent more time with the nannies than she did with her mother. She had memories of running into her mother's bedroom, finding her mom laying on her side staring out the window, saying nothing. Her mother had fallen into a deep depression after she had Stella, and never quite recovered. When Stella was twelve, Christina had gone down to Marcus' gun cabinet while he was on a hunting trip, stood in front of it, and shot herself. The house manager called Marcus, who ordered the room to be cleaned, the body to be removed, and the entire room to be redecorated by the time he got home twenty-four hours later. There was no funeral.

Stella tried to control the memories that were flashing in her mind and concentrate on the problem in front of her. "I thought you told me that there would be no search for drugs."

"That was my impression, ma'am. Apparently, my source got it wrong."

"This is unacceptable. Fix it." She threw the phone against one of the pillows on the couch. Bobby had been someone who'd been with his family since he was a boy, starting by running errands in the neighborhood where her family lived. Not that you could really call it a neighborhood -- there were just a smattering of small houses dotted across the valley floor. Marcus and his family lived above all of them in an estate perched on a Romanian mountainside. That was before her father had bought a second home in Switzerland.

Now, Bobby was in London with Stella. He had come to work with her once her father had given her the import-export business. He said it was for advice and protection. Stella knew it was more than that. She was sure Bobby was updating her father on exactly what she was doing, probably on a moment by moment basis.

She started to pace in front of the fireplace. A drug dog alerting on her newest way to ship drugs through Europe could represent a significant impact on her work. In her position, she couldn't have any failures.

GROWING up with two older brothers who were destined for the family business had been difficult. No matter what Stella did, no matter how hard she worked or what she accomplished, it wasn't enough for her father. Their nightly dinners growing up were a rundown of what everyone had done for the day, even before the boys started working for their father. John would talk about his success at school, while Stefan told of the wrestling moves he'd learned at practice. Her father would laugh and instruct and praise the boys, while all she got was, "How was your day, honey? Did you and your friends have fun?"

The feeling of being minimized stuck with Stella from the time her mother died. It never left her, except for the moment that Marcus had given her control of the import-export business. John had taken over the real estate business, the family holding properties all over Europe and South America. Stefan was working with Marcus on the gambling side of the business.

The day came when Marcus told Stella to get ready. They had somewhere to go. She got in the car with his driver and Bobby in tow. At the warehouse, a dusty, old building that had barely been used for the last decade, Marcus walked her to the office. "This is now yours. Honestly, I haven't done much with it in a long time. You can make it something." She could still feel the warmth of his hand on her cheek, "You are a smart girl. You've done well at school." Marcus glanced over at Bobby, "You'll help her."

Bobby nodded, "Yes, sir. Whatever she needs."

Stella was starstruck for a moment, walking around the building. She had been in it many times as a child, sitting in the corner of the office while her dad did some work, getting shooed out if a business associate came to visit. Stella could still hear the sounds of the forklifts and men working, the smell of their lunches as they stopped midday, pulling out paper sacks their wives had packed for them.

Stella felt excitement growing within her as she walked away from her father and Bobby. She'd redecorate the office first and get an assistant. She'd travel, looking for new opportunities her father had never found. She'd rebuild the business. She was sure of it.

Marcus and Bobby were talking when she walked back. She came up behind them. "It's just something to keep her occupied. Keep an eye on her..." her father said.

Stella stopped and swallowed. The truth crashed down over her. Her father hadn't woken up and started believing in her. Nothing had changed. As her father turned, she smiled, "Papa, thank you. I'm so excited!" She gave him a kiss on the cheek, though her lips felt cold and bloodless.

He patted her on the arm. "Of course, honey. This will keep you busy until you are ready to have babies."

A rage she had never felt before bloomed inside of her. He hadn't changed. What would happen if she fell in love and got married? Did he think she'd walk away from the business so she could be at home caring for her children day and night? A coldness passed over her. Any love that she had for her father disappeared at that moment. The feeling of respect and duty lingered, but that was all.

. . .

STELLA STOPPED in the middle of the living room, the warmth from the fire soaking through her legs. In the distance, she could see the lights from Big Ben. She had gotten used to dealing with problems on her own. The first couple of times that issues with the business rose up, she tried to call her father for advice. He told her not to worry about it. The problems disappeared without her doing a thing. When she had an issue with an employee or a contractor, they tended to disappear or came to apologize as if their life depended on it. She knew Marcus was pulling the puppet strings behind the scenes. He was a master manipulator.

She walked into the kitchen, considering her options. Out of the refrigerator, she pulled a bottle of white wine. She needed something stronger than a cup of tea. From a cabinet above the sink, she reached for a long-stemmed wine glass, filling it up nearly to the top. She took a sip, the liquid warming her insides better than the tea.

The drug dog could be a problem, she thought, sitting down on a chair facing the fire, covering her legs with the afghan again. The bigger problem was if they could find the drugs. She sighed. The drugs themselves were worth more than a million dollars on their own. They had started with a small shipment, not much more than a kilogram, because there was no guarantee if they would be able to get it through. Either way, she didn't want to lose that amount of money. Stella took a long sip of wine, the alcohol burning the back of her throat.

The art was another issue entirely. On their own, the canvases she had acquired through Christopher were worth nothing. They were the work of a gifted, but unknown, art student. But sold on the market as real pieces, they were each worth hundreds of millions.

Art wasn't something that her father had ever been involved

in. Marcus had stuck to more traditional imports and exports. In the early days, he smuggled things like alcohol and other prohibited items into the Eastern Bloc countries of Europe. People would pay a huge premium in order to get the things that they wanted. Rationing and governmental requirements never allowed cigarettes, cigars and alcohol to hit the market. The black market was the only place to get them.

As times changed and the Eastern Bloc countries opened up, everyone had to evolve. That included the importers and exporters. Stella twirled the wine glass in her fingers, the light of the fire shimmering through the amber liquid, thinking about her first days running the business. She learned to follow her instincts quickly. Her father assigned her crew to clean up, paint and redecorate the office. It had been done in just a couple of days. Stella, unlike other members of her family, wasn't that interested in the trappings that the business brought. She was more interested in the business itself. That was something she discovered as she started to work. Though her father had said that the business was working, one quick look at the books told her that there was nothing there that could be leveraged. Though she had been a philosophy major at university, she had taken some classes in economics. The basic principles of the market served her well. Supply. Demand. That's how all businesses ran. In fact, Stella learned quickly that was how the world ran, too. If you had something that someone wanted and there wasn't much of it available, you could command whatever price you wanted.

Stella stood up and paced, taking another sip of wine. She remembered right after Marcus had handed the business over to her. One night, she was at the warehouse late. It was only about two months after her father had given her the business. The floors had been swept, the lights updated, and she had people who were in the building all day long every day to protect the things that were coming in and out. The imports and exports had started up like a trickle, but it wasn't enough. She knew she wanted a bigger business, but how?

Sitting in her office that night, she realized that if she could find things the people collected but couldn't get anywhere else, she could command whatever price she wanted. It might no longer be cigars, but there had to be other things that were hard to get. With her father's business contacts, she had at her fingertips plenty of people willing and able to pay whatever she asked.

The next weekend, Stella visited a friend back in Romania. The friend was an art student, someone that Stella had met while she was at university in London. There was a new exhibit of Dutch Masters being shown near her family's home. The two of them decided to go see it, stopping for lunch along the way. Pointing to a portrait of a young man and a woman standing together by Vermeer, she asked her friend, "What's a piece of artwork like this worth?"

The friend shook her head. "It's priceless, Stella. There's no way anyone would ever have enough money to pay for something like this."

Though it was a nice piece of art, Stella wasn't attracted to the design. She was, however, attracted to the value.

STELLA SAT DOWN and crossed her legs in the chair where she was sitting, feeling the muscles in her legs start to cramp. She needed to get some sleep before her meetings in the morning. The fire crackled in the background. Artwork had become the basis of her import-export business. It had evolved over time, of course. First, she moved small shipments of real art. Now, she moved hundreds of millions of dollars in forgeries. No one knew. Not even Marcus.

Stella shook her head. Now the drug portion of the business had gotten her in trouble. She'd never been that interested in taking drugs herself. She wanted to be in command of her senses. She knew that her brother Stefan had experimented with cocaine when it was fashionable a decade ago but quit when some of his father's men took him out back and taught him a lesson. It was the harsh reality of being Marcus Rusu's son. Fun was allowed, but it had to be under control. In a way, Stella was glad that her father had put a stop to Stefan's drug habit. Stefan could have easily gotten addicted. He could've taken the whole family down with him.

Stella stared off out through the window. It was dark. The only thing she could see were lights glowing in the distance from the city. She knew the real reason that Marcus had stopped her brother's drug addiction wasn't out of love. It was a business decision. Drug addicts tended to get themselves into trouble and take the people down around them. Marcus couldn't afford that.

Stella took a deep breath and held it in her chest, the way that she used to do when she would swim in the lake near their chalet in Switzerland. The water had always been ice cold, no matter what time of the year they were outside. She let her mind wander for a moment, knowing that it was working on its own to solve the problem of the drug dog. She swallowed, let the breath out and realized that even if they lost the drugs and the art, it could be replaced. It would be a serious loss to the business, but she would survive. She always did.

By the time Carson got back to his house, it was late. Knowing that the artwork Kat tracked to London included a drug shipment changed everything. No matter how hard he tried to sleep, it wouldn't come. After tossing and turning, he got up, leaving the bed wrinkled. He was restless.

He went downstairs, opened the refrigerator and got out a bottle of water. This case was keeping him up nights, something that he wasn't used to. It felt like someone had dumped two separate jigsaw puzzles out on the same table. There was no telling which piece belonged to which puzzle and no telling what the final picture was supposed to look like. Carson didn't like being confused, and yet he was.

He picked up his phone and stared at it. It was the middle of the night. He was due at the police station in just over four hours to start his morning shift. His gut told him that going into the office wasn't going to solve any of the problems he was having. He quickly scrolled through his contacts and tapped the phone number for Chief Jackson. He stood stock-still waiting for the call to connect.

"Yes?"

"Chief, I'm sorry to bother you in the middle of the night. This is Carson."

"Yes, Carson. I know it's you. You're in my phone."

"Sorry about that, Chief. Listen, I have a problem. There's been a development in the Hailey Park murder case." Carson could hear the sound of the chief getting out of bed, a little grunting coming from him.

"Something happened in the middle of the night?"

"Not here, sir. Beckman, the journalist, called. She's in London with Scotland Yard. They found the art that had been stolen from Hailey Park's apartment."

"Son, that sounds like news you could have told me at the beginning of the shift."

Carson flushed, "Sir, that's not all."

"Yes?"

"It turns out there was a shipment of carfentanil included in the shipment."

Carson could hear rustling in the background. It sounded like the chief was making himself some coffee. "Hold on for a second, Carson. I need some coffee if this is going to get serious."

Carson could hear water running in the background. "Okay, I'm back. Now, what were you saying?"

"It seems like this case has taken a turn, sir. I think that we are talking about more than just an art student getting murdered."

"All right. I'll bite. Run me through it."

Carson started to pace again, giving his boss all the details that he had yet to pass over in his completed report. He started to piece the puzzle together, from the initial stabbing to the expensive attorney hired to protect the boy that had been accused, to the stolen artwork, to the fact that Kat and Eli had found the art in London, Kat's escape and now the drug stash and Oskar Kellum's death. "Sir, I think we're dealing with a much larger issue. I think that Hailey's death was just the cleaning up of loose ends."

"What are you suggesting, Carson?"

"I'm thinking I need to go to London." The words hung in the air for a moment. Carson swallowed hard, not knowing how Chief Jackson would react. Joe had been a longtime supporter of his but asking to go to Europe to follow up on what could easily be viewed as just a local case might be a bit of a stretch.

"If I sent you to London, and I am saying if," Joe responded, "What would you hope to find?"

Carson sucked in a breath. He hadn't gotten a no yet from the chief. That, at least, was good news. "Well, I could go and help Scotland Yard and Kat and Eli try to figure out what happened, and how it's connected to Hailey. They might need our local perspective in order to finalize the case." Carson knew this was a bit of a sales job. A little weak, even. He was hoping the chief would buy it.

"I don't know, Carson. That's a big expense for a small department like ours. Don't you think that Scotland Yard can handle it?"

Carson needed to think quickly if he had any hopes of getting the approval to go to London. "I can see your point, sir. What I'm concerned about is that Scotland Yard will solve the larger case of the art and the drugs, but we won't get a resolution about Hailey's murder. If we don't, then it may become a cold case and still be on our books for years to come." Carson hoped that the idea of having a cold case hanging around Joe's neck would be enough to motivate him to let Carson go.

Carson heard what sounded like a chair being pulled away from the table. The chief didn't respond. "Let me think about this. I'll call you back in a little bit."

"Okay. Thank you, sir. Again, sorry to wake you." Carson ended the call not sure if he should feel hopeful or defeated.

He couldn't tell from the tone of Joe's voice if it sounded like he was leaning towards letting Carson go or keeping him at the department. Carson stood and stared, not sure what to do. It was really too late to go back to bed. Even if he did, he knew he wouldn't sleep.

Carson had left his laptop on the counter charging for the night. He flipped the lid open and pressed the button to wake it up. Within a few seconds, it came to life. Carson typed in the word carfentanil. He had learned about it at training they had attended as a department about eight months before. Scrolling through the information he realized that this powerful drug was incredibly valuable. Smugglers would move it throughout the world, cut it with items like cleanser, and then sell it on the streets. No matter where it went, it left bodies in its wake. Whoever was moving the drugs, was clearly someone without remorse. They would have a lot of blood on their hands.

Carson leaned back on the stool he was sitting on, feeling the wooden back cup his shoulders. He let his mind wander, hoping that he could somehow see a path forward that would explain all the different parts of the crime. The drugs added a very different twist to what had been going on. He squinted, hoping that his thoughts would come into focus. The fact that valuable drugs were tied in this case explained a lot. The life of an art student wasn't worth much in the face of a smuggling ring. Where the artwork fit in though, he wasn't sure. Was it just a front to ship the drugs?

He didn't have time to fully complete his thought. His phone rang. "All right, Carson." Chief Jackson started talking without even saying hello. "Take a trip to London. Let's see if we can figure out how Hailey Park ties into all the other pieces. Go make Savannah proud."

"Thanks, Chief. I'll let you know when I land."

Carson quickly looked up the next available flights to London. He found a connection through New York that left

Savannah in five hours. It was more time than he would have liked, but it would do. He looked at the clock on his cell phone, realizing that with the time change, it was well into the decent hours of the morning in London already. He called Kat.

"What are you doing?" she said.

"Packing. I'm on my way. I'll be in later on today, or tonight."

"Sounds good. I'll see you then."

BY THE TIME Carson landed in London, it was dark out again. His body told him it was dinner time, but the clock said otherwise. He took a cab to Henry's house. The door opened before he even got out of the car. "Welcome!" Henry said, grabbing for Carson's bag, "How was the flight?"

"It was a lot of hours of sitting still. That's for sure."

Carson followed Henry into the house. Kat and Eli were sitting at a small kitchen table, Kat at her computer, Eli with both hands wrapped around a cup of tea. "Hey, Carson," Kat said.

Eli nodded, "Hello, Detective Martino."

Henry looked at Carson, "Make yourself at home. Would you like some tea?"

Even though Carson had literally done nothing except walk from plane to plane and sit, he was exhausted. "Yes, please." He sat down at the table next to Eli, "How are you two?"

Kat chewed her lip. "I'd be better if we could figure this case out."

Carson blinked, "Me, too. That's why I'm here."

For the next two hours, the group sat at the round, white dinette. Kat brought Carson up to date on what they had learned, and Henry provided some background on customs practices in England. Eli updated Carson on the status of the artwork, and they discussed how the drugs had been found inside the peanuts. "One of the investigators will let us know as soon they have more definitive information," Henry said. "But I think we have the general gist from what William said." Henry lifted his hands above his head, stretching, "I don't know about you all, but I am spent. How about if we call it a night and regroup in the morning?"

Everyone nodded, each one of them standing up and finding a place to sleep. Carson followed Eli upstairs, lying down on the other twin bed that was in the room Eli had slept in the night before. Carson didn't even bother to change his clothes. He just curled up on top of the bedspread, hoping that when he woke up, they would be able to find the answers they needed.

31

Outside of Henry's house, a shiny black cab pulled up across the street wedging itself between the work van and a small sedan that had been left there by their owners. David lifted the cap off his head and pushed his hair back, resettling the hat. He had been told to watch the house. For what, he wasn't sure. He saw the lights go off, one by one, as though whoever was in the house was settling in for the night. A cold front had moved through London, dropping the temperature. He was glad for the thin jacket before he left earlier in the day. Pulling the collar up tight around his neck, he slid down in the seat, so that anyone passing at a glance would think the cab was empty.

It was going to be a long night...

32

C hristopher had slept well on the flight to London. One of his most powerful clients had requested to see him and had sent their private jet to collect him. It was his favorite way to fly.

Flying privately was a much simpler process than commercial. With commercial flights, there were all the security checks and long walks to the gate, the horrible cups of coffee, and the cramped seating for hours at a time.

Flying on a private jet, however, was actually quite pleasant. There were usually few people on the flight, and the pilot and the crew were generally ready to leave as soon as their guests arrived. When he had gotten a call to go to London, he had been given the name of a private airstrip and the tail number of the correct plane. It didn't take him long to pack. Christopher never stayed for an extended period and any place. He checked out of his penthouse and asked for a driver to take him to the airport. As soon as he got there, he saw a bright white jet gleaming in the sunshine. The tail number matched the one that he had been given. He gave the driver a generous tip and carried his own bags to the plane.

On the plane, he was met by a tall flight attendant, wearing a red dress. Some of the flight attendants provided additional services for their guests. Looking at her, he wondered how many men had gotten tangled up in her long black hair on a transatlantic flight. He wasn't interested though.

As Christopher settled in his seat, the stewardess, who he'd found out was named Michelle, brought him a scotch on the rocks. He reclined in his seat trying to relax. His mind raced ahead. He didn't know why the Rusu family Had called him to come to London. He had done work for Marcus, the father, for decades, nearly since he started working as a broker. In the last five years, he had done work for Stella, Marcus's youngest daughter. She had proven to be a challenge. Moody, temperamental — all the things that made high-powered clients difficult. She would say one thing one day and the next completely change her mind.

Christopher laid back in his seat as he watched Michelle prepare a bed across the aisle with sheets and a blanket. Unlike flying commercial, the seats converted on a private plane to a proper bed.

Michelle looked at him as he jiggled the ice in his glass. "Would you care for another, sir?"

"Yes, please. And I'm ready for my dinner if you have anything available."

"Of course. We have a choice of salmon or beef tenderloin tonight. Which would you prefer?"

Another side benefit of traveling on a private plane is that the food was much better, generally prepared by either their own chef or a restaurant chef and brought on board just before departure. The stewardess did the final cooking for the guest. The portions were larger, and the food wasn't as salty as on a commercial plane. "I'll have the tenderloin, please."

Michelle took his glass from him. "Certainly. How would you like that prepared?"

"Rare." He watched her as she walked away, toward the cockpit of the plane. Christopher hadn't seen the pilots other than to give them a quick wave when he boarded the plane. After 9/11, all planes, even the private ones, had cockpit doors that were secured during the flight. They had a small peephole and a small opening where a flight attendant could push food through. The pilots even had their own private restroom. Christopher nodded to himself, making a note to investigate a new flight service for his own use. Flying private was the best option for travel. He didn't believe anyone could argue that point.

While he was waiting for dinner, Christopher's mind wandered to Stella Rusu. He didn't know why she had called him to London. It was possible that she was unhappy with the shipment of art that Hailey had provided, or the solution he had come up with in order to tie up loose ends.

A FEW MONTHS BACK, while he was traveling through France, Stella had asked him to come to the Rusu's chalet in Switzerland. The meeting had been brief. Stella sat to the right of her father at a long table, her small, athletic body, curled up on the chair next to him, like a child. But she was no child, Christopher knew that.

Marcus's gravelly voice was still etched in Christopher's memory. "Christopher, you've done good work for the family for a long time. We need to switch gears and find another option for Stella's art import business. I hope you understand."

Christopher could feel sets of eyes boring into him, ones that belong to Marcus, Stella and Bobby, a lieutenant that had been with the family for decades. "Certainly." He hesitated for a moment, not sure if he should ask, "May I ask a question?"

Marcus didn't say anything. He just nodded.

"So that I can serve you better in the future, if you'd

consider letting me continue on, that is," Christopher phrased the question carefully, "Was there an issue with the quality or the delivery of the product?"

Marcus looked at Stella as if he were encouraging her to answer. She cleared her throat, "No. It's simply time to change directions."

Christopher nodded, knowing that they wouldn't tell them anything more than they already had. It was up to him to get the job done. His job wasn't to know why they wanted something done. His job was to do it. That was how he got paid. Even more, that was how he stayed alive.

In the end, Marcus called a week later and told him that they did want to continue on. Christopher was relieved... sort of.

MICHELLE BROUGHT a tray of food to him, the steam curling in the dry air of the plane. She set the white bone china plate and silverware out in front of him after she had covered the tray table with a starched linen cloth. The food smelled delicious, the scent of roasted beef tenderloin, spring vegetables and rice pilaf filling his nose. "Would you like another scotch now, sir? Or would you prefer wine with your dinner?"

Christopher nodded, chewing his first bite of the tenderloin. "Yes, please. A red would be fine. Whatever you have on board."

He took another bite, thinking about the Rusu family and the fact he was being called to London as he ate his dinner. Normally, if the client was upset with you, they suggested that you fly commercial. They might say that the plane wasn't available or not even offer it. In this case, the family had sent their own private jet to get him. That was a good sign. Maybe they had another project for him.

He knew there was one problem he would have to face, and

he hoped they weren't looking for an immediate answer. He would need to replace Hailey. Finding talent like hers was difficult, if not nearly impossible. In a way, that's what made it fun.

There were literally thousands of art schools internationally. He used artists from all corners of the globe — Asia, Africa, North America and Europe. But this was the first time that a client had asked him to end someone's life. He wanted to think that he felt upset about it, but he didn't. Finding a way to kill Hailey had just been another part of the game. Once he had found the bookie that handled Oskar's debts, the rest had been easy. The bookie had provided him with the names of several people that owed him a lot of money, and when he found out that Oskar was a psychiatrist, it seemed to be a perfect fit. The rest of the problem was on Oskar.

Realistically, Oskar should have been able to walk away without a beating and without being killed. But, for some reason, the bookie had taken extreme action. Christopher was aware that the Rusu family knew of the plan. They approved it before he acted. He had been prepared that Hailey would die. He didn't realize that the family might do an end-run around him and kill off Oskar as well.

He shrugged, putting a piece of baby carrot in his mouth, the taste of balsamic vinegar and ginger plus the sweetness of the carrot, running across his taste buds. Oskar could have been useful in the future, but now that wasn't an option. Christopher realized he might have to reevaluate his relationship with the family once this transaction was over. Not that getting out of these arrangements was easy, especially given the fact that he had worked for Marcus for so many years. Christopher was an independent man, or at least he liked to think so. With five different passports with five different names, he could literally disappear anywhere in the world and no one would be able to find him. Or at least he hoped that was the case.

33

K at heard Henry rattling around in the kitchen. It was early. As she turned over, she heard his phone ring. "Yes?" he said with a whisper, probably trying not to wake her. Kat yawned. There was no point in him being quiet now. She was up.

She swung her legs out over the edge of the couch and sat up, stretching her arms up overhead. Sleeping on the couch hadn't been too bad. She looked at her phone. It was six o'clock in the morning. That meant it was one o'clock in the morning at home. She sent a quick text to Van, wondering if he was still awake. He texted back. "Heading to bed. How are things?"

"Just waking up. It's going to be a long day. The detective from Savannah arrived last night. I'll keep you posted."

"Okay. Going to bed. Love you. I'll kiss Jack."

Kat got up and walked to the bathroom, anxious to brush her teeth. It seemed that no matter how much water she drank she couldn't get herself hydrated. It felt like she had slept with a sock in her mouth, the fuzz sticking to every surface.

Kat used the bathroom and brushed her teeth, the mint taste making her feel better. She washed her hands and walked out, turning her head to see where Henry was. He was still on the phone, pacing back and forth, his black hair in a swirl, as though he had gotten caught in a windstorm while he slept. Kat smiled. She had only known Henry's ex-wife Bev for a day before she had passed away, but she could very well imagine Bev scolding Henry for his wild hair.

He pulled the phone away from his ear and tapped the screen ending the call, "Sorry about that. I didn't mean to wake you."

"No problem. I'm a light sleeper." Kat blinked and swallowed trying to fight off the last bit of drowsiness from the sleep that she did get. "What's going on? Did you get any news?"

"In fact, I did. We need to go to the office as soon as we can get everyone up and ready." Henry picked up the teakettle from the counter, "But before we go, I'll start some tea. We can pick up breakfast on the way into the office."

Kat nodded, "I'll leave it up to you to wake up the guys." She walked back over to the end of the couch, knelt down, and tipped over her suitcase, tugging at the zipper. She pulled out a clean change of clothes. She needed a shower before they could start their day. The last one that she had had was in Savannah, which felt like a lifetime ago. She glanced at Henry, who was fussing with mugs and tea bags. "I'm going to get a quick shower before we go. I'll be no good to you otherwise."

"That sounds lovely."

By the time Kat got out of the shower, she heard more voices in the kitchen. Eli and Carson were sitting on stools, sipping hot mugs of tea. It looked like Carson had grabbed a quick shower too. "Good morning," she said, pushing her blonde hair behind her ear. It was still wet from the shower.

"Morning," Carson muttered. He seemed uncomfortable.

Kat put her old clothes back in her suitcase, zipped it closed and stood it up in the corner of Henry's living room. "So, what's the plan?"

Henry took a small sip of his tea, blowing on the edge of the cup, trying to cool it. "Well, when all of you are ready to go, we will head to my office. There is a little café on the way we can stop to get a few breakfast sandwiches."

Carson frowned, "I don't understand. I'm all for getting an early start, but why the rush to get to your office?"

"Ah, yes. That piece of information might be helpful. The problem is I'm not exactly sure. Mary, the customs official we met last night, has asked to meet us. She said she has information."

Kat nodded. She was hoping that Mary could shed some light on what had been going on. Hopefully, that would help them to put all the pieces together.

Within a few minutes, the four of them had finished what they needed to do at Henry's house and set out for the Scotland Yard offices. It wasn't a long drive, just about ten or fifteen minutes. As Henry backed the car out of the driveway, Kat spotted a cab parked across the street. "Henry? Do you see that?"

"What?"

"The cab. There is a cab parked right across the street." Kat's heart started to beat a little faster. Was it the same cab from before? She stared at it, not sure. It appeared to be empty.

"Oh, that. Yes, my neighbor is a cab driver. He sometimes parks there when he's not at work." As Henry turned the sedan down the street, he glanced over his shoulder. "Strange thing, though. The number that's on that cab isn't the same as the one he drives. Maybe he's driving a loaner..."

Although Henry didn't seem to think that the cab parked across the street was anything of a threat, Kat's gut told her otherwise. She swallowed hard, trying to keep the bile from racing up her throat and into her mouth.

It didn't take long for the four of them to grab some breakfast at a local café drive-through and get to the office. By the time they got there, Mary was waiting for them in Henry's office.

Henry gave her a nod, "Why don't we move down to the conference room? There's more space."

The conference room was spacious compared to the offices that were in the building, Kat noticed. She sat her backpack down against the wall and pulled up one of the chairs that were on the far side of the table. The room itself had been painted in an off-white, the flag of England framed at one end of the room and the seal of Scotland Yard on the opposite wall. There were two windows on the widest wall, facing the parking lot. Eli sat next to her, with Henry and Carson on the other side of the table. Mary put down a stack of files at the head of the table that was closest to the door.

There was a crinkling of paper as the group started to eat their breakfast. Henry took a bite of his sandwich, and said to Mary, "Why did you call us all here so early?"

"Yeah, sorry about that. We had some findings overnight that I thought might be critical to get to you. It could influence your investigation. Didn't want to wait on that."

Henry nodded, "All right, go ahead. We're all ears."

Mary took a deep breath and flipped open the file that was on the top of the stack. Kat watched. From what she could tell, Mary was careful and highly detailed. Her uniform was almost as neatly pressed as Carson's suit. She tried not to giggle. This was a serious situation but noticing people's idiosyncrasies was funny at times. She looked back down at her sandwich and took another bite, forcing herself to concentrate. The thought of laughter made her think of Jack. She wondered how he was doing.

"As you know, we discovered a shipment of highly toxic carfentanil hidden within the packing peanuts of the crates that you followed here from New York. In addition to the crates, we isolated more than thirty oil paintings that your art expert identified." Mary gave a brief nod to Eli, who nodded back. "As of the last time we spoke, we were still working on how the drugs got into each peanut and figuring out how much drug material we could recover."

"And you figured that out?" Carson asked.

Mary looked at him strangely for a moment. Kat realized that they hadn't met before. "I'm sorry. Carson, please meet Mary. She is our contact for the investigation. Mary, please meet Detective Carson Martino from the Savannah Police Department."

Mary blinked. "Pleasure." She reshuffled the papers for a moment, clearly looking for information so that she could answer Carson's question. "We did. William figured out that there were approximately three grams of drug material in each peanut. From our initial testing, it looks as though each peanut was first injected with a hot solution to melt the interior of the peanut followed by another injection of the drugs. As of this morning, we had recovered three kilos of the drugs."

Kat frowned for a moment. "Mary, what is the value of those drugs?"

Mary lifted her eyebrows, "That's an excellent question. Whoever sent them probably paid about one million US. There's a difference though with the street value."

"And that is? I'm not super familiar with putting drugs on the street." Kat looked at Carson. He was smiling.

"You aren't? I'm surprised by that," he quipped.

Henry closed his eyes for a moment. "Sorry, Mary, you'll have to forgive these two. You know, Americans. Please continue."

"Yes, of course. Kat, to answer your question if we found one million worth of drugs, they would likely be worth three to five million on the street. That would be in US dollars of course. The chemical content of the drugs that we recovered is pure. That was the reason that William used the isolation chamber in order to test them. Even the slightest whiff of carfentanil could kill you. Drug dealers generally cut the substance with other drugs, things like cocaine and heroin. They've also been known to use toxic substances like cleanser and even icing sugar."

Eli leaned over to Kat and whispered, "Icing sugar is our powdered sugar."

Henry balled up the paper that his breakfast sandwich had come in and pitched it towards the wastebasket, missing. "Were there contaminated packing peanuts in every crate?"

Mary nodded. "Yes. All three crates had packing peanuts that contained drugs. We are still testing the last batches, but it looks like most of them were contaminated."

Carson stood up from the table, pacing behind the chairs. "I just don't understand how all of this fits together. So, what did they do? Do they hire Hailey to paint the canvases just to use them to send the drugs overseas? That doesn't make any sense. They could have purchased anything to ship with the packing peanuts."

Eli nodded, "I agree with Detective Martino. Each one of those canvases could have taken weeks to prepare. There had to be a more efficient way to ship things across to Europe other than artwork."

Kat looked down squeezing her hands together. She felt like they were on the verge of something, but she didn't know what. "I think Carson and Eli are on to something," she said. "Honestly, if the goal was just to ship the drugs, why not use something that was pre-manufactured and easy to get?"

Mary glanced at each of them, "We came to the same conclusion. That's where things get interesting. It's the real reason I called you into the office this early."

Kat felt like Mary had buried the headline.

The room was silent, everyone looking at Mary. Kat hoped she would be able to shine some light on how the pieces of this case fit together. The frustration had gone on long enough.

Mary cleared her throat. "It seems there is a link between the artwork and the drugs. Detective Martino," she glanced at Carson, "I'm not sure how this ties into your case in the States, but let's see if this starts to fill in some blanks." Mary passed a yellow manilla file out to each person. The front of it was emblazoned with the crest of the British customs unit. Mary continued, "If you open the file, on the left-hand side you will see that I've placed information for you on typical issues that we see with imports and exports in and out of England. This is background information, but I thought it would be helpful. As you can see, the fourth-largest group of imports and exports that come in and out of the country are pieces of art. It's not unexpected that we see crates of art come through. We deal with them nearly every single day. What happens to them afterward is where things start to get interesting."

Kat stared down at the file, scanning the list. On it were items you would expect to see an import list, things like foods, wine, furniture, rugs, and clothing. She knew many of these things never made it to the warehouse. Larger shipments of things like medical supplies, tools and electronics in shipping containers were generally checked at the port. At least that's how it was done back home. One day, she had taken Jack down near the ports in California. While they couldn't go inside, Jack loved looking at the enormous cargo ships offloading their colorful containers.

"I checked back to see if we've had other shipments from this particular import-export company. If you'll flip the page over, still staying on the left side, you'll see that the company Romanian Imports, Inc., was started roughly fifty years ago by Marcus Rusu."

Eli sucked in his breath, "Do you mean Marcus Rusu?" The color drained from his face.

Kat scowled. "Eli, what has you spooked?" She glanced at Mary and Henry. "I'm sorry, who is this Marcus person?"

Mary nodded, "If you'll flip to the next page, you'll see a photograph of him and his children. I'll give you a quick rundown. Mr. Rusu is the head of what we believe to be one of the largest family organizations in Romania. They work throughout Europe."

"Are you saying they're an organized crime family?" Carson asked.

Mary nodded. "Definitely. Marcus and his brothers started the family business about five decades ago. The other two brothers were killed in organizational squabbles, you could say. If you review the page in front of you, you'll see that Marcus has three children: John, Stefan and Stella."

Kat stared down at the pictures of them. Marcus looked to be a distinguished older gentleman with salt-and-pepper gray hair, square glasses and a mustache. His sons had jet black hair and yet his daughter was blonde. "Where is the wife?"

"Christina? She's deceased. She committed suicide when the children were little. Marcus never remarried, but I heard he has had a string of girlfriends."

Kat bit her lip. "I just want to clarify. You are saying that the drug shipment and art that we found belongs to the Rusu family?"

"That's our suspicion."

Carson cleared his throat. Kat glanced over at him. He was flipping through the pages on the right side of the folder even though Mary was only walking them through the pages on the left. When she looked at Henry, he was doing the same. Mary was about to say something, but Carson interrupted. "How far of a reach does this family have?"

"Excellent question. As far as we can tell, it's global. I've reached out to the FBI to get more information, but they are being notoriously slow about responding. You know, Americans."

Kat smiled, appreciating the fact that Mary was trying to joke with them while they were in the middle of this serious briefing. "How do the art and the drugs tie together? I'm still not seeing a connection."

"Another layer to the story, I suppose," Mary said. "Based on the research I was able to do, it looks like Marcus gave significant portions of the business to his two sons about fifteen years ago. They are a few years older than their younger sister. Stella went to university here in London and graduated with a degree in philosophy. She was a particularly good gymnast, from what I can tell. She almost went to the Olympics for Romania but injured her ankle during the trials and was unable to compete. Apparently, the family money was unable to buy her a spot on the team." Mary raised her eyebrows, "Once Stella graduated from college, we believe she joined the family business. There is no record of her having any other job that we can find."

Henry lifted his head, brushing his hair away from his eyes. "What part of the business did Marcus give her?"

"The import-export business."

No one said anything for a moment. It seemed that Mary was giving them a chance to absorb the information she had thrown at them rapid-fire. Kat flipped back through the pages in the folder. It was a lot to digest in such a short time. "Well, I think the picture is starting to come into focus. This certainly makes sense with the threat I received."

Mary cocked her head to the side, "Threat?"

Henry cleared his throat and quickly told Mary what had happened to Kat outside the hotel. "The lot of them have been staying with me ever since. Makes for cramped quarters, but at least everyone is safe."

"Interesting," Mary said. "If that's the case, then that's just another layer to the story, but it could be a dangerous one. The family must know that you are here looking at the shipment they sent."

Carson squinted at the file, "You are sure that the shipment is linked to the Rusu family?"

Mary nodded. "Yes. The family has made no effort to hide the fact they own the company. As I said, it looks like the business was handed over to Stella after she graduated from college. Before that, we have little record of the business doing anything significant. My guess? I believe Marcus originally put the business together as a shell corporation to allow him to move goods in and out of Europe. They probably moved things through back channels but used the company to generate false papers in case they got stopped at a border."

Eli tapped his fingers on the table, "The artwork? How does that fit in?"

"It seems the company has been moving artwork in and out of England for about five years. That fits with the timeline we have on Stella. I believe they are bringing forged artwork in and then moving it to auctions throughout the world."

Eli didn't give Mary a chance to finish, "That makes sense. Selling forgeries is big business. And the ones with the quality that Hailey created? Those could be worth a fortune."

Henry turned to look at Eli, "Any idea, Eli, how much those paintings might be worth?"

"Well, it depends on the story they sell with the piece of art. They are very well done. It would be difficult for anyone except for an expert to know whether those are originals or forgeries. The brushwork, the colors, the aging of the canvas both front and back... put in the correct frame, no one would know the difference. They could each be worth hundreds of millions of dollars if they were passed off as originals."

Kat swallowed, "Hundreds of millions of dollars?"

Eli nodded, "Art is a supply and demand business. The supply is exceedingly small, especially when you want works from old masters. After all, they are all dead. Much of the work was lost during the world wars. We've all heard about what the Nazis did to private art collections. Each piece could be worth even more if it were passed off as a newly discovered canvas." Kat let her mind wander for a moment. Eli was right. The stories about private art collections all over Europe being stolen and taken back to Nazi headquarters was something, even with her limited art background, that she had heard of. "Lost" pieces of art were found on a regular basis. Locating their original owner, commonly called the provenance, could be nearly impossible. Kat chewed her lip, lost in thought. If Stella Rusu had taken over the import-export business and was looking to make her mark, that was certainly a way to generate a significant amount of profit for the family business. Kat wondered if it had anything to do with her brothers.

While the rest of the team talked, she flipped back to the page where their pictures were. The whole family was attractive, especially Stella. She had fine features and was pale, with porcelain skin. A quick glance looking at the entire family made Kat wonder if she favored her mother, Christina. She didn't look anything like her brothers or father.

Kat twisted in her chair, "If we start with the fact that all of this is about Stella trying to make her mark in the family, then it makes better sense. Maybe Hailey wanted more."

Carson frowned, shaking his head. "What do you mean, Kat?"

Kat stood up. She started to pace back and forth behind the table. She felt everyone's eyes on her. "If we take what Mary found out and add it to the information we have from Savannah, you could say that Stella is behind all of this."

Henry looked at her, "Even the murder?"

Carson corrected him, "You mean murders. Don't forget two bodies were left in Savannah."

"Yes, yes. I'm sorry. Forgot about that for a brief moment."

Kat didn't wait for them to speak again. "Imagine this... Stella gets out of college, with a degree that isn't worth anything at all. She's had a pretty good run as a gymnast but couldn't get the job done. She never made it to the Olympics. Apparently, her family money or influence wasn't enough to get her on the team. She's got two older brothers who are already successful and probably have their father's respect. This is an old Romanian family, after all. The boys would get respect naturally. What if Stella wanted more? She wants her father's attention, and not just in the good-girl way she might have learned growing up. So, to placate his daughter, Marcus gives her the import business, which he's never really used. She sounds like a smart girl. Wouldn't she realize she was being played?"

Henry nodded, "I would guess so. She would have to be blind to think otherwise."

Kat started to pace again, "So, Stella has something to prove. She takes the import business and builds it. She bet on something that is more valuable than her brothers could possibly have." She glanced at the group, "I'm guessing here. I don't know what the brothers do for the business."

Mary interrupted, "One of them handles their real estate and the other one handles gambling. Both very profitable, from what I can tell."

Kat nodded. "That makes sense. The father would give them the more valuable parts of the business. So, Stella takes the import business and turns it into something to try to show her brothers up and get her father's attention." Kat paused for a moment, looking at Mary, "What do we know about Stella's mom?"

Mary cocked her head to the side, "Not terribly much. We know she was a dancer, married Marcus, had three kids and then killed herself. The information is sketchy beyond that. We don't have any other background."

Kat glanced at Henry, "Any chance that Scotland Yard has more background?"

"I can check, but I doubt it. We use the same databases, so I'm sure Mary has pulled all the information that would be available to British-based agencies."

Eli cleared his throat. Kat glanced at him and noticed that he was staring down at his hands. His fingers were interlaced, the knuckles white. "Eli? Is there something you'd like to add?"

He looked up at the group and then back down at his hands again. "I know that family."

Kat furrowed her eyebrows, "How?"

Eli unclasped his hands and put them in his lap. He straightened in his seat. "I've had dealings with them. For my art business, of course." He glanced at Mary and Henry. "They can be rough if they don't get what they want."

A smirk crept over Henry's face. "Would that be from personal experience, Eli?"

Eli nodded. He pulled up his shirt sleeve on his right arm. Kat could see a set of scars about halfway up. "They left me with these. It was a long time ago, but I'll never forget it."

The tension was thick. The fact that Eli had scars to show left a knot in Kat's stomach.

Carson shook his head. "Regardless of what's happened in the past, we have a murder to solve. What's our next step?"

In Kat's mind, she saw Hailey's mom and dad the day this all started. She remembered walking through the parking lot at the police station, catching them as they got into their car. The look on Hailey's dad's face was something she would never forget. His anguish helped her to refocus. "If we put this all together, it looks like Stella decided to get rid of Hailey. Maybe she asked for more money?"

Henry nodded and leaned forward in his chair, staring at the top of the table. "I think the pieces are starting to fit together. We've got the daughter of a powerful family trying to make her mark in the world. She's importing forged art, probably sending it to art auctions and bringing in drugs at the same time. It would make sense that she would want to clean up loose ends. Hailey would be the only one who would know for sure those were forgeries."

Kat sat back down at the table, "You're saying that Hailey was a loose end? A liability to the business?"

Henry tilted his head. "As much as I would not want to say that about anyone, in Stella's mind, she probably was."

Fury started to rise in Kat's chest. Hailey had been nothing more than a young girl trying to pursue her dream. All she wanted was the opportunity to express her talent. It wasn't her fault that her grandmother had died and the funding for college had dried up. A question started to form in Kat's mind, "Carson, when I was in Savannah with you, I met a professor. Do you remember? She said she was the one who had given Hailey the job. But she never told me who the client was. Did you find out?"

Carson nodded. "Yeah, I remember that you told me about it. I didn't have a chance to follow up on that before I left. I was busy wrestling with the attorney of the kid we think stabbed Hailey."

"If we could find that person, we might be able to put the rest of the story together."

Mary tapped on the table. "Well, you might not have to wait too long. The one thing I haven't shared is that there is another shipment coming in from the same company in just a few hours. That might be your chance to find who hired Hailey and who ended her life."

34

S tella was attempting to stay calm. Unfortunately, she had inherited her father's temper. She would be relaxed for long periods of time and then the slightest thing would ignite her rage.

She hadn't slept well the night before. She knew there was another shipment coming in from New York. This time it was from another artist, one that Christopher had found for her. The fact that the drugs had been discovered was a costly mistake, one she blamed on him. It was his responsibility to find someone who could pack things without them being detected. He had failed. What that meant was in her father's eyes, she failed. That wasn't acceptable.

When she had heard that the drug dog had found the test shipment, she immediately sent the jet to go get Christopher. She didn't want any arguing from him that he couldn't find a flight. She checked the watch on her wrist as she got dressed for the morning. He was scheduled to land shortly along with a few items stashed in the small cargo hold. In between the hills of anger that were growing in her chest, she tried to decide what to do with him. Overall, he had been a good provider of quality art. He knew what she was looking for and he had good contacts in the community. But Stella wondered if he had outlived his usefulness. Only time would tell. She swallowed hard, pushing the anger down back into a place she could control it. She needed to be clear-headed. She didn't want to eliminate someone without giving them a chance to explain the situation. She felt she owed him that at least.

Down in the kitchen, she poured herself a cup of coffee that the housekeeper had brewed for her. She sent a text to Bobby, letting him know that she wanted to go to the hanger to meet Christopher and inspect the shipment before it was sent to customs. Normally, that wouldn't be allowed. The law required that imported items go straight to customs for inspection without the owner having an opportunity to look at them. She knew why they did it. The government didn't want people to be able to go in and take things of value out of crates and boxes that had been shipped overseas before they had a chance to look at them. It made sense, but not in a business like hers.

Bobby texted back that he would be at the front door in five minutes. Although he had been placed by her father to be her shadow, over time she had grown to respect Bobby, for the most part. She liked the fact that he was useful. He dealt with the dirty parts of the business, the parts that she didn't want to deal with. She always had a feeling that Bobby had orders from her father to not let her do anything that would put her in jeopardy. She didn't know whether to be grateful or angry.

She walked back into the master bathroom and dabbed on a coat of dark red lipstick. Today would be a defining day for her business. She liked the way it sounded. Her business. When her father handed over the reins to her, she was sure he didn't think she'd be able to do anything with it. Now her profits rivaled those of her brothers. She knew that being able to successfully move drugs in and out of the country would take things to another level. She had counted on Christopher. That might have been a mistake.

Her phone beeped. Bobby was waiting out front. On her way out, Stella yelled to the housekeeper, "I'll be gone for most of the day. Text Bobby if you need anything." The housekeeper waved, lifting a rag in the air as she polished the granite countertops in the kitchen.

Outside, the day was cool for summer in London. She was glad she had a jacket on. Her heels made a tapping noise on the front walk as she approached the Mercedes sedan that Bobby drove. She slid into the backseat, Bobby closing the door behind her.

For this shipment, she had selected one of the out-of-the-way airstrips. There were several private airstrips in the London area, but this particular one was favorable to her family. That meant she could have a look at her imports or talk to her passengers without the normal governmental paperwork. At best, she could completely avoid any government interference. At worst, her family had bribed many of the workers at the airstrip to turn the other way, which bought her valuable time.

Neither she nor Bobby said anything in the car on the way. Bobby had learned long ago not to speak unless spoken to. That was one courtesy Bobby had always extended to her. She was grateful for that, especially today. Her mind was swirling with options and possibilities. The question still lingered in her mind about what to do about Christopher. She would have to decide what to do with him, and soon. Time was running out.

35

I t didn't take long for Kat, Henry, Eli and Carson to get ready to head out. Henry assembled a team of officers from Scotland Yard to accompany them to the airstrip. Mary was bringing her own team with her. All in all, it looked to Kat like there would be nearly twenty officers ready to help them with the shipment.

As Kat got in the backseat of Henry's Scotland Yard sedan, she started to feel anxious again, butterflies forming and flocking in her stomach. She didn't know what would happen next. None of them did. In a way, she hoped it was a dead end. On the other hand, she wanted to get this case wrapped up so that she could go home to Van and Jack. Just thinking about that made her heart ache. She sent them a quick text. The pinging from Henry's phone caught her attention.

"The plane is scheduled to land soon." Henry set his phone down and looked at Carson, who was sitting in the passenger seat, "Guess it's time to go see what we can find out."

Kat did a quick calculation in her head. Would they have enough time to get in position? "Henry, how long will it take to get to the airport?"

"We will be there in about eight minutes, depending on traffic. They're landing at an out of the way airstrip that's primarily used for private airplane traffic."

Kat hoped they had enough time to get into position. It would be close. She leaned forward, between the two front seats, her knee accidentally touching Eli's. He pulled away quickly. She almost smiled. She had gotten used to his quirkiness. "What's the plan when we get there?"

"We've been approved for a surveillance operation. If anything goes poorly while we are there, then our authority escalates. But for now, all we can do is watch."

Kat leaned back on the seat, making sure not to touch Eli as she slid back. She understood the orders, but she wondered if it would be enough. Her heart started to beat harder in her chest. Would they be able to get the information they needed just by watching? She shook her head if only to herself. She wasn't sure. "Where's everyone else?"

Henry glanced in the rearview mirror. "We've got a few teams on the outskirts of the airport. The customs agents will go through the main entrance. Mary wanted us to come through the back entrance. If anyone asks, we are just here to collect some paperwork."

It was a weak cover story. Kat wasn't sure would hold up if anyone really asked, but that wasn't her problem. Henry and Mary were in charge. She and Eli were just along for the ride. If anyone had extra authority, it was Carson, but Kat realized he didn't really have any power either. They were all guests of the British government at this point.

As they approached the back entrance to the airport, Henry slowed the car to stop at the guard shack. A man appeared and looked at the group of them. Everything about him was round — round eyes, a full round, brown beard. Even the tip of his nose seemed to be round. "Can I help you?"

"Just here to pick up papers at the office. Need me to sign in or anything?"

"Papers?"

Kat's stomach clenched. She wasn't sure if they would be able to get through the gate without Henry showing his identification. Why he hadn't, she wasn't sure.

Henry nodded, "Yes, sir. There is a pack of papers for me at the office. These are just my trainees."

The man coughed a little, "All right. Have a good day."

Carson looked over his shoulder as they pulled through the gate. "Well, that wasn't exactly the tightest security I've ever seen."

Henry chuckled, "Some of these airstrips, they make you wonder."

Eli leaned forward, "He didn't ask for identification or anything!"

Henry turned the wheel aiming the sedan close to the buildings that were on the right side of the airport. "Well, Eli, that should tell you a little bit about the type of people that come in and out of this airport. They aren't the kind that want their identification checked. That's for sure."

As the car moved towards the hangers, Kat leaned forward, trying to get a good look at what was ahead of them. There was a row of buildings, all painted in the same light blue color, as though whoever had been hired to do the painting got a great price on the paint. It wasn't a color she would have chosen for an airport. Some of the hangers looked closed, their tall garage doors touching the ground. Out of the row of hangers, two of the doors were open. One of them was low and wide, the other hanger was tall, probably three stories, Kat realized.

Outside of the hangers, there were stacks of crates. A forklift had been abandoned near the office. Kat guessed that the operator was probably at lunch. There was a single car parked at the office, an old white sedan with a dent in the back bumper. The blinds on the office door and window had been pulled down. If there was anyone in the office, they certainly didn't want to be seen. Henry pulled the car up to the office, leaving a space between his sedan and the white car that was parked there. "Let's go."

Kat got out of the car behind Eli, Henry and Carson. Henry walked quickly, staying close to the side of the building. A few seconds later, Kat realized that he was focused on a stack of crates that were stacked by the large hanger door. "Mary said they would be going into hanger three." He pointed to the tallest of all the hangers. "That looks like it over there."

Carson moved behind Kat and Eli. She couldn't help but think that he was covering their backs. "Nice of them to leave the stack of crates there for us, huh?"

The group moved quietly to the stack of crates. As she got closer, Kat realized that it wasn't just a single stack. In fact, there were probably at least thirty in piles. Kat followed Henry between the stacks. She knelt down. As she did, she heard the sound of wood grinding on concrete. Carson had pulled one of the crates in front of the spot where they were hiding, preventing anyone from seeing them as they went by. Henry did the same on the other end, leaving slight space so they could get out if they needed to.

Kat sat down on the concrete and looked at Henry, "What do we do now?"

Henry fumbled in his pocket and pulled an earwig out, shoving it in his ear. "Nothing. We wait." Henry whispered into the microphone attached to his radio, "In position." Kat watched him as he paused, listening. He whispered, "ETA on the plane is four minutes."

Henry slid down next to Kat, his back pressed against the crate. Carson had taken a position watching the open door. Henry glanced at her, "How are you holding up?"

"Well enough."

"Managed to get yourself involved in another scrape, I see."
Kat scowled. "For some reason, trouble seems to find me."
Henry nodded. "Indeed."

From the distance, Kat could hear the thrumming of a jet engine. She whispered, looking at Henry, "Is that them? Are they coming?"

Henry nodded, putting his finger up to his ear as though he was trying to hear information coming in through the earpiece. "They are taxiing to the hangar now." He motioned for everyone to get down. Eli sat with his back against a crate right on the tarmac. He didn't seem to want to watch what was happening. Kat wondered exactly what his relationship had been with Stella's family. The rest of the group knelt behind the cargo crates, staying out of sight, peering through the cracks. Kat leaned towards Eli, "Are you okay?" she whispered. He nodded.

As Kat glanced up, she could see the gleaming white jet make its way toward them, the pilot and copilot just small dots behind the windshield. The whine of the engines bounced off the front of the hanger. A man wearing blue coveralls emerged from inside carrying two orange flags. He waved the jet right into the hanger.

The engines powered down inside the hangar. From where Kat was watching, she had a good view of how it was positioned. The door on the side of the fuselage popped open exposing a ladder. There was no movement for what seemed to be a long time, although it was probably just a minute or so. Kat waited, her heart beating in her chest. From inside the hangar, a man in a dark suit approached the plane, climbed the steps and disappeared inside. He didn't reappear. Instead, Kat saw the pilot and the copilot leave the plane. As they walked across the tarmac, she saw they were both carrying briefcases and chatting as though it was a regular day at the office. It certainly didn't feel that way to her. "Henry, is there anyone else in the plane?" she whispered, not wanting to blow their location.

"I dunno. Mary said there was a shipment, but she wasn't sure who else was on the plane."

"Maybe they're just waiting to unload cargo?"

Henry scowled. "Well, if they are, it's gotta be something small. They couldn't move anything large with this size plane."

Kat knew Henry was right. The information Mary had given them was that there was a shipment coming that was tied directly to Stella's family. But the size plane it was delivered on was way too small for it to be anything large. Kat frowned, "Is that normal?"

"I have no idea. I don't usually work on the import side of enforcement." Henry glanced down at Eli. "Eli? Do companies use small jets for imports?"

Eli shook his head, his eyes wide. "I have no idea," he stammered. "I suppose it's possible. Maybe they're just moving something little like diamonds or cash, or something."

The minutes passed by. Kat looked to her right. Carson was staring directly at the hangar, although nothing was happening. The man in the suit still hadn't reemerged from the airplane. Eli was still sitting on the tarmac, staring straight ahead. Henry alternately looked towards the hangar and down at the ground, as though he was listening to someone on his radio.

Kat slumped down next to Eli, feeling frustrated. She had no idea what they were waiting for. Why didn't the man in the suit come off the plane? Was there a flight attendant? She imagined that most flights require not only a pilot and copilot but someone to service the cabin. They hadn't seen anyone come off the plane who would fit that description.

Carson tapped her on the shoulder and lifted his head, directing her to look back at the hangar. The same young man that had guided the plane into the hangar was back, this time carrying chocks for the wheels. He placed them behind the landing gear and walked away. Kat sat back down shaking her head. They were wasting time. "Shouldn't we do something, Henry?" she asked him, although she knew the answer. "No, love," he glanced back at the hangar. "The job right now is to wait and see who comes off that plane."

Kat scooted back up so she could get another look. The plane was still sitting in the hangar, basically unattended. What they knew was that a man in a suit had boarded but he hadn't come off. Who else was on that plane? "Henry, I think this is a waste of time," she said.

Before Henry could answer, she saw him quickly turn his head and look back behind them, sinking down even further. He put his hand on her shoulder pushing her back down behind the crates. Carson did the same. He didn't say anything, but he looked at her and gave his head a little bob which told her she needed to look in the other direction. From between a sliver of a gap between the crates, she could see a car approaching, a shiny black Mercedes sedan. "Who's that?" she whispered.

"We will find out in a moment," Henry said.

Kat pivoted around so that she could see the hangar again. She stared between a gap in the crates that faced the hangar. She could peer through with one eye and see most of what was happening. Carson hadn't moved. Neither had Henry.

As she watched, the black Mercedes pulled up right next to the plane, stopping near the steps. As soon as it stopped, the driver exited, moving to the back seat and opening the back door on the passenger side. A woman, slight and blonde, got out of the car and walked around to the side of the car that was closest to the plane, her high heels clicking on the polished concrete floors.

Kat's eyes got wide. Could that be Stella Rusu? Was she meeting the plane personally? Kat wanted to ask Carson or

Henry but thought better of it. Making noise of any kind could blow their cover. She glanced back towards the hangar. From the inside of the plane, a long woman wearing a bright red dress exited, the handle of a purse in her right hand. She walked past the driver, the blonde woman and the Mercedes with a brief head nod. She didn't say anything but simply left the hanger. At least Kat assumed that was the case, as she couldn't see her anymore.

If their count was correct, and there is no guarantee it was, that meant that only the man in the suit, and possibly someone else, was on the plane. Or maybe it was something else, Kat wondered. Before Kat had a chance to think too much, her stomach completely clenched, she saw a man walk down the jet's steps. He was a large man, tall and blonde, wearing a pale suit. His hands were empty. No suitcase and not even a brief-case. "Who's that?" Kat whispered to Henry.

"I don't know," Henry spoke quietly into his radio.

Kat peeked her head up over the crates to see if she could get a better look. She had no idea who the man was. It was too far to get a very good look at him. Kat hoped that Henry's other officers were taking surveillance pictures. She imagined they were, but she wasn't sure.

The man who'd gone onto the plane when it arrived walked right behind the big blonde man that came off first. He took two steps down the jet's ladder when Kat saw something in his hand. "Gun," she whispered as loudly as she dared. The man standing behind Christopher clearly had a pistol in his hand. It was pointed, for the moment, downward, but the fact that he had it all sent a wave of nervous energy through Kat's shoulders. She slumped back down behind the crates, peering out through the crack. As soon as she did, the man with the gun lifted his finger to his ear, as though he was wearing the same kind of earpiece Henry was. The man turned, glaring out the door of the hangar, and started running toward the blonde woman.

From behind them, Kat heard tires screech on the tarmac. The noise was close, so close that it made the hair on the back of her neck stand up. Henry and Carson ran out from behind the crates. Kat scrambled up to a standing position, "Come on, Eli," she yelled, extending her hand. "We've gotta get out of here!" As Kat made her way out from behind the crates, she saw Carson and Henry sprinting towards the hanger door. Kat started running, trying to keep up with them, but she only made it a few steps before a strong hand grabbed her and spun her around. A large man with black hair held her arm so tightly she felt like the blood wasn't getting to her hand. "Whoa, there. Where do you think you're going?" She started to yell, but the man smashed a rag across her face that instantly made her feel dizzy. As she felt her body slump, she caught a glimpse of the blonde woman driving away. The world went dark...

"What the hell was that?" Stella yelled, holding onto the handle built into the door of the Mercedes as it screeched around the corner and sped away from the airstrip.

"I'm sorry, ma'am. I don't know. I'm waiting to hear."

Stella slumped back in her seat. Her meet with Christopher had gone south. She had just been getting ready to confront him when one of the guys that worked for Bobby had yelled something. She hadn't heard what. She only felt Bobby's hand pushing her into the back seat of the car and slamming the door shut. As they had peeled away from the hangar, she saw one of her father's black vans and another sedan driving towards a pile of cargo that had been left on the outside of the hangar doors. Two men had been running towards the hangar. She didn't know what happened to them. She smoothed her hair, quickly putting it in a braid.

Interruptions to their meetings happened occasionally, but not like this. Her mind raced. Who were those men that were running towards the hangar? Before she had a chance to think about it, Bobby glanced in the rearview mirror. "Ma'am?" he asked.

"Yes?" Stella tried to sound as calm as possible although her legs were shaking from the rush of adrenaline. She looked down at her hands and realized she had broken a fingernail when Bobby had thrown her into the car. If that was the least of the damage, she could live with that.

"I still don't know exactly who those people were that were watching us, but Anton just radioed in and said he's taking two of them and Christopher to the warehouse."

"Very well." Stella smoothed her pant legs with her hands and pulled a compact out of her purse. She checked her makeup. It was still acceptable. Anton was one of her most trusted men, right next to Bobby. He would do what needed to be done.

Being properly dressed for meetings with something her father had taught her. He never showed up to meet anyone, whether friend or foe, without being dressed in a suit and dress shoes. He had told her long ago that dressing up for meetings gave the impression that you deserved respect, whether you had earned it yet or not. When Stella took over the import business, that was one of the few things that she took from her father's teaching.

"Bobby? Let's go to the warehouse now. I want to know who was following us as well as have my conversation with Christopher."

"Yes, ma'am."

Bobby didn't say any more. She couldn't tell whether he approved of her request to go to the warehouse or not. She didn't really care. She was sure the minute he had a chance, he would reach out to her father if Anton hadn't already. She shook her head slightly. Although she ran her business, she knew it wasn't exactly hers. Her father's specter always hung over every move she made.

She took a deep breath, looking out the window, trying to allow her body to relax. It was no use to go into a business negotiation upset. They would cause her to make rash decisions that weren't the best for her business. She knew that.

She glanced down at her shoes, realizing that one of the nude pumps had gotten scuffed. She would have her housekeeper take care of it. The woman was a wonder with shoes. As soon as she finished the thought, she chastised herself. She should be less concerned about her broken nail and her scuffed heel than what was happening in front of her. She needed to focus, and focus fast. "Bobby?"

"Yes, ma'am?"

"Please have Christopher put in the office and keep a guard with him. I'm not sure who Anton picked up, but please put them in the back of the warehouse in the stock cage. I will deal with each of them separately."

"Yes, ma'am."

She saw Bobby reach for the earpiece he was wearing. Her father's company had invested in encrypted communications for its staff. It had been expensive but was worth it.

"And one other thing. I want to know who was watching us. I want to know before we get to the warehouse." Stella knew that only gave Bobby and his team a few minutes to figure out who was there. She wasn't sure that would be enough time, but she had found that putting a little bit of pressure on them helped them to work more efficiently, whether they liked it or not. The odds of them being able to get identities before she arrived at the warehouse was small, but it was worth trying.

By the time Bobby pulled up in front of the warehouse, a black van and a small black sedan were already parked out in front. Each of them was nearly as shiny as the Mercedes. Her father insisted that the teams that worked for him take good care of the equipment they were given. Severe consequences had been known to happen for items that were not maintained. Her father felt it was part of running a disciplined organization. Stella didn't wait for Bobby to let her out of the car. She opened the door and got out herself, walking towards the office entrance. Once inside, she paused at the doorway, allowing her eyes to adjust. As she looked straight ahead, she could see Christopher pacing in her office, one of her father's men standing in the corner, his jacket off, his pistol exposed. Christopher would be no threat. Her father's men were so well-trained that if Christopher tried to make a move, he would be dead before he took one single step out of line.

She weighed her options for a moment and decided to walk to the back of the warehouse first. Her curiosity about the people that Anton had scooped up outweighed her desire to deal with Christopher. He could wait.

Her heels clicked on the concrete floor, the noise bouncing off the high walls in the warehouse. She walked quickly, Bobby following behind her. She heard a noise coming from the back of the warehouse, where the stock cage had been built.

From time to time, there were some high-value items that came through the warehouse–antiques, statues and even a 1955 Jaguar she was shocked to find out was worth more than twenty million. She had had a cage erected in the back of the warehouse to give those items an extra level of protection. It was made of cyclone fencing, the sides and the top covered in heavy wire with a locking door. There were no important items in there right now, save for the people that Anton brought in.

As she rounded the corner, she glanced ahead of her. The lights were on, long black shadows wriggling on the floor. Two people were seated in chairs. Anton looked to be finishing tying a woman's hands behind her back, her head lolled to the side. There was an older man next to her who seemed to be out cold.

"What did you do to them?" she asked Anton. Of all of her father's men, she liked Anton the most. He was at least six foot three, with an enormous frame and a shock of the same black hair that so many Romanians had. His nose was crooked, the result of being broken too many times. He was loyal and had been kind to her when she was a teenager. Not all of her father's men had been.

"Chloroform. They both went down like rocks. The woman is starting to wake up now."

"Any idea who they are?"

Anton shook his head slowly from left to right, like a tree moving in the wind. "No. I'll be able to get more out of them as they wake up."

Stella nodded. Though she would like to know who the people were before they were conscious, she wanted to be reasonable. She turned, walking back to the office, Bobby following. "Any news on who these people were with?"

"It looks like it was police surveillance, ma'am. One of our guys spotted a team up by the perimeter fence. Looked to him like customs enforcement."

Stella gritted her teeth. The last thing she needed was British customs enforcement breathing down her neck when she was trying to launch a new transit line for opioids into Europe. That could stall her efforts by weeks, if not months, if she could ever get it moving again.

Stella walked back towards the office, the blood rushing to her face. It was time for her to have a conversation with Christopher. It would be one he wouldn't like.

37

C arson turned around, assuming Kat and Eli were just behind them. They weren't. He spun, scanning the tarmac only to see the taillights of a black van and two black sedans screaming away from the airstrip. "Henry!"

Without a word, the two men ran back to the area where the crates were stacked. There was no one there. Only a pair of glasses were left on the ground. Henry bent over and picked them up. "Are these Eli's?"

Carson nodded. "What just happened?" He glanced back towards the hangar and saw two men in handcuffs being walked out to police cars. The woman in the Mercedes was gone and so were Kat and Henry. His heart started to pound in his chest. It had been his job to help protect them and he and Henry had failed. And now, at the hand of the Rusu family, it might cost them their lives...

38

S tella stared at Christopher from the doorway of her office and then walked behind her desk, sitting down in the leather executive chair that she had purchased for herself. She sunk into the cushions and crossed her legs before looking up at him, "Sit."

Christopher glanced behind him at the man in the corner of the room. The man raised his eyebrows and Christopher immediately sat down as he had been told. He didn't say a word.

A sense of satisfaction wound its way through Stella. She liked being in control. She had a troublemaker in front of her and two more in the back. It was her choice to do with them as she wanted. "Mr. Lavaud, I've been a little disappointed in your services. That's why we brought you here."

Christopher didn't say anything for a moment, his lips pressed so tightly together that they turned white. He drew in a sharp breath, "I'm sorry to hear that. What can I do to make it right?"

Stella tilted her head to the side before she spoke, wanting to make him squirm a little bit, "I am not sure there is anything you can do."

Christopher shifted in his seat as though he was terribly uncomfortable. "Could we at least discuss what you are unhappy about? I'd like the opportunity to make it right if that's okay with you."

Stella turned in her chair away from Christopher, looking out a window that was behind her. Mirrored film had been put on it so that she could look out but no one on the outside could look in. Privacy was paramount in her business. She had learned that early on when a valuable shipment had been stolen from her. A collection of old gold coins that belonged to an Italian diplomat disappeared. In her naivete, she called the police. Then she had gotten a late-night call from her father, "Stella, come to me with your problems. Not the police. Not ever."

She turned back, almost facing him directly, but not quite. "You've cost me a lot of money this week," she said, "And worse, you have attracted the attention of the authorities. That is never helpful for my business."

Stella watched Christopher for his reaction. She was sure that with his clientele he had been in this position more than once. She was curious how he would respond. As she waited, she noticed the color drain from his face. He was looking down at his lap holding his hands together in a tight grip. "Well?"

He drew in a sharp breath, "Let me start by saying that I'm deeply sorry. I apologize for any difficulty this has put you in. I hired the absolute best people I could find to handle the shipment."

Stella stood up, feeling the boil of anger in her gut. "Do you understand that we lost a million dollars' worth of product overnight? Your little plan to fill the packing peanuts didn't work."

"I apologize, ma'am. What can I do to make this right? I

would be more than happy to forgo my fee for this shipment. I really do appreciate my relationship with you and your family. I would hate to see decades of good work be lost over a bad shipment."

"A bad shipment? I've got customs and law enforcement breathing down my neck. They've got the art that is scheduled to go to auction as well. I'd say that's a little bit more than a plan that didn't work!" Stella felt like walking over to her guard, pulling his gun and shooting Christopher right at that moment. But that wasn't the type of work she did. She had never gotten her hands dirty before. The thought made her nauseous. She preferred when her problems just disappeared.

She sat down in her chair again, feeling the cushions supporting her back. She would need a good massage after all of this tension. Christopher's offer to forgo his fee was definitely a sign of good faith, but she wasn't sure if it was enough. His fee for the latest shipment would have been two million, twice what she had lost. She spun in her chair to look out the window again, not sure what to do. She needed time to think, and the answers weren't coming quickly.

Stella got up from her chair, looked at the guard and said, "Keep him here." She walked out of the office without another word. Time wasn't on her side. She knew she needed to make decisions about what to do with Christopher and the two people in the cage, but she wasn't ready to, not just yet...

39

Kat woke up, a funny taste in her mouth and her shoulders aching. As the fog lifted, she realized she couldn't move her hands forward, they were bound behind her. She tried to move her legs and realized they were bound as well. Fear pulsated inside of her as she gasped. Where was she? What had happened?

She looked to her right and to her left. She was strapped to a chair inside of a metal cage. Standing to her left in the corner was a man, one she didn't recognize. He was an enormous, bigger than any man she had ever seen. She looked to her right and saw Eli, his head still slumped to the side, his hands and feet bound as well. "Eli? Wake up!" she whispered, even though she knew the guard could hear her.

Eli started to stir, blinking. His eyes grew wide as he realized the situation he and Kat were in. He didn't say anything, but Kat could tell from the rise and the fall of his chest that he was nearly hyperventilating.

Kat tried to draw in long deep breaths, the kind her therapist had taught her, to fend off her PTSD. Worse than how anxious she was feeling was not knowing if she could keep her

PTSD at bay. She had been known to hyperventilate so bad that she passed out, enough times that she learned to just sit on the floor. That wasn't an option here. Emotions started to well up inside of her. All she could think about was Jack and Van and wanting to be home. How had she gotten into this mess? Where was Henry? Where was Carson? Did they even know that she and Eli were missing? Her mind raced ahead of her with questions, emotions rolling over her like high tide on a beach.

She glanced up at the man in the corner of the cage. He wasn't moving. He didn't say anything. He just kept staring at her. Silent.

Kat desperately needed to stay calm. She closed her eyes for a moment. A memory flashed before her. Right after they had moved to California, there had been a rash of wildfires. Some of them natural, some of them set by a madman. Her family had nearly gotten consumed by the fire when it had raced up the hillside below them. Afterward, she had commented to Van that they never would've gotten through it without him being so calm. She could see his face in her head, his eyes staring at her, his head shaking from side to side, "That's just not true, Kat. You are strong."

His voice rattled in her head, the words pushing back against her fear. She took a deep breath and focused, taking an inventory of what she saw around her. There was the metal cage, yes, but she could also see crates of goods behind her. Wherever she was, it didn't look much different than the customs warehouse they had visited. Just beyond the cage, she saw some canvases leaning against one of the stacks of crates. Could those be Hailey's? Maybe from another shipment? She didn't know. They were too far away. She scanned the inside of the cage. There was nothing in it she could see except for herself, Eli and the gigantic man in the corner. He had looked away and was picking at the cuticles on one of his nails.

Kat looked at Eli. His breathing had slowed, which was a

good sign. She could tell by his posture that he had retreated inside. Even if she could do something, she wasn't sure he would be able to help. She hoped that Henry and Carson were looking for them, but there was no guarantee that they would get to the two of them in time.

As she started scanning the room again, she heard the clack of high heels on the concrete floor. They were approaching and approaching quickly. The guard turned and pushed the door open just as a petite blonde woman came in the cage. She looked at them for a minute without saying anything. Fear rose in another wave inside of Kat. Henry and Carson didn't know where they were. There was no help coming, or at least no help coming quickly.

"Get me a chair," the woman said. The guard disappeared for a moment and came back with a folding chair that he set up for her. She sat down, crossing her legs. "So, you decided to do a little spying today."

Kat wasn't sure what to say. One wrong word and she was sure the woman would instruct the guard to kill them. A prickle ran up her spine, "You could say that."

The woman raised her eyebrows, seemingly surprised that Kat would be that forthcoming, "So, you admit you were there?"

Kat shifted in her seat, trying to get comfortable with her arms and legs bound. "There's no point in lying. You know we were there."

Stella looked at the guard, "Anton, do you see this? This is someone who isn't wasting my time." She looked back at Kat, "Do you know who I am?"

Something inside of Kat clicked. She decided to push forward. "You're Stella Rusu, the youngest daughter of Marcus Rusu."

Stella tilted her head to the side, "Very good. And you are?"

"Kat Beckman. This is Eli Langster." Kat didn't offer any

more information. She wanted to see what Stella would do with what she said.

"Okay, Kat Beckman, what were you doing at the landing strip?"

Kat decided she had nothing to lose. There was no point in trying to hide from Stella the reason they were at the airport. "I have a friend that works for Scotland Yard and another that works for the Savannah Police Department. We were there waiting for the shipment that we were told would arrive. That's when you found us."

Stella squinted for a moment. "Why were you there? You are in law enforcement?"

"I'm a journalist. Eli is an art importer."

"Eli Langster, why does that name sound familiar?"

Kat waited for a moment, but Eli didn't answer, his eyes wide. "Eli said he had some dealings with your family years ago. He showed us scars on his arm."

Stella gave a brief nod to the guard, who walked over to Eli and pushed up his sleeve, Eli leaning as far back in his chair as he could to get away from the guard.

"I'm sorry about that, Eli. Sometimes work requires sacrifice." Stella nodded at the guard. He pulled Eli's sleeve back into place.

Kat felt something inside of her shift again. Anger started to well up inside of her. She had been through so much — Jack had been kidnapped, she had chased a sex trafficker across the country to save a young girl, she'd exposed a terrorism ring and gotten through massive wildfires. It didn't seem that today should be her day to die. But how she would get out of Stella's grip, she wasn't sure. "What do you want from us?"

Stella got up and started pacing, walking behind the chair. "I'm not sure. Do you have anything to offer?"

"Probably nothing you'd actually want," Kat answered

sarcastically. "Tell me, were you the one that ordered Hailey Park's death?"

Stella paused and stared at Kat, her dark eyes boring a hole right through her. "And why would you want to know that?"

"Because I was living a relatively normal life until I heard about Hailey Park's murder and went down to investigate. Now, I'm here." The more Kat talked the angrier she got. It was a new feeling, one that she wasn't accustomed to. The fear that had chased her had been replaced by fury.

"Fair enough. You could say I ordered it in a way. There was a failure by one of our providers. Ends needed to be cleaned up. And, that little girl was demanding more money."

"Was one of those ends the man that came off the plane?"

Stella looked at Kat as though she was amused, "You are quite perceptive, aren't you? The man you mentioned? He's sitting in my office right now. I'm trying to figure out what to do with him."

"That's the question of the day, isn't it? What are you going to do with all of us?"

"I don't know yet. I haven't decided."

Kat swallowed. She knew in her heart that the odds of her getting home to Van and Jack were shrinking by the moment. She pushed the thought out of her head. She couldn't afford to get emotional. "So, tell me, how did you get a ten-year-old to stab a girl?"

Stella leaned back in her chair, laughing. "You don't pull any punches, do you?"

She paused for a moment. "That wasn't exactly my doing. The man in my office was responsible for that piece of work."

"And the psychiatrist?"

"He was a loose end. He couldn't be trusted to keep his mouth closed. He got the boy to do the deed but was weak-willed. The man in my office should have known that. He didn't and so I had to handle it." Stella stood up. "You know, it's always that way. From the time I was little, people have underestimated me, they've tried to hold me back, to protect me. Let me tell you something, I don't need protecting. See all the stuff around you? When my father gave me the business — which was a total joke — he was just trying to placate me. He was sure I would never amount to anything, just like my mother."

"What happened your mother?" Kat asked.

"My mother?" Stella shook her head. "She was weak. She could have been great if he would have given her a little encouragement, but that's not what he wanted. He favors the men. You know that feeling, right? My brothers, they got everything handed to them. I didn't. I've had to work for all of this, and I've surprised everyone."

"I can relate to that."

Stella stood behind the chair, her hands on the back of it, "You can? And how's that?"

"I was in Afghanistan as an embedded journalist a long time ago. Got blown up in an IED attack. After that, no one thought I would amount to anything. They thought I'd be broken for the rest of my life. We're stronger than we think we are."

"Afghanistan? You?"

Kat nodded, suddenly feeling angry that she was being challenged by someone who had spent her whole life being questioned. It was ironic at best, hypocritical at worst. "Have your guard pull my sleeve up. You'll see the scars from the surgery after my wrist was shattered. I've had PTSD ever since."

Stella nodded and the guard came over and pulled up her sleeve. Stella peered around the back of the chair Kat was bound to, just close enough to see the scars. As she walked back to the doorway of the cage, she glanced back at Kat, "You could be lying, but I don't think so." Her eyes narrowed.

Heavy footfalls came running towards the cage. It was a

man. It looked to Kat like the same man that had driven Stella's car. "Bobby? What is it?"

"Your guest in the office," he said breathlessly, "He's escaped."

"What! How is that possible? One of the guards was standing right behind him when I left the office!"

"I'm sorry, ma'am. I don't know what happened. I walked by and saw the guard on the floor. The door was open. I ran outside, but your Mercedes is gone."

Kat watched as the blood flooded Stella's face, turning her cheeks bright red. "Are you kidding? You left the keys in the Mercedes?"

Bobby stammered, "We always do, ma'am. Just in case we need to leave quickly. It's something your father…"

Bobby didn't have a chance to finish the sentence. "My father! Don't talk to me about my father! This is my business. Mine. I have built it from the ground up. I didn't tell you to leave the keys in the Mercedes. Now Christopher is gone. What are you going to do about that?"

Bobby didn't say anything. He just stared at the ground for a moment. "I can track him, ma'am. The car has a locator on it through the GPS. Would you like me to go and do that?"

Kat's heart was pounding in her chest. She could barely breathe, waiting and watching to see what would happen next.

Stella hissed, "Yes, you moron. Go take care of it!"

Bobby turned and walked away. He got about ten feet before Stella called to him. "Bobby!"

He turned slowly as if he was ready to be screamed at again. Before he could say anything, Kat saw Stella reach behind her back. From underneath her coat, she pulled a pistol and fired off three rounds, the explosions echoing off the sides of the building before Bobby's body ever hit the ground.

Kat sucked in her breath, her heart pounding in her chest.

Eli was motionless, pale and drawn. She had no idea that Stella had a weapon on her. That changed the equation dramatically.

She turned back to Kat and Eli, "I bet he never saw that coming," she said smugly. "Anton," she motioned to the guard standing in the cage with her, "He's been training me. No one thought I'd be strong enough to kill someone. Well, I just proved them wrong." She looked at Anton, "Get him out of here."

Stella stuck the gun behind her back again and sat down on the chair as Anton walked away to deal with Bobby's body. "So, Ms. Beckman, here are the answers to your questions. Yes, I am the daughter of the man that runs a powerful family business. However, as you can see, I am powerful on my own. I have built an import-export business that moves both legal and illegal items. I was the one who came up with the idea to sell forged art. Most of the idiots out there have no idea what they are buying. I've used that to my advantage. The man you saw come off the plane failed me. I will deal with him later. As far as your artist, I'm sorry she had to be eliminated, but we are moving in a new direction and I can't afford to have any evidence left behind. She was becoming demanding. The people that work for me have to be adaptable and grateful. She was neither. Stupid girl."

As Stella gave Kat all the information they had been searching for, she felt an eerie silence fall over the warehouse, where she and Eli were strapped to chairs. Now Kat and Eli knew everything. Would Stella shoot them the same way she had shot Bobby? A wave of nausea went over Kat. Any bravado she had was gone.

Before she could say anything else, Kat heard a scuffle near the front door. Stella must have seen Kat gaze down the long aisle way between the stacks of crates. There was movement, low and fast. A growl came out of nowhere. Stella jumped up out of her chair as a big German Shepherd charged into the cage and at her. Stella backpedaled as she got pinned in the corner, the dog growling and barking. Kat could hear men's voices yelling as they approached.

"Kat? Eli? Are you there?"

Henry and Carson burst through the door of the cage and quickly cut them out of their bindings on their chairs. The dog handler came in right behind them, shouting "Aus!" the German word for off as he cuffed Stella Rusu.

Carson lifted Kat out of her chair to a standing position, "Are you okay?"

Kat sighed, "Yes, I think so." She glanced at Eli, "Eli, are you okay?"

Eli stammered, "Yes. Yes."

Kat stood for a second in place, her knees weak from the adrenaline rush. She looked at Henry, "How did you find us?"

He pointed at her pocket. "We tracked you through your phone. Sorry that it took a little time. We had to reach Van to get your account information and then deal with the British government. Nothing moves fast for the Brits."

Kat started to laugh. "Who knew not forgetting my phone today would be the thing that saved me?" She looked at Carson, Henry and Eli, suddenly feeling very grateful. "Well, the good thing is Stella admitted to everything. She's the one that orchestrated Hailey's murder, Oskar's death, the forged artwork and I think even the drugs." She glanced down the aisleway, seeing people move back and forth throughout the warehouse. An officer was standing over Bobby's body. "She shot him, too."

Carson looked at her, "All right. Let's get both of you outside and get you some fresh air. I think the medics should take a look, too."

He reached to grab her elbow, but she shrugged away. "Wait. What about the man in her office? She was upset because someone got away. He took her Mercedes."

Henry furrowed his brow, and spoke into his radio, "Anyone see a black Mercedes parked outside?"

"Negative."

Henry looked back at Kat. "Do you know who it was?"

"It was the same man that was on the plane. She called him Christopher. I think he was the art broker that sold the forged canvases on the open market."

Henry nodded. "We'll find him. Don't you worry about that, love. Let's just get the two of you outside, get this wrapped up, and get both of you on a plane home."

Kat nodded. She liked the idea of going home...

EPILOGUE

I t took another twenty-four hours of debriefing and travel arrangements before Kat and Eli could get back on a plane to the States. Carson decided to stay for an extra day or two just to make sure he had all the evidence he needed before going back and reporting to his chief. Officers from the Savannah Police Department had detained Dr. Abibi Roux from the art school but had to release her because of a lack of evidence. Her only crime was accepting an offer. She said she thought the art was properly marked as a copy. There was an ongoing investigation, but Carson wasn't optimistic they'd get any charges to stick.

The one thing that Carson's department had been able to do was to place Miles in a new home and with a new psychiatrist. There would be a trial for the stabbing of Hailey Park, but Carson wasn't optimistic about that either, "A ten-year-old? He will end up in juvy for a while and then out with a new family. We probably haven't seen the last of him."

Kat called and texted Van and Jack every couple of hours until the plane took off from London. The few days she stayed there had been so hectic she only texted when she could. She knew they understood. But now, each time she saw their faces on video, she felt like she got closer to breaking down, but held back. She was strong. She knew that now.

When she and Eli landed in New York City, she gave him a heartfelt hug. "I'll miss you," she said. "That was quite an adventure, wasn't it?"

He squirmed away. "It was. I'll be glad to get back to my quiet life in Savannah. Please feel free to come to the shop again if you would like to buy something. Otherwise..."

Kat laughed, "Of course, Eli. I understand."

On the flight between New York and California, Kat slept. She had never been so tired. The whine of the engines and the low hum of people talking didn't disturb her at all. She woke up about an hour outside of the airport, drank a little bit of water and listened to some music. As the plane touched down, she felt a sense of joy well up in her chest.

There was a long line of passengers getting off the plane, and then a long walk to the carousels where the suitcases would be delivered. Kat moved as quickly as she could, going down the escalator to baggage claim. Right at the bottom, she spotted them. Jack was jumping up and down holding a sign that said, "Welcome Home" in red and blue lettering. Van was standing right behind him, wearing a baseball hat, a rumpled T-shirt, jeans and flip-flops. She dropped her bag and ran, never being so happy to be at home.

Two days later, after getting out of the shower, Kat got a text from Henry. Scotland Yard had tracked the art dealer, Christopher Lavaud, to Bulgaria. He had landed at their main airport just an hour before and was now in custody. "Thanks for your hard work, love. You made all the difference on this one."

Kat smiled.

Can Kat stop a serial killer before it's too late? Check out the Sauk Valley Killer today! Get it here!

Get Kat's prequel short story -- FREE exclusive content and announcements on new releases — here!

A NOTE FROM THE AUTHOR

Thanks so much for taking the time to read!

After reading "The Bloody Canvas," I hope that you've been able to take a break from your everyday life and join Kat on her latest adventure. There are more to come! In fact, while there's a sneak peek of the next book in the series right after this page, you could just jump right on over and take a look at "Sauk Valley Killer" here.

Enjoy!

KJ

P. S. Would you take a moment to leave a review? Reviews from readers like you mean the world to me!

"SAUK VALLEY KILLER" — BOOK 6 OF THE KAT BECKMAN THRILLER SERIES

Chelsea Atkinson and Daniel Arthur are gone.

Two high school seniors have disappeared without a trace.

The Sauk Valley community is on edge, frightened for themselves and their children.

But Chelsea and Daniel aren't the only ones missing...

Kat Beckman, an investigative journalist, starts the hunt for a serial killer that's in her own backyard. Can she find him before he kills again?

The trail to find him takes Kat back through her own dark past, a past she would have rather never visited again.

If you like Tom Clancy, James Patterson and Lee Child, then you'll love this fast-paced, action-packed psychological thriller – book six of the Kat Beckman series.

Click here to get it now!

EXCERPT FROM "SAUK VALLEY KILLER"

The SWAT team breached the side door of the garage, Kat right on the heels of the last man in the line. Two officers charged Joseph and tackled him, flipping him over while he kicked with his legs and scratched at them with his hands, as they yelled, "Hands up!" Two more officers joined them, securing him and flipping him over. Within seconds, the takedown was over.

Kat ran past the officers who had piled on top of Joseph and came to a stop, facing two enormous Plexiglas boxes over-flowing with water, two bodies of what looked to be young girls floating in them. Her heart jumped in her throat, "Van!" she screamed, "Van!"

Unlock all of the Kat Beckman adventures now by clicking here to visit the series page or check out my website.

Made in the USA
Las Vegas, NV
08 December 2021